"I meant it when I said we should move on," Rafe said.

Olivia's stomach knotted with anxiety, but Rafe's hand on her shoulder felt warm and protective. He searched her face for her reaction. Apparently, she had struck some chord in him. He didn't want to stay mad at her and he needed her to acknowledge that they were adult enough to forgive and forget. Was he asking her to be friends?

His eyes were the color of the bluest spring sky, filled with unspoken promises. At that moment, Olivia realized she was lost in him. Did he know she would give anything to feel his lips against hers? Could he sense her heart thrumming in her chest? Why wasn't he saying anything? And why was his hand moving so achingly slowly from her shoulder to the nape of her neck?

His mouth was so close to hers, his breath warmed her nose. "Wish me luck," he said as he closed his eyes and leaned in.

Dear Reader,

Fear of Falling is one of those novels that comes to an author from their own life experiences and memories.

Back in the sixties and early seventies, our town was in great need of a new hospital. My mother and the other ladies in her group initiated the Hospital Horse Show to raise money for the construction, and for years the show was a huge draw.

My mother grew up going to harness racing in Florida and accompanied her father to Hot Springs, Arkansas, in the 1930s to watch horse racing. She adored Thoroughbreds, and as I grew up, she hosted a Kentucky Derby party at our house every year. I carry on that tradition with joy and a lot of mint juleps with the mint my mother planted in our garden. My mother could pick winning horses nearly every year. It was uncanny.

When the time came for my story about Rafe Barzonni, the brooding, handsome farmer who worshipped his father and adored horses as my mother did, I knew he was the perfect match for Olivia Melton, the caterer and amateur photographer whose father gambled away the family savings at the racetrack.

Fear of Falling was a joy for me to write. I hope you enjoy it, as well. Please write to me at cathlanigan1@gmail.com, or you can find me on Twitter, @cathlanigan, Facebook, Pinterest, Goodreads, Amazon, LinkedIn, at catherinelanigan.com and heartwarmingauthors.blogspot.com.

All my very best and God bless,

Catherine Lanigan

HEARTWARMING

Fear of Falling

—

Catherine Lanigan

H HARLEQUIN® HEARTWARMIN

Recycling programs
for this product may
not exist in your area.

ISBN-13: 978-0-373-36781-8

Fear of Falling

Copyright © 2016 by Catherine Lanigan

ⁿted in U.S.A.

HARLEQUIN®
www.Harlequin.com

Catherine Lanigan knew she was born to storytelling at a very young age when she told stories to her younger brothers and sister. After years of encouragement from family and teachers, Catherine was brokenhearted when her freshman college professor told her she had "no writing talent whatsoever" and she would never earn a dime as a writer. He promised he would get her through with a B grade *if* Catherine would promise never to write again.

For fourteen years she didn't write until she was encouraged by a television journalist and wrote a 600-page historical romantic spy-thriller set against World War I. The journalist sent the manuscript to his agent, who got bids from two publishers. That was nearly forty published books ago.

Books by Catherine Lanigan

Harlequin Heartwarming

Love Shadows
Heart's Desire
A Fine Year for Love
Katia's Promise

MIRA Books

Dangerous Love
Elusive Love
Tender Malice
In Love's Shadow
Legend Makers
California Moon

Harlequin Desire

The Texan
Montana Bride

Visit the Author Profile page at
Harlequin.com for more titles.

This book is dedicated to my beloved husband, Jed Nolan, who fought a valiant battle against leukemia. It was a torturous journey, but you were gallant and brave. Sail away to that land of peace and joy.

Acknowledgments

Cutting and polishing diamonds to brilliance is the work of skilled geniuses. That is what Claire Caldwell, my valued and cherished editor, does for me. Our work together to bring The Shores of Indian Lake into existence has been a construction of monumental proportions because our little town now lives like Glocca Morra, that mythical, magical realm in the ethers. To me, it's very real. Thank you, Claire, for helping me bring all these people to life.

And to Victoria Curran, for raising the bar each time I send in a proposal, making me think and push harder and explore the best part of myself.

And as always to Dianne Moggy, who has believed in me and my God-given talent for over twenty years. You never gave up on me.

And I want to thank my parents, Dorothy Lanigan and Frank J. Lanigan, who left a massive imprint on our community and who taught me that legacy is important.

CHAPTER ONE

THE EARLY-SPRING DEW glistened as dawn struck the lush grass of the Barzonni training paddock. The only disturbance in the chilly air was the heavy snort, rhythmic breathing and thundering hooves of Rowan as Rafe urged his father's prize Thoroughbred around the second quarter mile of track.

Rafe was far from a professional jockey, and at six foot one, he'd never aspired to the career, but no one knew Rowan's talent, spirit and desire to run like Rafe did. Every beat of Rowan's heart matched his own. Blood pulsed through his veins, suffusing his body and mind with oxygen, and Rafe's lungs filled and exhaled the crisp, clean morning air like an elixir. His exhilaration grew as the horse sped up, and Rafe leaned his head closer to Rowan's neck, shouting encouragement. He knew Rowan sensed his pride, his own need to push them both to their physical limits. No run was a test or trial. Each one was the end game. It was for the win.

At moments like this, Rafe and the horse were one, moving fluidly through space and time, gobbling up track as if they weren't part of the real world. Together they were magic.

They were coming up to the third turn, so Rafe pressed his thighs into Rowan's sides and dug in his heels just enough to communicate it was time for Rowan to unleash all his power.

Rafe and his father had built their home track together, board by board, truckload after truckload of precisely mixed sandy loam, clay and base soil when Rafe was only fourteen. Angelo had always dreamed of owning a Kentucky Derby winner, so they'd fine-tuned their track to the exact specifications of Churchill Downs in Louisville. And no ordinary racehorse would do. Angelo wanted fame, but not necessarily fortune—though his farm had yielded a fairly large one over the years. His four sons were his legacy, but a moment in the winner's circle would erase all his beleaguered childhood experiences, or so he'd told Rafe. Rafe never once forgot what he was racing for.

Rafe's father had come to America after

living most of his young life on the streets in Sicily. Angelo had told the boys he worked hard because he never wanted anyone to take his land from him. As long as he tilled the earth and watched vegetables grow, he knew he'd never have to scrounge through garbage for a meal. Some townspeople said Angelo was a thief, that he'd stolen bankrupt farms from their neighbors over forty years ago. But Rafe never believed his father had done anything wrong.

The fact was that Angelo was a driven man. His need to control his future and that of his sons overrode everything else in his life. Angelo was not demonstrative or thoughtful. He didn't often tell his sons or his wife that he loved them. Instead, he toiled from dawn till long past dusk to keep the farm solvent. His hard work had made him wealthy over the years, but Angelo never saw it that way. He was always one failed crop away from destitution. He taught his sons to keep their sights on the abundance that came from the earth.

Angelo was also a man of contradictions. Though he loved horses, he never bet on a race in his life. To him, gambling was the same as burning money. A waste. But the thrill of being victorious at a race, the prestige that came from owning a winner and the possibility that his name would be attached to a horse that made history was Angelo's dream. And he didn't believe in half measures. When he realized Rafe shared his love for horses, Angelo did everything he could to encourage Rafe's passion and involvement in the sport.

Rafe had raced over a dozen Thoroughbreds around this track, but no horse had ever measured up to Rowan. He was the son of a Preakness-winning sire and a mare that had won over a million dollars at Santa Anita, Arlington and other tracks in her lifetime. Rowan had been born to race, and Rafe believed that with the help of their trainer, Curt Wheeling, they were finally about to triumph.

As Rafe and Rowan headed down the final stretch, Rafe tried to imagine what it would be like to be the jockey on Rowan's back during a professional race. Thousands of spectators would be watching him, critiquing his skills, the nuances of the tugs he gave the reins, the directions he shouted into Rowan's ears and the lean of his body in the saddle. They would cheer and yell for him, and his boyhood dreams would become reality.

The sound of Rowan's hooves as they

pounded the dirt filled Rafe's ears. In the distance he could hear his father's voice rolling toward him like an oncoming storm.

"Push him out, Rafe! Put your knees into him!" Angelo shouted. Rafe could see his father out of the corner of his eye, holding his stopwatch at eye level, and he smiled to himself. Angelo never let that stopwatch drift a quarter inch out of his sight, always fearful he'd miss a split second of vital clocking.

Curt Wheeling pulled off his ever-present cowboy hat and smacked it against the white fence. His thick salt-and-pepper hair sprang into a half-dozen spiky cowlicks. "Let him free, Rafe! Let him take you to the limit!"

Curt also held a stopwatch, the one his father had given him fifty years ago on his sixth birthday. Curt had come from a long line of horse trainers, and the Barzonnis were lucky to have hired him. Curt had been let go from his last job in Texas because the owner wanted a younger man. Since coming to Indian Lake, Curt had fit right in and had bonded with Rowan just as Rafe had.

Rafe heard their instructions and leaned his chest against Rowan's withers, keeping his head low to reduce wind resistance. When he got this close to the finish line, Rafe always wondered how many seconds faster Rowan would be with a jockey who was sixty pounds lighter and nearly a foot shorter. At the same time, this ride was so thrilling that Rafe couldn't—wouldn't—dream of relinquishing the track to anyone else. Angelo always said that if Rowan could run with a lanky, hard body like Rafe's in the saddle, he could race to the stars with a professional jockey. Training Rowan with an anvil on his back was good for the horse, his father had said.

"C'mon, boy! This is it! Now—fly!"

That was all Rafe had to say. Rowan's strong legs beat out a rhythm that Rafe had never heard from any horse before. His hooves hit the ground and carried them so fast over the finish line that Rafe wasn't quite so sure the horse hadn't sprouted wings and left the earth.

Then something happened that Rafe had never experienced with his horse. He kept going. With each stride, he moved even faster.

Instead of pulling him back, Rafe let him run. And run he did. Rafe felt as if he was shooting through space. The air stung his eyes and he admonished himself for not wearing goggles, but he couldn't have anticipated this. Last week Rafe had pushed Rowan to nearly thirty-eight miles an hour, but today he knew they were moving much faster. Most Thoroughbreds' stride was twenty feet, but Rowan's was twenty-six. He was a highly unusual horse, and it was becoming more apparent to them all that this year Rowan was about to meet his destiny.

But what confused Rafe was the fact that Rowan had never displayed this kind of power before. Why had he held so much back?

They were nearly halfway around the track before Rowan's speed diminished even a millisecond. The horse was breathing so hard, it sounded as if his lungs would explode, though Rafe knew well that Thoroughbreds had exceptionally efficient cardiovascular systems. Breathing through his nose, Rowan drew in air when he extended his long legs, and he exhaled when his legs came together.

Finally, without any instruction from Rafe, Rowan slowed, turned around and galloped back to the fence gate where Angelo and Curt were clapping and grinning at them.

"That was unbelievable, son!" Angelo shouted with both arms raised jubilantly over his head, his stopwatch still in his right hand.

Curt opened the gate so Angelo could walk through and hug his son.

Rafe jumped down and wrapped his father in a tight bear hug. "Did you see that? Amazing! There aren't enough words." Rafe unfurled his arms from around his father and threw them around his horse's neck.

Rowan stamped a hoof and bobbed his head as if he was taking his rightful accolades. "Way to go, boy! You are the best. The best!"

Angelo hugged Rowan, as well. "I knew this was a special horse the first day we saw him in Tennessee." Angelo held the reins and stared into Rowan's deep brown eyes. "He has soul, Rafe. You remember that. This is no ordinary horse. He deserves your time."

"Time." Rafe snorted. "It's spring. Just when I should be helping Curt train him, we're working twenty hours a day to get the tilling and planting done. If only Gabe were here."

"He's not," Angelo ground out. Gabe's marriage to Liz Crenshaw was a sore subject with Rafe's father. Angelo believed the marriage was an excuse for his eldest son's defection, but Rafe understood Gabe's need to have a career of his own.

Rafe, on the other hand, couldn't imagine a more perfect life than what he had here on the farm. Though the work was backbreaking and exhausting at times, he couldn't conceive of any other way to live. And it was worth it for the horses, which had been part of the farm since before Rafe was born. Though Angelo hadn't begun purchasing Thoroughbreds until Rafe was in his teens, Rafe couldn't remember a time he wasn't riding. Gabe and Mica were enamored of sports cars, and though Rafe appreciated their passions, animals occupied that special place in Rafe's heart.

Over the years, Rafe had gained every bit of knowledge and expertise he could about Thoroughbreds. Until Curt Wheeling came along, Rafe and his father had not seriously considered entering races to win a purse. The horses they'd been able to afford weren't "star" material. But Rafe understood his father's strategy to keep buying horses and trading them "up" until he was able to afford a quality racehorse.

When they'd driven to Tennessee to see Rowan, the owner wasn't much interested in the young colt who took up space in his stable and time with his trainers because he already had an entrant in the Kentucky Derby. But though Rowan was only a year old when Rafe met him, he would never forget the way the horse seemed to sense his presence. Rowan had been grazing in a grassy paddock with his mother. The owner had pointed him out to Rafe, and while Angelo and the owner talked, Rafe had wandered over to the fence to take a closer look.

Rafe was still yards away from the fence when suddenly, Rowan lifted his head from the grass and looked directly at him. There was no fear in Rowan's eyes as he turned away from his mother's side and strode slowly toward Rafe.

Rafe reached the fence at the same moment as Rowan, and when he reached out to touch his snout, Rowan eased his head under Rafe's hand. Then the horse curved his neck around Rafe's shoulders, as if he was hugging him.

Rafe got chills. "You'll be coming home with me," Rafe had whispered. "I'll care for you all my life."

Rafe put his arms around Rowan. Then he kissed him just as his father and the owner walked up. Rafe was shocked at the lump in his throat. He'd barely known this horse and yet he felt he'd known him forever.

He remembered the compassion and understanding in his father's eyes as Angelo considered the purchase. His long pause filled Rafe with dread that the owner was asking too much for Rowan and that Rafe's strong reaction might have negated the sale. "Is he the one, son?"

Knowing that his father was a shrewd businessman, Rafe tamped down his emotions and found his voice. "I need to ride him, Pops. See what he can do before we decide."

Angelo remained stoic and nodded as he turned to the owner. "That all right with you?"

The owner agreed and signaled to his trainer to saddle Rowan. Then he explained that Rowan needed training. He could run, but he wasn't making any promises. Angelo and Rafe would have to provide substantial instruction.

Rafe put Rowan through a few paces on the training track, but it only took one turn for Rafe to realize the potential that the Thoroughbred packed.

Angelo made the deal. Neither of them ever looked back on the drive home to Indiana.

Rafe returned to the present and looked at his father. "Dad, remember when I rode Rowan for the first time?"

"Never forget it," Angelo replied, folding his arms across his chest.

"Well, something happened out there on

the track today. You saw it." He glanced at Curt, who was giving him a wary expression. "Hear me out. All this time, we've been racing Rowan on a track like Churchill Downs. That's adequate for places like Arlington and such, but I think it's too short for him."

"What are you saying?" Angelo asked.

"I think he's a Preakness-type runner. That race is a mile and three-sixteenths, not just the mile like the Kentucky Derby. Rowan didn't hit his stride until we passed the finish line. I want to take him on another round right now and see what he can do. He should be tired out, but he isn't. And to keep him running these shorter races is a disservice to his talent."

Curt scratched his head. "How could we have missed this?"

Rafe put his hand on Curt's shoulder. "How could we have known? It was a brutal winter. He hasn't had a chance to let it rip for months. Two weeks ago he was running through muck and mud. This is the first time the track's been in decent shape this season."

"Logical," Angelo said with an odd grimace. "Listen, you take him out. I'm tired. I'm going up to the house...to see if breakfast is ready." He hugged himself again.

"But, Dad, you gotta see this. You have the best eye ever."

"Oh." Angelo stared at the ground. "All right," he said quietly.

Rafe couldn't understand why his father wasn't sharing his enthusiasm, but he wouldn't let Angelo's attitude get to him. "Excellent!" Rafe smiled broadly and slung himself up onto Rowan's back. He pulled on the reins and turned the horse around.

Rafe and Rowan waited at the starting line while Angelo leaned against the fence and held his stopwatch. Curt did the same. As usual, Curt held up the red bandanna he used to signal the start of the trial, which was easy for Rafe to see.

Curt dropped the bandanna, and Rowan shot ahead. Rafe could tell that Rowan had made the first turn in a shorter time than the first trial. The second turn breezed by. So did the third. Coming up to the finish, Rafe glanced over at his father and Curt as he always did. Curt was screaming something at Rafe, though he couldn't make out the words. Angelo still held his stopwatch at eye level, but he was not cheering or shouting like Rafe thought he would be. He'd expected his father to be bursting with enthusiasm; instead, he appeared to be watching with a very steady gaze.

Rafe glowed with pride as he leaned forward and pushed Rowan to cross the finish line and not stop. Rowan poured on the power and left the finish line far behind him. They were around the first turn before the horse's stride slowed.

Rafe's suspicions were confirmed. They hadn't begun to tap Rowan's power and abilities. As Rafe slowed the horse, his mind filled with visions of great races, superb wins…and making history. Rafe was nearly euphoric as they galloped back toward the gate.

Instantly, his smile melted off his face. Angelo was lying on the ground, and Curt was still yelling at him. Rafe couldn't make out the words over the pounding of his heart. He urged Rowan to the gate and jumped off.

"What's wrong?" Rafe shouted as he opened the gate and stooped over his father.

"I called 911 from my cell," Curt said. "He clutched his chest and sank to the ground just as you passed the finish line. There was no way you could hear or even see me then."

Angelo's eyes were closed, his face a ghastly, frightening gray.

"He's not breathing," Rafe said, placing his

cheek next to his father's nostrils. He started CPR, pushing on Angelo's chest with all his strength. His mother had made sure all four of her sons kept up-to-date on first-aid courses. On a farm, they needed to be prepared for all eventualities. Rafe knew his father had heart issues, but Angelo refused to talk about his ill health—ever.

Rafe should have seen this coming.

Thinking back, he'd had a warning of sorts. At his brother Nate's couples' shower at Mrs. Beabots's house, Rafe learned his father had been prescribed Coumadin. Nate actually hadn't known anything about Angelo's heart condition. Nate had told Rafe and Gabe that it was time for Angelo to slow down, perhaps even retire. But it hadn't happened.

Then Gabe had married Liz, and that caused Angelo an extreme amount of stress, which Rafe didn't truly understand. Apparently, something had happened between Liz's grandfather and Angelo decades ago, but Rafe, Nate and Mica had no clue what that "thing" was. But Rafe had noticed their mother hovering over Angelo this past winter, acting as if he was dying. It was ridiculous. As far as Rafe could tell, his father was as fit as him or his brother. He was just older, that was all. Angelo needed to knock off at four instead of six or seven like he and Mica did, but their father went on, day after day, as if he was still fighting to make his farm a success. Now Rafe realized with torturous hindsight that Angelo's refusal to take it easy was precisely why his mother had been making such a fuss.

Rafe continued to press on his father's chest so hard he was afraid he'd break Angelo's sternum.

"Come on, Dad! You can make it. Come on! I'll save you. Promise."

Curt placed a hand on his back. A comforting hand. An empathetic hand. He barely registered the sirens in the distance. He would do anything to save the most important person in his life. Rafe loved his father with all his being, and he would trade his own life to save Angelo's.

"Rafe," Curt said softly. "Rafe. He's gone."

Rafe didn't hear Curt. He wouldn't. What he was saying was an absolute impossibility. His father was not dead. The paramedics would come. They'd stick some paddles on his chest and wake him up.

An ambulance and a fire truck drove down the long brick drive that Angelo had laid himself. The sirens echoed across the spring fields. Gina came running from the house still dressed in her robe and pajamas. Mica rushed down the back stairs.

Curt raced toward the ambulance, waving his arms. "Over here!"

Rafe was right. The paramedics placed paddles on Angelo's chest and shocked him with enough electricity to bring a dead man back to life.

Angelo's body remained quiet and still.

CHAPTER TWO

BENEATH A FLUTTER of pink crab-apple blossoms floating on the spring breeze, Olivia opened a café umbrella to welcome her patrons to the street-side tables at Indian Lake Deli for breakfast. A pair of robins flew to their nest in the white flowering pear tree. Spring was Olivia's favorite season. Winter storm windows were taken down and opened, tulips and daffodils filled the city planters and the tops rolled back on convertibles. Everything she saw and smelled was electric with promise. She always felt anticipation in the spring, but this season was different somehow. She could almost feel a burst of creative energy taking place inside her cells, igniting them into tiny, raging flares of ideas and dreams. She just hoped that this year they didn't all suffocate by summer's end like they usually did.

Before she thought herself into a downward spiral, Olivia took out the digital camera she always carried in her apron pocket and snapped a close-up shot of the robins in the tree. She caught the radiant and colorful male tilting his head toward the dowdy, demure-looking female. Their flirtatious behavior was nearly human, and the photo offered the kind of peek into the animal dimension that Olivia prided herself on.

Over the years, Olivia had been amazed at the glimpses of the natural world she'd captured on film. Butterflies in whirling masses around butterfly bushes. Spiders spinning opalescent webs. Dewdrops slipping off rose petals and onto the back of a crawling grasshopper. Iridescent dragonfly wings as the insects darted in and out of sunbeams.

Sometimes Olivia left her apartment long before dawn to go down to the lake. Or she came home late at night after taking sunset photos on Lake Michigan's beach.

Olivia had logged many hours perfecting her photographic skills, but she had yet to do anything significant with them. For years she'd told herself she wasn't good enough yet, or that her lack of formal training was a nonstarter. Then she became critical of others' work and realized that her photos were as good as those that were published. Sometimes they were even better. More insightful.

But Olivia was practical. She knew art and talent didn't always pay the bills. To put food on the table and pay her rent, insurance premiums and car note, she had to keep her day job, working with her mother at the Indian Lake Deli.

Just as Olivia locked the green canvas umbrella in place, Sarah, Maddie, Liz and Katia walked up and hugged her. They plopped down in the matching green canvas folding chairs. Liz looked exhausted but radiant and was starting to show her pregnancy in her spring-green tunic.

"Olivia, we need a round of your raspberry iced tea," Sarah said, pushing her blond hair away from her flushed face. "We're pooped."

"You can say that again," Maddie groaned. "My cappuccino is good, but your teas are absolutely vital for people in our ragged condition." She swiped her palm across her neck. "I'm so out of shape," she said under her breath.

"What have you been doing?" Olivia asked, taking out her pad and pen from her apron.

"Walking. Fast walking, to be exact. Liz

has to exercise every day—so says her ob-gyn," Maddie explained.

"Yeah," Liz grumbled, smoothing her long hair into a ponytail. "As if working the vine-yard isn't enough."

"It's not the right kind of exercise," Katia interjected. "Half a dozen of my Chicago girlfriends have been where you are. Walk-ing is mandatory. I should loan you my tread-mill," she said with a flick of her wrist as if the decision didn't require any more discus-sion.

"Spare me!" Liz raised her hands in mock horror. "I walk my hills every day!" Liz looked at Olivia. "Who knew I would have so many mother hens?"

"You need us, Liz," Olivia insisted.

Sarah snapped her head in agreement. "Be-sides, walking together is a great stress re-ducer for all of us. The best part is that it gets me out of the office."

"Me, too," Katia chimed in. "I swear I could easily miss the whole spring if it weren't for you, Liz. Olivia, you better make that six teas. Gina and Charmaine are supposed to join us in a few minutes."

"Where are they now?" Olivia asked.

"Gina's meeting Charmaine at Kid's Corner to pick out the linens for the nursery," Liz said. "I assume they're there now."

"You're a lucky girl, Liz." Olivia winked. "Gina and Charmaine have the best taste in just about everything."

"So true. They almost make me feel guilty. Gina has been so generous. I asked Sarah to design the nursery, but…"

Sarah threw up her hands. "But oh, no! Charmaine wouldn't hear of it. She practically stole one of my best friend's accounts from me. Just teasing. Charmaine was dying to do that nursery."

Olivia nodded. "I get that." Charmaine had never been married, and with no kids of her own, she had to be over the moon about it.

Sarah chuckled. "Her real problem was reining in her ideas. You should have seen her design boards." Sarah slapped both palms on her cheeks. "It was like every kid's fantasy— from castles and dragons to little sailboats flying to the moon."

Liz lifted her eyes to Olivia. "I went with the sailboats, by the way. Over a vineyard, of course," She beamed happily. "The ceiling has glow-in-the-dark stars with glittery comets. It's adorable."

"Sounds magical." Olivia sighed. This was

what spring was all about. Looking forward to changes and new perspectives. Liz was living proof that something unexpected and wonderful could happen at any minute. Last spring she was tending her new grapevines just like she did every year. Then *boom*! Gabe Barzonni trespassed on her land, she nearly shot him and now here was Liz, married to Gabe and having his baby. Olivia would swoon over the romance of it all, if she was the swooning type. Which she was not. Olivia was much too practical for rhapsodic thoughts.

Olivia smiled at Liz. "I'm so happy for you, Liz. Really happy."

"Thanks, Olivia." Liz squeezed Olivia's hand then looked around the table. "Friends like you—all of you—are so rare. We're all very lucky."

"Yes, we are," Katia said. "Moving back to Indian Lake was the best thing I ever did."

Olivia nearly hooted. "No kidding! And we have you to thank for putting the smile back on Austin's face. I've always liked him. My mom and I have catered in his home several times. He's always been kind to us." Olivia smiled. "We're sure glad you're here, Katia."

"Thanks." Katia returned Olivia's smile.

Just then Liz's cell phone chimed. She took it out of her pocket and checked the caller ID. "It's Gabe. I gotta take this."

"I'll get the iced teas," Olivia said, heading back inside the deli. She'd just stepped behind the pastry case when the phone rang. "Indian Lake Deli," she answered.

At first she could barely understand the woman on the other end of the phone because she was crying so much. Olivia put her left hand over her left ear to shut out the din of voices inside the deli. "How can I help you?" Her mouth fell open as she realized it was Gina Barzonni. "Gina. Slow down. Tell me again what happened."

Olivia was stunned by the news. Angelo was dead. Heart attack. Gina was planning a funeral for Saturday, five days from now, because one of her sisters was flying in from Sicily. Gina wanted a formal sit-down luncheon after the burial, and she wanted Olivia and her mother, Julia, to handle the entire event. She promised to call the next day to go over details, but she needed to make sure that Olivia was free at such late notice.

"I'm so, so sorry to hear all this, Gina. I had no idea Angelo was sick. Don't worry about a thing," Olivia assured her. "We'll put together some ideas and I'll call you tomorrow. You take care of yourself. This is a very stressful time, and I know your entire family will be leaning on you."

Olivia hung up and glanced out to the window. From the stricken looks on her friends' faces, she guessed Gabe had just called Liz with the news. Liz was still on the phone, nodding and looking compassionately at Maddie, now her sister-in-law. Sarah was holding Liz's hand. Katia's expression was solemn.

Olivia rushed back outside to be with them. Maddie's phone rang just as she reached the table. She answered it, rose and walked to the curb to have privacy while she spoke to her husband.

"Liz, I'm so sorry," Olivia said once Liz hung up, standing over her friend and putting her arm around her shoulder. "How is Gabe?"

Sarah glanced up at Olivia. "You were inside. How did you hear about it?"

"That was Gina on the phone."

"How did she sound?"

"Devastated. I could barely make out what she was saying."

Liz nodded. "Gabe said he was worried about her. I guess he should be."

Olivia had to agree. "She told me the funeral and burial are set for Saturday. She wants me and Mom to cater the luncheon. I'm in shock. You must be, too, Liz. And Maddie. Angelo seemed so healthy to me."

"To be honest, Nate told us that Angelo had several heart issues, but he just wouldn't take care of himself," Liz explained sadly.

Maddie hung up her phone and came back to the table. She looked at Olivia. "Nate was in surgery since nearly daybreak. He just got the news from Rafe. Nate told me he's been expecting this exact thing to happen, but he's still shocked. I don't think there is any way we can prepare ourselves for something like this."

Olivia couldn't help thinking that only a few minutes ago, she'd sensed that something was about to change and that her life was about to alter its course. She shivered. To Olivia, Angelo Barzonni was a legend, the immigrant from the streets of Sicily who came to Indian Lake and built one of the most successful family-owned farms in the Midwest. She admired him. He'd taken the raw fabric of his life and created a mini-dynasty with his wife and four sons. Olivia could feel the void opening up in Indian Lake with his passing, like a rip in the universe. Already, she could tell that a lot would change with his death.

"Maddie, I'm so very sorry. Please tell Nate I'm praying for the whole family."

"I will."

Katia took out her phone. "I should call Austin. He needs to be with Rafe. They're so close, and I'm sure this is devastating for Rafe."

Maddie's gaze swung to Katia. "I hadn't thought about that. Rafe will be the most affected. Nate always said Rafe was Angelo's favorite. And Rafe and Mica were the last ones left on the farm. They've been sharing Gabe's duties since the wedding."

Liz pressed her hand to her forehead. "I feel so sorry for all of them. They were a close family. I can't imagine what it would be like if my grandfather—"

"Don't even go there," Olivia admonished her. "Sam is fine, and he does see Nate when he's supposed to."

Liz nodded glumly.

"I just had a thought," Maddie said to Olivia. "Could you do me a favor and put together a tray of sandwiches and maybe a bowl of potato salad—the yogurt kind Nate likes—so I could take it out to the farm? It's my bet people will be stopping by all day today."

"All week, you mean. Sure. Absolutely." Olivia went over to hug Maddie.

Liz rose. "I better go. Gabe's going to meet me at the farm. You want to drive with me, Maddie?" she asked her sister-in-law.

"Sure." Maddie paused and looked at Sarah. "Will you tell Mrs. Beabots or do you want me to call her?"

"I'll go over to her house. I'll call Luke from my cell. Charmaine, too."

Olivia hugged each of her friends one more time and as they walked off in separate directions, she was struck with the significance of the moment. In one way or another, big and small, they'd each been touched by Angelo's life…and now death. Maddie and Liz had married his sons. Katia's fiancé, Austin, was Rafe Barzonni's best friend. Though Olivia didn't know Angelo all that well, her best friends were part of his family now and that affected her. Olivia had always believed that all living organisms were connected, somehow. This sad event was a kind of proof.

The rupture in her friends' world was overtaking them. And the tragedy touched Olivia, too. But Angelo was an inspiration, and Olivia couldn't help but wonder whether there was a lesson in the life he'd lived.

Olivia dreamed of taking her photography skills and talent to the next level, but she'd never done much about it. She left her ability buried and untried, never giving it a chance to flourish. Angelo had never compromised on his ambition, working dawn till dusk to achieve his goals and build a legacy.

She went back inside the deli, taking out her pad to begin making a list of what they'd need to cater the funeral. She could ponder the meaning of Angelo's death on her life, but this coming week would be brutal and heart-wrenching for her friends. She could only hope to give them support and words of solace. She would be the loving friend they needed.

CHAPTER THREE

THE DAY OF Angelo Barzonni's funeral dinner sounded like the clanging of requiem bells as Olivia and Julia slammed pots, pans and metal trays into the back of their eight-year-old Chevrolet minivan. With her hair shoved into a tight knot on top of her head, wearing little makeup and comfortable black leggings, a chef's jacket and running shoes, Olivia's only concession to fashion were the gold hoop earrings in her ears.

"Did you get the copper chafing dish and the Sterno?" Julia asked.

"Yes. Did you remember the warming tray and the plug?"

Her mother's dark eyes grew wide. "The plug. I never remember the plug."

"I taped it to the back of the tray after we catered the Halsteads' brunch last Sunday. I just wanted to make sure it was there."

Julia turned the heavy electronic tray over. "Here!"

"Great. Also, I packed the three-tiered epergne for my *macarons* and napoleon pastries. The gingerbread cookies are in tins, and I'll put those in the scoops of cinnamon ice cream right before we serve the desserts."

Julia looked around the inside of the van. "Where's the chocolate mousse?"

Olivia gasped. "What mousse? Was I supposed to make chocolate mousse? I didn't see it on the menu. Oh, no. What'll I do?"

Julia dropped her chin to her chest but then looked up in relief. "Silly me. We used the mousse for the *macarons*."

Olivia's exhale could have set sail to a Yankee Clipper. "Thank goodness! We don't have time for mistakes, and I want this to be as stress-free for that family as possible."

"I agree." Julia paused thoughtfully. "Angelo was only five years older than I am. This has made me sit up and take notice."

Olivia shoved a bowl of ambrosia into the van. "Notice what?"

"You know. Life."

"I know what you mean, Mom. I guess death always does that to the rest of us, huh?"

Julia shook her head. "Somehow this is different. Did you see the cortege that drove past here on the way to the grave site? I counted sixty-five cars."

"Sixty-seven," Olivia corrected her, checking her watch. "Fortunately, not all of them are invited to the house. The family will be back from the cemetery by now. Still, we need to hustle."

"You're right," Julia said. "Why don't you drive out and get started. I'll gather up the rest of the salads, the fruit and casseroles and bring them out in a few minutes."

"Good thinking. I'll meet you out there." Olivia patted her pockets to make sure she hadn't forgotten her camera. Olivia never went anywhere without a camera of some kind. Though it was important for their catering business that she take photos of the food for their website, Olivia was always on the lookout for the exceptional photo, the surprise shot that one day, someday, she could submit in a portfolio for a major magazine.

As Olivia drove off, she glanced in the rearview mirror in time to see her mother wave to her, as she always did when she left her mom's sight. It was just a little gesture in a long day of catering, planning…living, but it meant a great deal to Olivia. Her mother was right. Death always made people stop and think about their own lives. She smiled at the reflection in the rearview mirror. Olivia loved her mother a great deal; Julia was her best friend. She couldn't imagine what the Barzonni sons were going through right now.

HALF A DOZEN cars were parked along the winding path to the Barzonni villa. The dinner guests weren't due for another two hours, but Olivia knew it would be almost impossible to find a spot on the drive by then.

Olivia continued past a two-story carriage house, with garage doors on the ground level and what she guessed was an apartment up above. She parked outside it, close to the back door of the main house, then followed a short hall past the laundry room and into the kitchen. Easy access was always a plus for Olivia when she was hauling large chafing dishes, food and serving pieces. Her marble-and-silver epergne was lovely, but it weighed thirty pounds.

The aromas of garlic, basil, tomato and baking bread hit Olivia when she entered the enormous, Tuscan-style kitchen. Gina had conferred with Olivia and Julia about the menu and in the end, Gina had decided she wanted to cook a few of her signature Italian dishes for her family.

Gina was dressed in a black silk sheath dress with long lace sleeves and a white apron that was smeared with what looked like red sauce. She was stirring something in an industrial-size stainless-steel pot. She lifted a huge spoon and said to Olivia, "You have to taste this. My cream-of-tomato soup. I froze the tomatoes last fall and dried the basil from my garden. I think it's my best ever."

Olivia put the plastic crate she was carrying on the floor next to one of the two granite-topped islands and crossed to the six-burner gas stove. Gina offered her a teaspoon and Olivia dipped it in the soup. "It's incredible. Sweet," Olivia said when she tasted it.

"That's brown sugar. My secret. You can tell your mother but no one else. By the way, where is Julia?"

"She's on her way with the rest of the food. But may I ask, why aren't you with your guests and visitors?"

Gina lowered her eyes and looked at the pot. "This was Angelo's favorite soup. He would have wanted me to make it for the family." She stirred the soup absently. "I'm better when I'm busy. It's hours until we eat. I even told the boys to stop hovering. Gabe took Liz for a walk. I think Mica, Nate and Maddie are playing cards with my sister, Bianca. Most of the guests are in the living room. Rafe went out for a ride on Rowan."

"Rowan?" Olivia asked.

"His favorite horse. We have quite a few horses, did you know?"

Olivia felt a knot form in her stomach. "Oh, yeah. Workhorses. Sure. Makes sense. This being a farm and all."

"We have those, but I'm talking about Thoroughbreds."

Olivia's mouth went dry with an all-too-familiar, though long-buried fear. Gina was talking about racehorses.

"Rafe and Angelo think they have a winner in Rowan. They're hoping to enter him in some Graded Stakes races for the Kentucky Derby. They changed all the rules two years ago. Even the Illinois Derby isn't part of the qualifying trials anymore. Angelo—" Gina's voice hitched.

Olivia reached out to console her.

Racing horses. She said racing horses.

She froze and dropped her arm to her side. She felt the *thrum thrum thrum* of her heart in her ears. Olivia tried to formulate some kind of empathetic sentence. Nothing happened. Her stomach roiled. The fear she'd felt earlier gripped her. She knew she wouldn't escape this time.

Gina wiped the tears from her eyes and kept staring at the soup. "Sorry. They won't be doing that this year. I don't know what Rafe will do."

Anger and fear rooted Olivia to the spot. It had been years since she'd been confronted by the demons of her past. Those dark, sinewy fingers of dread that crippled her mind and soul had returned. She felt as if she were tumbling backward through the years. Through a tunnel of black terror.

Olivia's father had been addicted to gambling. Horse races, in particular. Any horse race: those he listened to on the radio, those he watched on television. But the ones he loved most were live action. His thrill meter soared the highest when he was in the crowd, cheering and stomping for his horse to cross the finish line.

She choked back the sour taste in her mouth.

When she was very young, her father drove her to Arlington International Racecourse near Chicago and showed her how to place bets. He went into great detail about the strategy he used, the amount of money he would win and all the wonderful things he would do for her and her mother once he "hit the jackpot." Olivia hadn't cared about the betting, but she had been mesmerized by the horses: their gait, the way the sun glinted off their shiny coats as their muscles strained with each gallop. She admired their majesty and the tilt of their heads in the winner's circle, as if they knew they were the stars. They were the real trophies.

She'd revisited the memory of her first encounter with horses often in her life. She only wished it had not been juxtaposed with the disappointment and betrayal of her father's disease.

When Olivia was twelve, her father had drained the family savings account, surreptitiously taken out a second mortgage on their home and run up a mountain of credit-card debt by taking cash advances. All the rehabilitation meetings and counseling sessions that Julia had dragged him to hadn't made a dent. He continued to borrow from friends, claiming the money was for Olivia or some other lie he'd concocted. Finally, one night during a screaming match between her parents, Julia had asked for a divorce.

Olivia's father left the next morning and never contacted them again. Julia had no formal education, but she was an excellent cook. With the help of Ann Marie Jensen, who cosigned the lease for the space that would become the Indian Lake Deli, Julia began her catering business. It took every last cent Julia had hidden for Olivia's college fund to pay off her father's debts and to keep the deli open in those early years, but together Olivia and her mother had survived.

The shameful years. That was what Olivia had called them when she was younger. Kids often whispered behind her back or bullied her. But her real friends, like Sarah, Maddie and Isabelle, had stuck by her and got her through. It had been Sarah's idea to help Olivia get over her fears by forcing Olivia to accompany her to dressage classes.

She couldn't afford the lessons, of course, but Sarah had insisted she just come along and watch, maybe take photos of her. And it had been fun. Sarah had helped Olivia realize that horses were not just beautiful, but also intelligent and not to be feared. Eventually, Olivia realized that it was her father's addiction that terrified her, not the horses. In fact, Olivia believed she understood not just horses but all animals, too, more than she understood humans. What she wished for horses was freedom to run unencumbered by a rider, especially a jockey, whose sole purpose and drive was to win a race.

Olivia had never forgiven her father. She blamed him for all the difficulties she'd faced, and for having to stay home and work when almost all her friends went off to college. She'd developed an abhorrence for horse racing and anything associated with the sport. She despised gambling and though several casinos had opened nearby, she hadn't even driven past them.

As she stood in Gina's kitchen, Olivia was astounded that the Barzonni family was in league with what she considered the pond scum of all sports. But she was here for a job, and she had to stay professional.

"Gina, what can I do?"

Gina tapped the spoon on the edge of the soup pot then gently laid it in a blue-and-white spoon rest. "We should get on with it."

Olivia knew Gina's thoughts were just as much in the past as hers were. She could only hope the older woman's memories were not as bitter.

"The bartenders are serving the wine. Would you mind putting out more canapés?"

"Absolutely. I brought spinach dip in a round of rye bread. Boiled finger potatoes filled with sour cream and salmon, and stuffed cherry tomatoes with herbed cream cheese."

"Lovely. I got out some silver trays for you to use. Over there on the counter." Gina nodded toward the far side of the kitchen near the butler's pantry.

Just then Rafe walked in, wearing old jeans and a faded T-shirt that stretched across his broad chest like a second skin. His cowboy boots were scuffed. His black hair was wind-blown and ragged, but apparently, he didn't notice or care because he didn't make the first effort to smooth it.

"Hi," he said, going to the refrigerator and taking out a protein shake. He popped the top and slugged it, tilting his head back as he drank.

Olivia watched his Adam's apple bob up and down. Beads of sweat trickled down from his temples, past his strong jaw. When he finished, he wiped his mouth with his tanned forearm. Rafe was arrestingly handsome, yes, but there was also something dangerous and wild in his expression. *He must be hurting so much right now,* Olivia thought, remembering what Katia and Maddie had said about his relationship with Angelo.

"Raphael, did you wipe those boots outside?" Gina scolded him. Olivia got the impression her comment was out of habit more than necessity.

"I did," he replied flatly.

"I'm sorry, sweetheart. How was your ride?"

"Good. Rowan really poured it on. It was as if he was running to show Pop how he could measure up, you know?"

"I do," Gina replied, walking over to Rafe and putting her hand gently on his cheek. "He loved you a great deal."

Olivia felt like an intruder as Rafe's eyes filled with tears. She winced at the pain she both saw and felt. Gina seemed to have forgotten she was there, and she wasn't sure Rafe had noticed her at all.

Rafe squeezed his mother's hand. "I'll go change. I'm sure Aunt Bianca wouldn't think too highly of me in these clothes so soon after Dad's funeral."

"She always was a stickler for decorum. Probably another reason I was so anxious to leave home and travel halfway around the world to get away from her." Gina laughed softly at her joke.

"You shower," she said, pointing to the back kitchen door. "And then you can get Nate and Mica to help you with the tables and chairs for dinner."

"Will do." Rafe crossed the kitchen. As he stepped out through the back door, he glanced at Olivia. "See you later."

"Sure," she managed. She empathized with Rafe; he was obviously grief-stricken, and Olivia knew what it was like to lose a father. Yet Gina had just told her that Rafe was involved with horse racing, the evil of all evils. She should dismiss him. Dissolve the imaginary freeze-frame of him in his worn jeans and T-shirt, vulnerable yet masculine. But she couldn't. Then again, it made sense that his presence would affect her so strongly. She'd been thinking about her dad, and here was Rafe, suffering a similar loss. But at the same time, Rafe represented everything Olivia loathed in this world.

Death always made people think, muddled them up. Olivia struggled to clear the fog from her brain and get back to her work. "I'll get those appetizers for you, Mrs. Barzonni."

"I have a table set up near the bar in the den."

"I'll take care of it," Olivia assured her.

On her way to the van, Olivia suddenly wondered why Rafe would be going outside to take his shower. She looked over at the carriage house and saw that the door to the upstairs apartment was slightly ajar. That explained it.

Olivia had moved to her own one-bedroom apartment a few years ago, needing to get some space and independence from her mom, especially as they continued to work at the deli together. Now she lived on the first floor of one of the Victorian mansions on Maple Boulevard. It was a small space, but the twelve-foot-high, floor-to-ceiling windows filled her little kitchen and living area with light. There was a back entrance that was hers alone, and she'd lined the steps with pots of daffodil and tulip bulbs. The gardens in back were not as spectacular as Mrs. Beabots's, but the yard was ringed with blue spruce, maples and oaks, and it provided a secluded respite from the world. She could understand why Rafe had wanted a place of his own, even if it was only a few steps from where his parents lived.

OLIVIA SPENT THE rest of the afternoon putting out food and helping her mother clean up in the kitchen, stealing whatever moments she could to give her condolences to Nate, Gabe and Mica. Twice, she approached the table where Rafe sat with his mother, her sister, Bianca, and the priest who had performed the funeral service, and twice, she backed away, unable to talk to him.

After her second attempt, Olivia felt as if the walls were closing in on her. The room had grown stifling. She remembered these reactions from those years right after her father left. Her aunt and some of her mother's friends had told her she was being dramatic, but Olivia's symptoms were very real. Her words would be cut off midsentence, or she wouldn't be able to speak at all. She would sweat and her hands would shake—just like they were doing now. The cure was to simply avoid the triggers. In this case: Rafe. She had to stay away from him at all costs.

There were more chores waiting for her in the kitchen, and she needed to take photos of the elegant pastry display she'd created. But when she reached the kitchen, she noticed Gina had come in behind her.

"I want to serve the dessert and coffee

now," Gina said. "Come help me fill the coffeepots. Olivia, you'll pour the left side of the room, and Julia, will you take the right?"

"Of course," Olivia said. "What about the ice creams?"

Gina nodded briskly. "I'll serve them after we've put them together."

Olivia went to the island and opened the containers. "I got the ice cream from Louise." She took out a silver dish, scooped a perfect ball of ice cream into it, stuck a ginger star cookie in the middle and then sprinkled spun sugar "glitter" on top. "It was my idea to add the stars," Olivia said hesitantly. "I like to think of Mr. Barzonni being in heaven, walking among the stars."

Gina flung her arms around Olivia. "My sweet girl. That is the loveliest thing anyone has said to me all week. I'll remember it forever. Thank you."

"You're welcome." Olivia fought back tears as she glanced at her mother and saw pride and love shining in her eyes.

Gina took a deep breath and swept her fingers under her eyes. "I'll announce dessert. Oh, Olivia, don't forget the cream and sugar. I put it over there on that silver tray."

Olivia smiled. "I got it."

She watched from the kitchen as Rafe and Mica stacked their plates with her pastries. She wished she could take their photos; their smiles were the first she'd seen all day, and it warmed her to know that her creations brought them this little joy on such a sorrowful day. Once everyone had visited the dessert table, Gina began serving the ice cream, and Olivia followed her out with a china pot of hot coffee.

As she rounded Rafe's table, pouring coffee, Rafe reached out and clutched her hand.

"Is it true you made these macaroons?" he asked, holding up the colorful cookie with chocolate mousse filling between the layers.

"I did. Do you like them?"

"They're great," he said sourly. "But these aren't macaroons. There's no coconut in these."

"I didn't want to correct you, but yes, these are French *macarons*. Macaroons do have coconut." She leaned down to pick up his cup and saucer. Her arm passed very close to his shoulder, but he didn't move to give her more space. "Would you like cream or sugar?"

"Black. There's enough sugar in the cookies. I could eat a dozen of these. You're very talented."

"Thank you," she said, feeling a rush of warmth through her body. As she poured the coffee, she could smell his spicy cologne over the fresh scents of soap and shampoo.

He put his hand on her sleeve and she felt the strength of his fingers as they curled around her wrist. She turned her head slightly to meet his blazing eyes. "Thanks for helping my mom. You've been very kind to her. She told me what you said about my father walking among the stars. Thank you."

Olivia was tongue-tied. "I...I believe what I said."

Rafe nodded. "Well, it was what she needed to hear. I know Mom's still planning a baby shower for Gabe and Liz. We've all decided that from now on, we want you and your mother to cater her parties so she doesn't have to work so hard."

It was sweet that Rafe and his brothers were looking out for Gina, and Olivia tried to ignore the jab of disappointment: Rafe saw her as an employee. A hired hand.

But why should she care, and why should he think of her any other way? She was the hired professional for their dinner party. Period. Olivia tried to move on from the moment, but she couldn't. She was rooted to the spot. His intense eyes, his fresh, clean smell, the pressure of his hand on her arm were all causing sensual overload.

"I'm more than happy to help anytime," Olivia struggled to say.

He dropped his hand and looked at the coffee Olivia was still holding. "Thanks." She still didn't move. "I've got it," he said, taking the cup and saucer from her when she didn't put it down. His fingers bumped hers, and Olivia retracted her hand as if she'd been burned. Rafe was immersed in the world of horse racing. The one sphere in the universe she'd vowed never to enter again. Too many shadows and whispers of her father's addiction to overwhelm her. She didn't trust this man or his magnetism, and she knew that if she wavered at all, she would be lost.

"Cream? Sugar?" She heard herself ask perfunctorily. He glanced up at her with eyes that cut right to her core. She read honesty, friendliness, gratitude, sadness…and loneliness. Was that right? His eyes searched her face in expectation, but of what? She got the distinct impression that he wanted to ask her something, though she was unsure of his reasons or needs. What she did know was that he was making himself unforgettable.

"No. Like I said, I take it straight."

"Right. Gotcha," she said and backed away from his table. Gina asked Rafe a question and he turned to her. "I'm sorry, Mom. What were you saying?"

Olivia could hear the shutter snapping in her mind, taking dozens of mental images of Rafe as she walked from table to table. Normally, she liked the way she saw the world in photographs. But right now she wanted to focus on anything *but* Rafe. Besides, he wasn't paying the slightest bit of attention to her.

As she took a load of dishes to the kitchen, she reminded herself that Rafe Barzonni was a gambler. Like her father.

Actually, he was worse than her father, because Rafe was the horse owner. The kind of man whose pastime fueled the flames of spiritual and financial demise for others.

This night had unleashed a battalion of emotions for Olivia, and if she was smart, she would lock them up for good. Nights like this were dangerous because they tapped into what her mother called the "dark side of the soul." Too much introspection could be a bad thing.

Olivia should have expected this kind of

inner turmoil at a funeral, yet it had caught
her off guard. The only way she could put an
end to her consternation was to forget Rafe.
She relaxed a little. That would be easy; after
tonight, she probably wouldn't see Rafe again
for months. If ever.

CHAPTER FOUR

RAFE SLIPPED OUT of the house as soon as he could, knowing that most of the guests would hang around after dinner, devouring the remains of the desserts or sipping brandy with Nate, Gabe and Mica. The air in the house was claustrophobic. The walls pressed in on him as if he were the one in the coffin. It was all he could do to make it through dinner. He'd barely registered what had been served, except for those cookies the caterer had explained to him.

Macarons. He had to remember that. She had been nice. Pretty, too. Soft brown eyes. A guy could lose himself in eyes like that. He'd liked how genuine she seemed. He didn't actually recall much else about her—she'd been dressed in her chef's coat and black leggings. She looked official, he supposed, for a caterer.

His mother seemed to know her fairly well,

he thought, trying to rattle his thoughts into place.

Rafe rotated his neck from left to right. Everything seemed surreal. He knew people had been talking to him, but their voices seemed so far away. Words floated around him like kelp in the ocean. He felt as if he was half-conscious. Or going crazy.

Pulling the collar of his jacket up to ward off the early-spring chill, he made his way toward the stable. The sun was down and the warmth he'd felt earlier was gone. He shoved his hands into his pants pockets and held his arms close to his sides to keep warm. The cold was more than physical. It bored into his psyche and sat upon his soul. Suddenly, he felt alone. Abandoned. Adrift.

He supposed these feelings were to be expected when death came around. Rafe hadn't experienced death personally before, except when his chocolate Lab, Moosie, had died ten years ago. His father had been orphaned as a child, and his maternal grandparents had never come to America. He remembered talking to them on the telephone a few times, but all he'd ever said was *buongiorno*, since they didn't speak English. When they passed on, he and his brothers all stayed home. He didn't have any aunts, uncles or cousins in America—even Aunt Bianca had been a stranger to him before this visit.

He hadn't really missed having relatives around. Today, the house was filled with friends who had become like family. Austin McCreary was nearly a brother to him. He liked old Mrs. Beabots. But when he got down to it, his life had been wrapped up in his father, his mother and his brothers, this farm and his horses.

He'd never needed much else. Naively, he'd thought it would all go on forever. He'd never once thought about his father dying. Angelo had been the essence of good health and had always had a strong body. Sure, they'd been worried about his heart condition in recent months, but Rafe had chalked it up to a bit of aging. He couldn't believe there was anything seriously wrong with his dad. He was Angelo. The invincible Italian.

Rafe looked down as he neared the stables. His father had hand-laid the drive and pathways when Rafe was just a baby. Angelo had built half the house with his own hands and as the boys got older, they were expected to do the same. They'd all worked on the barns and the horse stable. Rafe had painted every board, shutter, gate, fence post and board in and around the paddock. He'd hauled dirt, raked loam and planted grass to make the horse arena the finest in the area.

He pulled his hands out of his pockets and looked at them. Rafe had believed he could build a dream with his hands, just as his father had. But they couldn't stop death. He'd pressed on his father's chest with all his might, and it hadn't made a difference. He felt incompetent and inadequate. In the days since Angelo's collapse, Rafe had wished over and over again that he'd been Nate instead. A heart surgeon. A man who could have saved his father. But he was just Rafe. A farmer. A guy who loved horses and horse racing.

Rafe went into the stable and closed the door behind him. To his left was the tack room and next to it was the office, complete with a sofa and television that Curt used. There were six wide horse stalls to his right. Years ago they'd installed heaters to keep the horses warm during the bitter Indiana winters. Warm, dry air blasted into the hallway between the stalls. It felt good on Rafe's back as he went over to see Rowan.

Curt must have just cleaned the stall because the concrete floor was strewn with fresh hay. Rowan's feeder was filled with food, and the plastic water bottle that fed into the trough had been replenished.

Rowan, hearing Rafe's approach, turned from the back of the stall where he'd been taking a drink and walked to the white half door. The horse raised his neck and bowed his head as he always did when he saw Rafe. It was their greeting. Rowan held his head still for a long moment, as if assessing his owner. Then he put his head on Rafe's shoulder.

Rafe curled his arms around Rowan's neck and wept. For three days Rafe had felt a burning inside him that cut off his breath and strangled his heart. Yet even as tears slid down his cheeks and soaked the horse's mane, the pressure didn't subside. It grew worse. He nearly fell to his knees but he clung tight to Rowan.

"Sorry, boy." Rafe didn't recognize his own voice, raspy and filled with a pain he'd never known. Rafe struggled just to open his eyes. But feeling Rowan's heartbeat surging through his chest and the warmth of his breath cascading over his shoulder, Rafe suddenly felt safe in a way he hadn't in a very long time. Rafe had loved his father, but Angelo had rarely shown him physical affection. He hadn't cradled Rafe in his arms when he fell off a horse, spraining his ankle; or when he nearly drowned in the swimming pool attempting a swan dive when he was eight; or when he'd broken his collarbone during the rival football game his junior year as quarterback.

Every time he'd needed comforting, it was his mother's arms that held him. Her hands that smoothed his sweaty hair from his face, and her lips that kissed his cheek, giving him the courage to try again.

He'd tried to prove himself to his father, but nothing he'd done had ever been good enough.

Except for Rowan.

This horse had saved Rafe in his father's eyes. By the time they'd bought Rowan, Rafe had learned how to ride like a jockey, though he was much too tall and at a hundred and seventy-five pounds, far too heavy; but he had the skills. Angelo had seen that and admired it.

But now Rafe's chance to show his father just what he could do with Rowan was gone.

There was nothing left to prove. Rafe's dreams were dust in his hands.

Rowan snorted and jerked out of Rafe's embrace. He backed up and stomped his foot.

"What is it, boy?"

Rowan whinnied. He cocked his head, and Rafe read challenge and chastisement in his eyes.

"You can't know what I'm thinking," Rafe said.

Rowan walked back to the door, lowered his nose and pushed Rafe. Hard.

Rafe stumbled backward and nearly slipped on the cement. Extending his arms out to his sides, he caught his balance and righted himself. He stared at his horse. "I get it. You think I'm feeling sorry for myself. Well, I was. I have a right to. Everything has changed." Rafe's voice rose as his emotions battled between grief and anger. "I don't know what's going to happen. There's just me and Mica now to run things. That leaves no time for you or for training. Maybe it would be best if I sold you to someone who could do you justice."

Rowan stood stock-still and leveled his eyes at Rafe.

Rafe rubbed his forehead. "I must be losing it. I wouldn't do that. I promise. In the long run, you may not like staying with me, but I won't abandon you." He put his arm around Rowan and then placed his face against the horse's neck. Rafe exhaled so deeply he thought he might have expunged all the sorrow and guilt inside him. But when he inhaled again, he felt the same painful barbs clinging to his ribs. Maybe he deserved it.

It was his fault his father was dead.

Just as his dark thoughts were about to overwhelm him, Curt Wheeling came through the door carrying a bucket of feed and a plastic jug of water on his right shoulder. Curt was wearing his familiar plaid wool jacket, faded jeans, Western boots and brown work gloves. He had a horse brush sticking out of his jacket pocket and a red bandanna hanging out of his back pocket like a warning flag.

"Hi, Curt," Rafe said, releasing Rowan's neck and swiping his hands over his face to clear any evidence of tears.

"Rafe. Thought you'd be up at the main house." He put the bucket down and squinted. His bushy gray eyebrows crept together until they were almost a single shelf across Curt's forehead. "Why aren't you with your friends and brothers?"

"I needed to get away in the worst way," Rafe said. Clearly, it was a night for confession.

Pursing his lips, Curt replied, "I understand." He lowered his head and picked up the tin bucket. "Gotta feed Pegasus. Your mom said she wants to ride in the morning."

Rafe looked at Rowan. "Yeah?"

"Capital idea if you ask me. Nothing gets the cobwebs out like a ride."

"Cobwebs?"

"Yeah. Those sticky echoes of all the 'should haves' and 'would haves' that death brings around."

"You sound like you know about this kind of…feeling."

Curt walked to the next stall where Gina's purebred gray Arabian mare stood. Pegasus was only fourteen point three hands high, just barely making it past the cutoff that distinguished a pony from a horse, but she was regal and strong-boned.

There were three other Arabian horses on the farm: Rocky, the black stallion his father rode, Gabe's chestnut, Merlot, and Mica's bay, Misty. Angelo preferred Arabians because they could carry a heavier ride, possessed great endurance and were suited to many types of riding. Thanks to centuries of domestication, Arabians were willing to please, good-natured and quick to learn.

Rafe opened the stall door for Curt and helped him with the water. Curt filled Pegasus's feed sack while Rafe snatched the brush from the trainer's jacket pocket.

Running his hands over the mare's smooth white coat, he cooed and spoke softly. Rafe wasn't aware of what he said exactly, but Pegasus stretched her neck and laid her head across Rafe's shoulders.

Curt stood up and laughed. "I gotta say, Rafe, you have a way with the ladies."

"Aw, Pegasus was my first girlfriend. Weren't you, girl? She'll always be my number one."

Pegasus raised her top lip in a grin.

"See?" Rafe turned to Curt. "She knows I'm her guy."

Curt slapped Rafe on the back. "She's a good friend to you, Rafe. She wants to make you happy. Ease your pain. That's what friends are for."

Rafe put his hand on Curt's shoulder. "Like you're doing for me now. That about it?"

"Trying," Curt admitted. "So, besides missing your pappy, there's something else eatin' at you. What is it?"

Rafe looked up at Pegasus. "The horses. Rowan, specifically. With Dad gone, I won't have time to train him, and he still needs work before we can even think about the Blue Grass Stakes."

"That's weeks from now. I'll double my time with him. We'll run him at night."

"Without lights? He could injure himself."

Curt scratched his head. "I thought of that. Know that old generator your Pappy bought several years back? We never did hook it up to the house. What say I get some light bars, set them on a couple tractors and position them around the track? I could light it up like a carnival."

"It might work." Rafe rubbed his chin with the back of his hand.

"I was thinking, too, that maybe we should lower our sights a bit. Try to get Rowan used to running real races. Maybe something a little more...small-town."

"What are you getting at, Curt?"

"In a few weeks there's a charity horse race here in Indian Lake. Only a five-hundred-dollar purse. Most winners give the money back."

"Money's not the issue. Running Rowan is."

Curt snapped his finger. "Just what I was thinking!" He smiled broadly at Rafe.

For the first time since Rafe had held his dying father in his arms, unable to save him, he felt release. A lightening of the guilt that had weighed him down like a lead vest. It was only a local horse race, probably thought up by some bored socialite who wanted her name at the top of a brochure. But whatever the reasons, it was happening, and it was happening here. They had an opportunity to run Rowan and see what he could do.

Rafe couldn't get his father back, but if he could train Rowan well enough to enter him in the Blue Grass Stakes, there was a chance, small as it was, that Rafe could fulfill the dream Angelo had held most dear.

The Kentucky Derby. It was a long shot, but weren't all dreams supposed to be impossible?

Rafe opened the door to Pegasus's stall and held it for Curt. "Tell me more about this Indian Lake race, Curt."

"I've got a brochure over in the bunk-house."

"Let's check it out together." Rafe approached Rowan one last time for the night. He hugged his horse.

"Don't give up on me, boy. We just might make it yet."

CHAPTER FIVE

OLIVIA LOADED THE last of her chafing dishes, trays and plates into her van. Her mother had already taken home the first load of glassware, linens and dinnerware that Gina had rented from them.

Olivia had stayed behind to make sure they had cleaned everything thoroughly and that none of the dishes were left in any of the rooms. Partygoers were notorious for dropping silverware on the floor and kicking it under a skirted chair or sofa. Many times, she'd found wineglasses on bookshelves or windowsills. She also checked all the potted plants. It was amazing what could be found in the philodendrons. After more than a decade catering funerals, weddings and countless other functions, Olivia could spot a missing teaspoon from yards away.

Several guests were still lingering in the den playing cards, talking and using every excuse not to be alone with their sorrow. She refilled water and coffee cups for Maddie, Nate, Gabe and Liz. Liz yawned and put her head on Gabe's shoulder. He slipped his arm around her and looked at Olivia. "I think I'll put my girl to bed."

"Are you driving home tonight?"

Liz opened her eyes. "We're staying in Gabe's old room for the weekend in case Gina needs us. Nate's got surgery in the morning, and Maddie has to be at the café for the early customers. Grampa said he'll drive back, though I worry about him at this time of night."

"He'll be okay," Gabe assured her. "Maybe he should have a cup of that coffee," he said to Olivia.

"Good idea," Olivia replied, glancing over at Sam Crenshaw, who appeared very wide-awake and engrossed in a quiet conversation with Gina near the French doors to the terrace.

Olivia excused herself and carried the silver coffeepot and tray with cream and sugar over to them. "Would you like more coffee?" Olivia asked. "This is decaf, but I can get regular, Mr. Crenshaw. Gabe said you had to drive back."

"I'm not at all tired." Sam smiled. "The

decaf is just fine." He held out his cup and saucer for Olivia. "How have you been, Olivia?"

"Very well, sir. Especially now that spring is here. I can't wait to get out to the lake."

Gina looked from Sam to Olivia. "Why the lake?"

Sam touched Gina's arm affectionately and allowed his hand to remain there, his thumb gently stroking her sleeve. It was a subtle gesture, but a telling one. What was going on between Sam and Gina? And did she want to know?

Sam followed Olivia's gaze and he immediately withdrew his hand. He rushed to speak. "Olivia is a wonderful photographer. You should see her work sometime. And she and Liz are on a rowing team together. Isn't that right, Olivia?"

Olivia's eyes tracked back to Gina, who was waiting patiently for an answer to her question. "Uh, yes. Exactly. Sarah, Maddie, Liz, Isabelle and I have been sculling for years. We can hardly stand these long winters, waiting for the ice to melt. Although, I have to admit to spending a lot of time out there taking pictures in the past few months. Did either of you see the frozen fog? I'd never experienced that before. I had a one-hour window to capture it before the sun melted those fuzzy stalactites. They formed on everything—bushes, tree branches. My shots were amazing." Olivia's voice held more energy and excitement than she'd anticipated. That happened whenever she talked about her photography. Adrenaline surged through her. She would have been perfectly happy to put down the pot and tray, sit and talk to them till dawn about the photos she took—those visions of nature she'd seen while combing the edges of the winter lake. Bass swimming under thick, frosted plates of ice. She'd zoomed in on a squirrel burying nuts from the walnut trees around the Pine Tree Lodges. She had taken over two hundred shots of beavers building a dam, cutting wood with their razor-sharp teeth and flapping their flat tails in the canal that connected Lily Lake and Indian Lake. She had photos that showed geese against the full moon, lavender ribbons of dawn rippling over the chunks of icy lake water and a clouded winter sun struggling to make its presence known through a snowstorm.

But Olivia's favorite subjects were animals. They were sweet souls that did not betray or bully unless they were hungry and on the prowl for food. That was the circle of life. That was survival. She understood that. Animals were peace and danger, calm and destruction, and they fascinated her. She strove to capture their essence in photographs though she knew it would be a lifelong, elusive effort.

She blinked, realizing Sam and Gina were staring at her strangely. "Um, anyway. I guess Liz won't be doing much rowing this spring."

"Don't count her out. She told me that as soon as the doctor tells her she's fit after the baby comes, she'll be out there at the crack of dawn with you girls," Sam said.

"I'm looking forward to that. You must be so excited about the baby."

"We are!" Gina and Sam exclaimed in unison. They looked at each other and laughed.

Then just as suddenly, the smile on Gina's face disappeared.

Olivia thought she knew why. "I'm sure Mr. Barzonni was looking forward to his first grandchild."

Gina cleared her throat and rose. "I see you need more cream," she said in flat, commanding tones that told Olivia not to object. "Let me help you."

Gina took the little tray of sugar and creamer

and headed for the kitchen. Sam's eyes were glued to her. He shook himself then turned to Olivia with a crestfallen expression.

"I'll be right back," she told him.

Olivia found Gina with a carton of heavy cream in one hand, holding the refrigerator door open with the other.

"I'll do it," Olivia offered.

"Angelo didn't sanction Gabe's marriage to Liz, which you probably already know," Gina began, handing her the carton. "You and your friends are all very close, aren't you?"

"Like sisters. Closer maybe." She shrugged. "I'm an only child, so I don't actually know what it's like to have siblings. My mom was always my best friend."

Gina lifted her chin. "That's how it is with Gabe and me. Best friends. Probably because he's the oldest. I was thrilled about the baby. But Angelo—he carried his resentments around with him like the wallet in his back pocket. Always at hand. He was an unforgiving man in many ways."

"But you loved him."

"Oh, yes. That's true. But I believe there are many kinds of love. Not all people are lucky enough to find true love. You know? Gabe and Liz. They have that. Maddie and

Nate do, too. I can see the difference now that my sons are so happy."

So that was it. The sparks that danced between Gina and Sam were romantic ones. Yet she was clearly grieving her husband deeply. Olivia had catered enough funerals to last a lifetime. She'd seen bizarre, out-of-character behavior at funerals that rivaled most reality shows. Death skewed human psyches like no other crisis.

She considered the cream. "Didn't Mr. Crenshaw have a heart attack last fall?"

"He did," Gina replied quietly. "It was a frightening time for Liz, as you must know."

Olivia stepped around Gina and eased the refrigerator door wide-open. "Then maybe we should give him the fat-free half-and-half I saw in here earlier."

Gina tilted her head and studied Olivia. "You're observant. And thoughtful. Thank you for thinking of him like that."

Olivia handed the cream to Gina. "He's always meant the world to Liz. He's a lovable man."

"He is," Gina replied, taking out a second cream pitcher. She glanced up at the digital clock on the microwave. "You're about done here. Everything is cleaned up. I'll write your check."

"It's okay. You can mail it."

Gina smiled. "Would you mind doing me one last favor before you go, Olivia?"

"Not at all." Olivia smiled. "Anything."

Gina turned to the stove and picked up a foil-covered dinner plate. "I put this aside for Curt, but he didn't have time to come up for supper." Gina slipped a dish towel under the bottom of the plate.

"Curt?"

"Our horse trainer. He's still down at the stables, and I don't want him to leave without something to eat," Gina said with a little shake to her head as she held the plate out to Olivia.

Olivia gulped back a lump of fear. Her eyes tracked over to the window, where she could see the lights still shining in the stable.

Olivia took the plate from Gina, hoping her hands wouldn't shake the roast beef right off. She bit her lip; maybe physical pain would jolt her out of the memory of her father shoving wads of bills at the betting-cage teller.

"Just follow the paved bricks down there. I see that Rafe turned on the walk lights. I'd do it myself, but I—"

Olivia interrupted. "It's no bother. Honestly, I'm happy to help." She forced a smile.

"Oh, and when you're down there, give a pet to my Pegasus for me, will you?" Gina put her hand to her cheek. "Silly of me. You're not afraid of horses, are you?"

"Horses?" No, she wasn't afraid of the most gorgeous creatures on earth. In fact, she adored them and had loved them all her life. It was the gambling they represented that she abhorred. "I like horses. They're some of my favorite photography subjects."

"Oh, my goodness. Then my Arabians will delight you and that talented eye of yours. My Pegasus is nearly pure white, though technically, she's a gray. Pink skin. Blue eyes. A vision."

"She sounds gorgeous. May I take a picture of her? I would be so grateful. I hardly ever get the chance to be around horses, though I went to Sarah Jensen's dressage classes when we were kids."

"You ride, then?"

"Oh, no. We couldn't afford the lessons, but I took my little camera and photographed Sarah. The instructor always let me pet the horses and talk to them." Olivia felt the rhapsody of those special times chime through her heart. She remembered country drives when she would cajole her mother to stop each time she saw a horse and let her take a picture. Even then, Olivia felt the conflict between loving the animals and despising the task they were forced to do. She wanted them to run free. "I've always wanted to learn, but I—well, I just haven't. I have my digital camera in my car..."

"Of course, dear. Just tell Curt that I said you could visit with Pegasus."

Olivia thanked her, and Gina left the kitchen with the cream pitchers.

Olivia took off her chef's coat and put on the black zip-up jacket she'd brought. All day she'd had her hair clipped up on top of her head. It kept her long, thick locks out of the way, but the tight twist always gave her a slight headache by the end of the day. When she pulled out the clip, the release was instantaneous. She shook her hair out and let it fall down her back as she massaged her scalp.

"That's better. Freedom," Olivia said to herself as she slipped out the back door and headed for her van. Her camera was in its case on the floor of the passenger side. The rest of the van was stuffed with catering utensils and serving pieces. There was only room for her to drive.

She checked her lens and looped the wide black strap around her neck, pulling her hair out from under it.

The single door to the stable was unlocked, so Olivia turned the knob and stepped inside. "Hello? Curt?" she said as she shut the door behind her. It was considerably warmer in here than it was outside. She was surprised at how roomy the structure was. To her left were a tack room and a meeting room of some kind, with dark, wood-paneled walls, green carpet, several red plaid wing chairs with matching footstools, a brown leather sofa and a large plasma screen television. There was also a roll-top desk and shelves filled with books and framed photographs.

"Hello?" Olivia continued walking down the corridor between the horse stalls. "Gina sent you some dinner."

At the sound of her voice, four horses came to the edge of their stalls and stuck their heads out over the closed half doors. Olivia put the plate down on a small table and moved toward them, smiling.

To her right was a midnight-black Arabian with a braided mane. He had a thick neck and wider chest than the chestnut horse in the stall next to him. Olivia placed her hand on the Arabian's neck and said, "Aren't you a handsome thing?" Then she noticed the nameplate on his stall. *Rocky.*

Olivia smiled. "I'll bet you're a real fighter, Rocky. The Italian stallion, huh?"

The horse neighed as if answering her question. He snorted and then backed away from her and went about eating his dinner.

Olivia clicked off several shots of Rocky, then she moved down to the chestnut horse, Merlot. Next was the bay, Misty.

She took photographs of all three before spinning around to see the strikingly beautiful, all-white Pegasus. "You do look like you thundered down from the heavens, don't you, girl?"

Olivia clicked a dozen pictures of Pegasus before she moved back up the line to Rowan's stall. Unlike the others, he had not displayed curiosity over hearing a stranger's voice when she entered the stable. He'd hung back and was standing in the shadows of his stall.

She leaned over the gate and peered at him. "Whose horse are you?"

Rowan stood very still, his brown eyes

assessing her, weighing her intentions with each word she spoke.

"You're quite the cautious one. I like that. You want to be sure before you make your move. I don't blame you. I've always thought it was wise to take my time. Size up the situation. And the opponent." She lifted her camera to her face. "Except that I'm not the enemy."

The second she peered through the viewfinder, framed him in what was to become her photograph, her breath caught in her lungs. Chills swept across her skin. She lowered the camera with stiff arms, too stunned to talk. He was magnificent.

Rowan lifted his snout a few inches and cocked it at an angle, giving her an imperious gaze. Haughty and self-assured, he sauntered toward her.

He was sleek and muscular, with eyes that were wise, intelligent and held no quarter for fools. Rowan had waited for her to move toward him first. He didn't seek her out just because she was human. He'd waited for her like a king awaits an audience with his subjects.

His eyes never wavered from her face as he slowly approached her. This was different from those moments in the wild when animals would pause to stare at her. She wasn't a curiosity to him. She wasn't just being observed. It was as if they were connecting on some deeper level.

Friends.

The single word skittered across Olivia's brain.

"I'll be your friend," she said aloud.

He hitched up his head.

"You're so beautiful," she whispered. Then she picked up her camera.

Olivia's finger clicked off a dozen shots so fast she knew she'd caught his every breath. He swished his tail and pressed his snout against her camera as if daring her to put it away.

She lowered the camera and without another thought, she put her arms around his neck and hugged him. Feeling her cheek against his throat, she was amazed at the emotions racing through her. "I meant what I said. I want to be your friend."

CHAPTER SIX

RAFE WAS STILL HOLDING the Indian Lake horse race brochure when he left the barn. He'd promised Curt he would close down the stable and lock up so the trainer could go straight to bed.

Rafe had just opened the stable door when he heard someone speaking.

He couldn't make out what was said, but it was definitely a woman's voice that lilted through his ears. It was a sweet sound, and it floated toward him like a lullaby. Then he heard the woman say Rowan's name with esteem and playfulness. He didn't understand. His mother, Liz and Maddie were all up at the house, and no other women knew his horse. And this voice was totally unfamiliar to him.

He inched forward, curious about the intruder.

Then he saw her. Her head was turned away from him, a waterfall of lush brown hair falling down her back, glistening with gold-and-red highlights. She was standing on her tiptoes, leaning far enough over the gate to Rowan's stall that he wondered if she knew she was in danger of falling right in.

He rushed up, grabbed her by the waist and pulled her back.

"Careful there!" he exclaimed as she tried to kick free of his grasp.

"What are you doing?"

"I thought you were going to fall," he said. She straightened up and yanked the waistband of her jacket into place, but not before he saw a band of creamy skin.

"I can take care of myself! And I certainly wasn't about to fall into a horse stall. I'm not stupid," she snapped.

Where was that musical voice he'd heard a minute ago? Was there someone else in his stable he didn't know about?

He fought a smile. He didn't know who she was, but her brown eyes blazed at him as if he was the one off base here. He lifted his palms apologetically. "Hey, I just wanted to help."

She snorted.

"I'm Rafe, by the way." He kept staring at her. She was familiar, but that gloomy fog in his brain refused to dissipate.

The woman gave him a strange look. "Your

mom wanted me to bring supper down here for Curt," she said slowly, pointing behind him to the table. He glanced back, and sure enough, there was a plate of food covered in foil.

Then it hit him. "The cookie girl!"

"Pardon me?"

"*Macarons*. Or whatever they're called. You're the woman my mother hired."

"Olivia," she said. He could swear her tone held disappointment.

He grabbed her hand and shook it. "I knew I recognized you."

"Um…you did?" She was staring at him as if he was nuts. Which he probably was at the moment. He hadn't carried on a coherent conversation with anyone since his father died. "What I meant was that I didn't know who you were when I first walked in here, but yes, I remember you now."

Those eyes. Who could forget those eyes?

She raised her arm and gestured toward the stalls. "Your mother told me it was okay for me to meet her horse and maybe take a few pictures. I didn't see Curt or anyone else out here, so I sort of…introduced myself to all your horses."

It was cute, the way she stumbled over her

apology. She had a pert mouth with a full bottom lip that was naturally pink. No lipstick. In fact, he didn't see much makeup at all on her. Her cheeks were red from embarrassment or being caught red-handed; he didn't know which. He'd have to get his mother to corroborate her story later.

"I love horses," she explained. "I've always thought they were God's most majestic animal."

"Don't tell that to any cat lover," he joked, shifting his weight. "So, you ride, then?"

"Your mother asked me the same thing. I don't. But I was around horses a lot as a kid with my friend Sarah Jensen—Bosworth now—when we went to her dressage classes." She lowered her gaze as if deep in thought. "There were other times I was around horses, too." She paused for a long moment.

Rafe couldn't imagine what was going on with her, but he noticed that her shoulders slumped and a frown plowed across her forehead. Whatever she was remembering, it wasn't good.

"I'm not sure I'd be good at riding," she continued.

"You just need instruction and practice," he said brightly, hoping to lift her spirits. "You certainly don't seem to be afraid of horses. For most people, that's half the battle."

"Afraid." She said the word as if considering its meaning. "Not exactly." She smiled at him, but it was forced. Her eyes were guarded; she was definitely holding something back.

His own curiosity surprised him. He wanted to know what that something was. Olivia was a total stranger to him, yet he was responding to her as if he'd known her for some time. Maybe it was their shared love of horses. Maybe his grief-torn heart just wanted a distraction from the reality of his father's death. If he was guilty of using her to ease his pain, he didn't care. At this moment he felt better. He felt as if he was breaking out of prison.

"Is it all right that I took a couple photos in here? I'm a photographer. An amateur. I mean, not professional by any means," she equivocated.

He took in the expensive-looking Pentax camera suspended from a strap around her neck. "I don't know anything about cameras. But I'm guessing you didn't buy that at Walmart."

Her ivory skin turned blotchy crimson-red. She touched the zoom lens daintily.

He didn't know what trigger he'd just pulled, but something had hit home. He was fascinated.

"This is my fourth trade-up since I finished high school. It's a 645D and has forty megapixels, and I know it looks big compared to a lot of cameras these days, but it takes amazing pictures." She glanced up at him and smiled sheepishly. "Sorry, I get carried away talking about my cameras and lenses. Equipment is critical to me. I'm constantly either adding to or improving my stash."

"Really? I just snap with my iPhone. That's it. Moment captured. I'm done."

The look she flashed him was simultaneously empathetic and condescending. He didn't know why he was trying to impress her, but he was. But he'd messed up on that one. He'd have to backpedal to cover up his mistake.

"Phones are good for those everyday moments," she conceded. "But if you're pursuing photography as an art—like Edward Burtynsky or Sebastião Salgado, not that I'm comparing myself to them—you need cameras so sophisticated and accurate that the photos they take bring the viewer into a world they never knew existed. That's what I'm striving for, anyway."

Rafe was speechless. She'd put him in his place. That didn't happen often. In fact, he couldn't remember the last time he'd cared what anyone thought about his opinions… aside from his dad. It had certainly been a long time since he'd wanted to impress a woman. Was that what was going on? He wasn't exactly sure. His thoughts were such a jumble, he wouldn't be surprised if he couldn't remember his birthday. "That's some kind of ambition," he responded, shaking his head and shoving his hand in his back pocket. "Did you study them in college?"

"I didn't go to college."

He guessed from the growing flame in her cheeks he'd hit on a sore subject. *Strike number two*, he thought. He had to recover this. "Apparently, you didn't need to. I'd say self-taught and self-motivated suits you."

"Thank you," she said, and the crimson in her cheeks faded to a blush. She lowered her eyes, and he could see the shadow of long, dark lashes against her skin. When she met his eyes again, he felt his breath catch. "I guess I do have high aspirations, but the way

I see it, if I don't shoot for the stars, I might never gain the moon."

"And what moon would that be?" He was delving into some intimate waters here. He didn't care. He wanted to know more about her.

"I'm hoping to become a photojournalist someday. I've been building my portfolio for years and perfecting my skills. I've taken some classes here and there at the college branches around the county, but it's hard to squeeze them in with the catering and keeping the deli going."

"The deli…" Rafe slapped his palm against his thigh. "The Indian Lake Deli. Now I remember my mom telling me. Sorry, I'm not a customer. Frankly, I don't get to town all that often. For fun, I mean."

"What do you do for fun?"

"Ride Rowan," he replied instantly, glancing over at his horse.

Rowan had come to the stall door when Rafe entered the stable and at the mention of his name, the horse snorted and whinnied.

"Hey, boy!" Rafe walked over to the stall and opened the door, letting him walk out and join the conversation.

"Are you...a jockey?" she asked with a tight set to her lips.

Funny, he could have sworn her hands had started to tremble, but she clamped them both over her camera before he could be sure.

What was it with this woman? One minute she was as effervescent as bubbles in champagne, the next she looked as if she was about to blow the cork off. Did the horses make her nervous, or was it him?

He decided to try some levity, so he chuckled and hoped it wasn't too forced. "I could never be a jockey. I'm too heavy and too long." He motioned to her, but she seemed to recoil. "Come pet him."

"I shouldn't." She remained glued to the spot.

Rafe leaned forward and smiled at her. "C'mon, you were practically throwing yourself at him before. It's okay. Really."

"Okay," she replied finally, stepping closer and lifting her hand.

Rowan moved his head under her palm, forcing her to pet him.

Rafe smiled appreciatively. "He likes you."

"He's not this friendly with everyone?"

"Quite the opposite. My mom has never ridden him and he won't even let her brush him. It's always been me, my dad or Curt. I've joked that Rowan is a misanthrope."

"Apparently not." Olivia laughed as she gazed lovingly at Rowan. "He's so beautiful. I've never seen a horse this gorgeous."

Rowan nudged Olivia's neck, forcing her to pay more attention to him than to Rafe. If Rafe didn't know better, he'd say that Rowan was jealous.

Olivia put her arms around the horse's neck for the second time that evening and kissed his nose. Her eyes traveled over his body, assessing him the way a sculptor would judge a model.

Rowan preened under her inspection, and Rafe allowed her the long moment of adoration for his horse. He watched her slowly make her way along his length, whispering and cooing to Rowan as she circled his haunches and tail. If she hadn't told Rafe she didn't ride, he never would have guessed. She was a natural. She reminded him of himself when he brushed or bathed Rowan. She even leaned down to lift his leg and inspect his hoof. He noticed how she used both hands to hold his leg, cradling it as if it was a precious treasure.

Of course, Rowan was Rafe's prize. But

Olivia didn't know that. She only acted in concert with what she sensed and felt. Rafe found that very endearing.

"You must have some kind of gift with animals," Rafe said as Olivia stood and looked at him over Rowan's back.

"Why do you say that?"

"He's never this quiet for this long. Usually, he's pushing me out the door to take him for a ride. Or a race."

Olivia's neck went stiff. "Race?"

Rafe chuckled. "You seemed so familiar with him, I thought you realized Rowan is a Thoroughbred. A racehorse."

"Right. Your mother told me," she replied with so much deliberation he sensed something was not quite right. "He's expensive, then." It was more of an observation than a question, so Rafe didn't take offense.

"He will be when he wins a few races. We got shut out of a few things lately because..." Reality reared its head again. Rafe felt that stone in his heart turn ice-cold. Heavy and foreign as it was, it had taken up residence and he didn't know what he could do to dissolve it. His eyes traveled over Olivia's lovely face; for a few moments she'd helped him forget. Brief as they were, he was grateful. He was amazed at the alteration he'd felt, like spring after an empty, frigid winter.

"Because of your dad?" Olivia finished for him. He nodded. "Angelo liked to race horses, as well?"

"Very much. More than me, actually. He was obsessed with racing."

"Obsessed," she repeated. The light in her eyes seemed to dim, and her smile disappeared from her face. Her demeanor reminded him of an animal reacting to a looming predator. Fight or flight.

What had he said? They were just talking about the horses. She folded her arms across her chest and gazed absently at the line of stalls, lost in her own world. Was it too soon for him to ask what she was thinking? Why would the mention of horse racing bother her?

She'd dropped her hands to her sides and was no longer touching Rowan.

"You look…sad," Rafe said carefully.

"I guess I am." She came back around and kissed Rowan's nose. She looked at Rafe with the unhappiest eyes he'd ever seen. "I have to go."

"You can come back," he blurted. "To see Rowan, I mean. I think he likes you."

"And I like him." She smiled, though it did little to decrease the melancholy in her eyes.

Who was she thinking about? Rafe's curiosity was dusted with a tinge of jealousy, which confused him. He barely knew Olivia—and that was the problem. He most definitely wanted to know a whole lot more about her.

"It's been a long day. I'm beat." She exhaled and rolled her shoulders.

"Sure," he replied. It had been a long day for the Barzonni family, too, but she'd been the one doing most of the work. He turned to walk her to the door.

"Thanks for introducing me to your... Rowan." She smiled again and this time there was no trace of sadness or tension. Just pure joy. He was mesmerized.

"Anytime," he managed to say. "You're welcome back anytime."

As she continued to gaze up at him, he found himself swimming in her brown eyes. He had no idea what was the matter with him, but he couldn't talk. He could only stare.

"Thanks again, Rafe," she said and walked out the door.

"Bye, Olivia."

As she turned, her camera flashed in the moonlight.

"Olivia," he called.

"Yes?"

He walked toward her. "Those photos you took. They're just for you, right?"

"Yeah. Just for me."

"Good." He smiled at her. "Enjoy them." He gave her a little two-fingered salute.

"I will. Thanks."

Impulsively, Rafe bent and kissed her cheek. Her skin was smooth and cool like fine marble, but soft as down. He closed his eyes. If he lingered, he could get addicted to this bliss.

"Bye," she whispered and walked into the shadows.

As she disappeared from his sight, Rafe felt lost again.

What was he doing? He should go after her. Walk her to her car. Maybe he could hold the door for her. Hold her. Maybe kiss her again. Really kiss her.

Rowan sauntered up and nudged him, pushing Rafe against the door. The handle slipped out of his hand and the door slammed shut.

Rafe turned around, hand on his hip. "So that's the way it is, huh? You like her, too?"

Rowan's head shot up and he whinnied.

Rafe burst out laughing. He patted Rowan's neck and led him back to his stall. "Come on, boy. I need to close up this stable."

CHAPTER SEVEN

OLIVIA PULLED HER van into her spot in the old carriage-house-turned-garage. All the lights in the main house were off, which meant Mrs. Osborn, her landlady, had gone to bed.

Olivia let herself into her apartment, dumped her purse on the little round table in her kitchen and turned on the light. Her camera still hung around her neck. Olivia often had to remind herself to remove the camera when she was at work or going into a store. It was like an extra limb, an appendage that brought her artistry into being.

Carefully, she slipped the strap off and set the camera next to her purse.

Next, she filled a glass of water from the antique faucet and watered the potted herb garden she'd been growing all winter in the large kitchen window. On Sunday she'd take her seedlings out to the raised garden she'd had Luke Bosworth build for her last summer and plant the herbs she and her mother would use in their special dishes all summer long. Picking up the rosemary bush and smelling its pungent leaves made her smile. Olivia loved rosemary, sage and mint, and often boiled them to fill her rooms with natural fragrance.

Olivia rubbed a few leaves between her fingers and then washed her hands with lavender soap to remove the horse smell.

She lifted her palms to her nose. There was still a trace of Rowan. She closed her eyes, but all she could see was Rafe. She pictured his arctic-blue eyes, flashing with a fire so fierce and compelling that it took her breath away.

When she'd seen him in Gina's kitchen, she'd thought he was good-looking. But between chatting with him at dinner and their moment in the stable, something had changed. She felt drawn to him like a magnet to steel. And she couldn't get him out of her mind.

She slumped down on the wrought-iron antique ice cream chair beside the table and dropped her head into her hands. "Just how big a fool did I make of myself?"

When he'd found her in his stable and she

was making friends with his horse...how had that looked, really? Like she was trespassing?

Even now, embarrassment flamed her cheeks. She'd been trying to get just the right light on Rowan as he "posed" for her in the back of his stall. She must have looked ridiculous.

He probably saw my butt hanging over the gate, hair swirling all over my face... I was acting like a complete idiot.

"That must have been attractive," she moaned sarcastically. Not that it mattered. She'd never date a gambler, anyway. She probably wouldn't even see him again. He'd said he rarely came to town, rarely did anything for fun....

Her breath clung to her ribs.

The baby shower. She'd see Rafe again at Gabe and Liz's baby shower.

She was filled with anticipation. And dread. She wanted to see him in the worst way, but she also hoped they would never cross paths. Somehow, meeting Rafe had unearthed the most painful parts of her past. Suddenly, she was sharing her every move with the shadow of the terrified child she'd once been. She remembered hearing her mother's sobs late at night, when there wasn't enough money for food or their rent was late. She despised the mean kids at school who had mocked her because her clothes came from the Goodwill and she'd outgrown her shoes. She didn't go to ballet or camp. She didn't join the Girl Scouts because the uniforms were too expensive. All because of her father's addiction to gambling.

Gambling had destroyed Olivia's young life. It had damaged her mother so greatly that Julia had never wanted to remarry. Julia didn't trust anyone, and she'd taught Olivia to operate in the same manner. They depended on each other. No others were allowed into their little circle.

There were thin scabs over Olivia's childhood wounds, and Rafe's presence was opening them up. He was more dangerous than any man Olivia could have conjured.

Rafe had been so quiet coming into the stable and she'd been so immersed in the friendship she was building with Rowan that a siren could have gone off and she wouldn't have noticed. It had always been that way with her and animals. Olivia couldn't go for a walk down Maple Boulevard without everyone's dog rushing up to her and begging for a pet as if they were long-lost friends. Her mother said it was because she was an only child and she didn't have enough human family or friends; according to Julia, animals were drawn to Olivia's lonely heart. Olivia wondered if Rafe had seen that her heart was lonely. Was his? Or was he content with his life with his horses, his family and the farm?

Underlying all her speculations was the sense that he was dangerous. Not to others, but to her. And he always would be.

Olivia rose and walked down the hall to her bedroom, switching on the two bedside lamps she'd bought at a garage sale. She'd remade the lamp shades using a red-and-white French toile and then rimmed the bottom edges with dangling red and crystal beads she'd found at a fabric store in Indianapolis. It had taken her two years to talk her landlady into letting her paint the walls deep raspberry-red, but she needed a dramatic backdrop for her photographs. Her best work from the past two years hung in black lacquered frames, but already she knew she'd improved from when she'd printed them.

Olivia had also sewn the red-and-white toile bedspread, Roman shades, pillow shams and dust ruffle on her double bed several years ago. She loved the pastoral depictions of country maids and gentlemen riding horses.

As she looked at the toile, her eyes zeroed in on a horse-riding scene. Rafe's face floated into her mind.

What was it with this guy?

There was some kind of connection between them. Olivia knew he'd felt it, too. The kiss he'd placed on her cheek had said it all.

Olivia flopped back on her bed and stared at the ceiling fan. "Rafe. Raphael. That's an angel's name," she mused. She hoped the angels were helping him now with his grief; no matter how silly she'd looked to him or what they'd shared tonight, Rafe was going to have a lot to deal with in the days and weeks to come.

Olivia had never been through a family death. Her mother's parents were still alive and her paternal grandparents had died before she was born. Her aunts, uncles and cousins were all alive and well.

But her father had left her.

Death was final, but abandonment offered the double-edged promise that things could change. The person could come back.

Olivia knew death was inevitable; she'd

have to deal with it one day. But she would never let anyone abandon her again.

That was why she couldn't even *think* about getting closer to Rafe. His love of horse racing made him far too much like her father. Although, if she was honest with herself, it wasn't just that superficial similarity that scared her. She hadn't seen any signs that he was a gambling addict. But Rafe was the kind of man who could mesmerize her and charm her and eventually, she was the one who would slide into addiction. She was her father's daughter, after all. Hadn't it been proven that the predisposition for addiction was genetic? If she was smart, she'd keep her distance. Play it safe. She imagined a band of caution tape marking the line she dared not cross.

She touched her cheek. She could still feel the zing that had gone through her when his lips had caressed her there.

Something had happened in that stable tonight. Something…magical. Life-changing. But what exactly was it?

She threw her forearm over her eyes to help her concentrate, but she couldn't figure it out. Her emotions had pinged all over the place from her initial reactions to Rowan to her last impression of Rafe.

"Hmm. Rowan," she mumbled, pushing herself up onto her elbows. She looked over at her computer, which sat on an old cherry-wood table she'd bought from Hazel Martin after her husband died. She wanted to upload her photos right away so she could revisit that enchanting moment in the stable.

Scooting off the bed, she went to the kitchen and retrieved her camera. Back in her room, she sat on a small walnut chair—also from Hazel's collection—and connected her camera to her laptop.

She clicked through shots of Rocky's imperious gaze, of Misty and Merlot. When her first shot of Rowan came up, she sat back with a gasp.

Rowan's eyes reached out to her from the screen as if he were in the room with her.

Goose bumps scampered across her arms, down her back and straight to her toes. This was no ordinary horse.

Her mother always told her not to ignore reactions like this. There were times when destiny came to call, Julia often said. Her mother was a strong believer in fate.

Olivia indulged her mother, but had never

really taken her seriously on this topic. Yet something about this moment—this whole night—brought her mother's words to mind.

Olivia glanced around the room, and her chills intensified. Hanging on her walls were at least ten black-and-white shots of horses. There were horses in her drapes and bedspread. And now there was Rowan staring back at her from the computer screen.

She opened up her email and typed in Sarah's address. It was only right that she share this auspicious moment with her best friend.

Sarah,
I want to thank you for including me all those years ago when you went to dressage class. I know now that my love of horses came from those days. Tonight I met Rafe Barzonni's horse, Rowan, who is the most special animal I've had the honor to encounter. I just wanted to thank you. I'm including the shot I took of him so you can see how magnificent he is. See you soon.
Love, Olivia.

She attached the photo and pressed Send. Olivia finished uploading the rest of her photos, then she yawned and stretched. She turned off the computer, went to the bathroom and took a hot shower.

Wearing blue plaid flannel pajamas—the old house was notoriously chilly until well into May—she climbed into bed.

Her last thoughts before sleep were not of Rowan, but of Rafe.

CHAPTER EIGHT

RAFE WIPED HIS sweaty face with the blue bandanna he had tied to the tractor's steering column. He'd been plowing fields since dawn and had only taken a half hour break for lunch. He was a bit surprised that his arms and shoulders ached as much as they did, but considering he hadn't been all that physically active this past winter, he should have guessed that spring plowing and planting would take a toll.

He took a long slug of water and then squirted some on his face. The sun had stayed out all day and warmed the spring air to nearly seventy degrees. Rafe was dealing with the upper slopes where they would plant soybeans this year while Mica plowed the flat fields for tomatoes.

Rafe finished the last row and then turned the tractor around and headed toward the barn. He was driving the old orange Allis Chalmers tractor his father had bought in

1979 before any of the boys were born. Rafe had oiled it, cleaned the engine and checked the tires himself. When he'd announced his intention to use it this season, Mica had laughed at him. Rafe had ignored his brother as he changed the spark plugs and put in a new battery. It had taken him twice as long as it should have because his hands were shaking.

Then Mica had touched his shoulder. "Sorry, man. I understand. You do whatever you want." Mica had slapped his shoulder again, walked over to the new John Deere tractor he preferred and started the engine. "I'll see you back here for lunch."

Rafe had waved then continued working on his father's old tractor. Once the spark plugs were connected, he'd climbed up into the seat, turned the key and smiled as the engine roared to life. Rafe had heaved a deep breath. His old man's tractor was going to plow a field or two once again.

Rafe had pressed his lips together to keep from releasing the sob that was perpetually stuck in his throat. Then he'd pushed the stick shift into gear, and the tractor leaped forward out the open barn door.

Now, at the end of the day, Rafe's heart was lighter. Hard work helped to ease his grief.

As he drove back to the barn, he couldn't help but think how out of character it was for him to be so sentimental. Until his father's death, his life had been about the present and his plans for the future. For him to spend an entire day plowing on his dad's rusty old tractor would have been unheard-of a few months ago.

For the first time ever, Rafe didn't want to think about tomorrow or next week. He wished he could go back. Not far back, but just far enough so he could tell Angelo one more time that he loved him; maybe push a little bit harder on his chest and revive him, like he'd done with the tractor. New spark plugs. Maybe that was all Angelo had needed.

"Stop kidding yourself, Rafe." He drove the tractor into the barn and turned off the engine. He banged his fist against the steering wheel. "He's gone. Gone!" he yelled. "And he's not coming back," he whispered, lowering his head onto the steering wheel.

A rumbling engine approached, and Mica pulled the John Deere into the space next to Rafe.

"Hey, buddy. You okay?" Mica asked, jumping down from his upholstered seat.

Rafe lifted his head and stared at his brother. "Sure. Yeah. Fine."

"No, you're not. I understand, Rafe. But we're all in this together. You're not the only one hurting. I miss him, too."

Rafe climbed down from the tractor and hugged his brother. "You're right." He released him. "How are you handling it?"

"About the same as you. I cry when I think nobody's watching." Mica tried to smile but failed. His eyes, the same clear blue as Rafe's, swept across the barn. "Nothing will be the same. I just hope we can keep the farm going. It won't be easy...."

"What are you thinking?"

"That we hire some help. I talked to Joe Ames over at the Grange meeting last night. His farm is west of ours. Well, he sold out last fall—you remember that, right? He and his son moved north of the Crenshaw vineyard, but now that it's spring, they're looking for work."

"It makes a lot of sense, Mica. They know the land around here, so they'd be familiar with the quirks of our fields. The rainfall, the soil makeup, the high winds we can get."

"They know it all. Their farm was quite

successful until Joe's wife got sick. He told me it was worth every penny because she's fine now."

"Thank God for that," Rafe said.

Mica put his arm around Rafe's shoulder. "We have to keep the farm going top speed, Rafe."

"I never said we shouldn't."

"I know, but I can tell how much you'd like to spend all your time with Rowan and Curt." He glanced toward the stable as they left the barn. "Dad sure would be proud if you put a trophy up on the mantel."

"He would," Rafe replied, his voice weighted with sadness. "I think about it all the time. How happy he was about Rowan making that turn and beating his time. He was so excited it brought on his heart attack."

"Rafe. You and Rowan had nothing to do with Dad's death. It was his time. Frankly, I was shocked he made it through Christmas."

"What?"

"Dad tried to hide how bad off he was, but I saw it. He couldn't make it up the stairs to bed most nights. He had to stop halfway to catch his breath. He pushed himself constantly. He was so stubborn. He wouldn't see the doctor, and he sure as heck wouldn't do anything Nate told him to do. It was that Barzonni defiance, you know?"

"Yeah, I do. No matter what it was, he always wanted to do it his way and no other."

"Thank God I'm not like that," Mica said, taking out his cell phone.

"Who says?" Rafe teased. He pointed at the phone. "What are you doing?"

"Calling Mom to see how long till supper and if she needs help with it. You should go visit your horse." Mica paused as Gina answered. "Hey, Mom. How's supper coming? Can I help? Sure… No, we're not in any hurry. Rafe's gonna ride Rowan for a bit. I'll be up in a minute." He tapped the screen to end the call.

"Give Rowan my regards," Mica said, grinning. His phone buzzed with a text and Rafe took the moment to saunter away toward the stable.

His heart lifted. He couldn't believe he actually had time for a ride.

He had almost reached the stable when his brother raced up to him, calling his name. Rafe turned around.

"I think you should see this," Mica said, waving his phone.

"What is it?"

"Scott Abbott sent me this link to his Facebook page. Seems some photograph of Rowan just went viral."

RAFE BURNED WITH anger as he wheeled his truck into the empty parking space in front of the Indian Lake Deli. The umbrellas were closed and the outside chairs had been put away for the night. He noticed the tables were chained to the two trees out front.

He frowned. Despite his anger, he didn't like the idea that any Indian Lake businessperson had to chain their equipment up, but it made sense. Criminals were everywhere.

He should know. He'd come here to confront a thief.

The sign on the front door read Closed, but the deli was unlocked. Rafe let himself in. Most of the lights in the dining section had been turned off, but the kitchen and grill area were brightly lit.

He saw Olivia behind the counter, sweeping the floor. She was whistling along to the music on the CD player as she bent down with the dustpan.

Rafe leaned over the front counter, watching her use a hand brush to get every grain of dirt and stray parsley leaf. He placed his palms on the butcher block, wondering when she'd notice him.

When she straightened up, her eyes went wide and she nearly screamed.

"I locked that door!"

"Apparently not," he said.

"I didn't hear you come in. Quiet as always," she said. "And since you've never stepped foot in our deli before, you must want something." She folded her arms across her chest and met him glare for glare. "Not a Reuben sandwich, I'm guessing."

He was restless and jittery as he held up his cell phone to show her the Facebook post of Rowan. "You want to explain to me what you think you're doing? I specifically asked you not to share your photographs of my horse with anyone. You lied to me. You told me no one would see them. They were for your personal enjoyment. Remember?"

"I don't understand," she said, reaching for the phone.

He snatched it back. "No, you don't."

"What is that?"

"My brother tells me Rowan has gone viral. He's being Tweeted all over the country. Facebook. Instagram. Pinterest. I don't use any of those sites, Olivia. So, you tell me how this happened."

She shook her head. "I didn't do this..." she started to say and then slapped her palm over her open mouth. "Oh, no. It was Sarah."

"Oh, so Sarah's in on this, too?"

"I mean, I sent the photo to Sarah when I got home from your place. I was just thanking her for introducing me to horses all those years ago. I was so excited about meeting Rowan that I guess I got carried away. I'm so sorry, Rafe."

"You should be! Do you have any idea the problem you've caused?"

"This is all my fault, I know."

"You're right about that!" He shouted so loudly that Olivia jumped.

"I said I'm sorry, Rafe. But this is a simple misunderstanding. I don't understand how my photograph could hurt you."

He swiped his palm over his face, making his frustration clear to her. "Rowan is very special to my father and me. We both knew the moment we saw him that with the right training, we might have a winner. Rowan was my father's dream. I intend to give my dad that win—no matter what." He exhaled so heavily, the stack of napkins next to the register fluttered. "The damage has been done."

"Rowan is special, Rafe. I saw that, too. But what damage are you talking about? I'm sorry I disrespected your wishes, but how is this a bad thing? I want to know so I can help make it up to you."

"My dad and I were hoping to enter him in trial races for the Kentucky Derby. I didn't want any kind of publicity or news about him coming out until I was ready. He still needs training and experience. He's not as lean as he could be. Not as muscular as he will be after Curt and I get through with him. On the day he makes his debut, I want to set the judges and reporters on their ear. I want him to be the best he can possibly be."

OLIVIA FELT WRETCHED. She'd promised Rafe she wouldn't share her shots of Rowan, but in her excitement she hadn't thought about the consequences. Then again, she'd never have expected Sarah to post her photo. On the other hand, Sarah, Maddie and Liz were some of her most dedicated and enthusiastic supporters when it came to her photography. Over the years, they'd done everything from featuring her collection at charity auctions to hosting a gallery show in downtown Indian Lake to putting her in touch with the editor of the *Chicago Tribune*. None of it had helped Olivia's career. The *Tribune* wasn't hiring photographers. The gallery showing only sold two photographs, and the charity auction didn't reach the kind of people who could advance her quest. Still, she appreciated her friends' dedication.

And as bad as she felt, Olivia had to admit that Sarah's mistake could be the biggest boost her photography career had ever had. *Her* photo had gone viral? What were people seeing in it that was any different than the hundreds of thousands of shots of horses out there? She herself had identified something ethereal and exceptional about Rowan. Racing potential aside, maybe it was that magical quality that Rafe wanted to keep for himself.

Olivia knew she deserved every bit of his anger. If someone had posted one of her private photographs, she would have been livid. But she wasn't sure she bought his argument about publicity.

"Rafe, most of the people who saw these posts aren't horse people or race lovers.

They're just people. Moms. Dads. Friends. I think you're getting worked up about something that may not impact you at all."

He looked as if he wanted to chop her head off. "I don't like it, Olivia! This horse was important to my dad."

There, she thought. So this was about his grief. If she was ever going to be his friend, it should start today. "Rafe," she said gently. "Rowan is magnificent already. A photo won't take that away."

"He can be better," Rafe retorted sharply. "Look, I can't expect a—a caterer—to understand what I've spent a lifetime learning. Rowan isn't just a horse. He's a champion. He has incredible genes."

"I believe that," she said, choosing to ignore his condescension.

"Good. Great. Then you'll control your urge to try to make yourself seem special to your girlfriends by using my horse."

Okay, that was it. Olivia put her hands on her hips and marched around the bakery case and right up to Rafe. "Look, you bonehead, I did nothing of the kind." She tilted her head back to glare at him. "Coming here to insult me doesn't get that post off social media. It doesn't help your horse win a race. What it does is tell me you chose me to be angry at today. Bingo! I'm the winner. I'm truly sorry that your dad died, but that doesn't give you the right to come into my restaurant and bawl me out for something unintentional. It was stupid—I'll give you that. And I can promise you it won't happen again. Ever."

Olivia stepped back. She had a crick in her neck from how close she'd been standing. It was the first time she realized how tall he was. "Now, please leave."

"Fine." He stomped away. Just as he reached the door, he swiveled around. "You're right. I am angry about my dad. And I did take it out on you. That wasn't fair. I'm sorry for that. Goodbye, Olivia."

"Goodbye, Rafe."

Olivia walked to the picture window, and through the gold lettering, she watched him get in his truck and drive off. She went to the door and locked it. Double-checked it to make sure it was secure.

Rafe had acted like a jerk tonight. Yet she didn't feel maligned. If anything, she felt compelled to run after him and give him a hug. He was obviously in a great deal of pain and didn't know how to deal with it.

Still, Olivia felt bad about the photograph. She'd call Sarah to make sure she didn't re-Tweet or repost it, though she wasn't sure she could bring herself to ask her friend to take it down. As selfish as it might be, Olivia was secretly thrilled so many people were seeing her work.

As for Rafe, Olivia's heart filled with compassion for him. At the same time, his visit had disturbed her. He'd been reactive and volatile, and running through all of it was the idea that his horse was "special." A winner. She'd heard those same words come out of her father's mouth. Too many times.

Olivia had bonded with Rowan, but she wasn't pinning her hopes and dreams on him the way Rafe was. It was possible that Rafe's grief was too deep for tears and he'd subconsciously convinced himself that winning the Derby or some important race would bring his dad back. Had Rafe fallen into that unhealthy mind-set? It was a common enough coping skill for those who'd lost a loved one. Olivia had certainly done her fair share of magical thinking when her dad was around.

Olivia turned out the rest of the lights in

the deli. Maybe she should stop at the hardware store on the way home, she thought. Maybe caution tape wasn't enough where Rafe was concerned. Maybe she needed razor wire.

CHAPTER NINE

JULIA'S HOME LOOKED like a doll's house. Surrounded by a white picket fence, it was only a story and a half with a bedroom and bath in the loft. The exterior was painted a New England blue with white shutters and a dark blue shingled roof. There were newly planted pansies in the flower boxes on either side of the small front porch.

In the summer the garden would be a sea of herbs, forty varieties of lavender, edible violets, nasturtiums and chrysanthemums. Julia had planted six raised beds in the back, where she grew tomatoes, shallots, lettuces, peas and beans. She'd lashed together tree branches into six-foot-high tripods, which would support squash, cucumbers and pumpkins and prevent them from rotting on the wet ground.

Olivia smiled as she pulled up to the house and pictured the garden in full bloom. At this time of year, her mother spent her nights in the potting shed under an electric heater, tending her seedlings and planning new recipes around the vegetables she was just starting to put in the ground.

After locking her van, she walked up the flagstone walk to the front door. Julia greeted her with a mug of coffee.

"Hello, darling." Julia smiled and kissed Olivia's cheek. "I made cappuccino. We'll need the caffeine."

Olivia took the mug and followed her mom into the living room, taking a seat on one of the floral love seats in front of the fireplace. On the mantel was Olivia's high school graduation photograph alongside two tennis tournament trophies she'd won in her senior year before breaking her ankle in the sectional playoffs. Olivia had asked her mother several times to put the trophies and photograph away, but Julia had been proud of her daughter's accomplishments, and so the mementos remained.

The main floor was open concept, with the kitchen taking up half the space, and a round walnut pedestal table sitting between it and the living area. Olivia had worked puzzles, completed homework and cut her high school graduation cake at that table. It had three leaves and could be extended when Julia needed space to assemble party trays or spread out order books and catalogs when planning a major event.

Like now.

Not only was the table extended to its full length, but it was also covered with magazines, boxes of invitations, two calculators, legal pads and catalogs for everything from tents to fabrics to flowers.

"What's going on?" Olivia asked, taking a big slug of coffee. She went to the table and lifted one of the catalogs, finding an issue of *Bride's Magazine* underneath. She whirled around to stare at her mother. "I came to help plan Liz and Gabe's baby shower. I brought some notes that Gina gave me. But these are wedding books..."

Julia beamed proudly. "I've been on the phone for hours with Katia Stanislaus."

Olivia's mouth fell open. "We're catering Austin and Katia's wedding?"

"No. We've been hired to help plan the entire event. From the rehearsal dinner to the reception."

Olivia lowered herself into a chair and held on to the back. She didn't know whether to be thrilled or run for shelter. "Can we do this? I mean, we've done small weddings, showers—sure. But Austin McCreary. He's…discerning, to say the least."

Julia burst into laughter. "You should see your face. I would think you would enjoy the challenge."

"Mom. I've seen those celebrity weddings you're always making me watch. I'm sure that Austin—"

Julia sat down next to her and took Olivia's hand. "That's the best part. They're only having forty guests."

Olivia was speechless. Austin had been a regular customer of theirs since the day they'd opened their doors, and she had no doubt he was the reason they'd been hired. But something wasn't adding up. "Forty? I don't get it."

"Katia told me she only has an aunt and two cousins in Chicago. Austin has no family left. Everything will be held at his house. The ceremony will be in the living room. The dinner outside on the tennis court." Julia picked up the tent rental catalog. "That's why we need this. She wants a Medieval-looking tent."

"Okay, so only forty guests, but exquisite."

"Her words exactly."

"Now I'm really worried," Olivia said, scanning the items on the table. She pointed to the box of invitations. "Katia wants us to help with the invitations, as well?"

"Actually, she's already got the invitation. She sent me a picture of it. Hold on." Julia picked up her iPhone and scrolled through her messages. "Here it is." She showed Olivia. "I thought I'd seen everything, but this is amazing."

The invitation was padded crème satin fabric overlaid with a gathered black sash. Sealing the invitation closed were two rhinestone "brooches" that looked to Olivia like Edwardian period reproductions. She swiped to the next image, which showed the black script lettering on the inside of the invitation.

"They want a June wedding? Is that enough time?"

"Not really. I told Katia that, but she said she didn't care. My bet is there won't be a tent available within three hundred miles of Indian Lake. We may have to rent out of Ohio."

"Every chair and table and linen will be rented. Not to mention glasses and china."

"I thought of that, but they're using Hannah's dishes, serving pieces and stemware. Even the tablecloths and napkins. They won't all match, but that's kind of the beauty of the whole thing."

Olivia grabbed a legal pad and started making notes. "Austin's kitchen is large enough that we can work there." She glanced up at her mother. "Has Katia talked about the menu yet?"

"We're batting around ideas. Nothing concrete yet, but she's leaning toward rack of lamb. With only forty people, it's not such a big production."

Olivia tapped the pencil against her cheek. "Staff. We're going to need a bartender and then two people for pickup and cleaning." She paused, thinking of Austin's housekeeper. "Will Daisy be a guest?"

"Yes. I didn't even ask. Katia made it clear that Daisy wasn't to work that day."

"Flowers. Cake? I assume Maddie will make the cake."

"Correct," Julia replied and finished her cappuccino. She scrolled through her photos. "This is the cake Katia wants. Isn't it gorgeous?"

The three-tiered cake resembled a stack of gifts, complete with white bows, icing roses and latticework decor. "It's magnificent. Have you talked to Maddie yet?"

"She sent me a text and said it was no problem."

"Maddie is so talented. She could create anything. After that Chanel purse cake she made for Mrs. Beabots's birthday party last year, I thought I'd seen it all. Apparently not."

"Katia is meeting with the florist this week. I've hired the musicians. That leaves the photographer." Julia stared at Olivia with a long, penetrating gaze.

Olivia knew that look. It was the one Julia threw at her whenever she elected Olivia for a specific job or task. It was decisive and final. Once Julia made up her mind, she was unwavering.

Olivia threw up her hands. "Oh, no."

"No one in town can shoot a wedding like you. That is, when you deign to do so."

"Weddings are so boring," Olivia groaned.

"Look, I'm not relegating you to a lifetime of wedding photography. I know you have high aspirations. It's just this one…"

"Impossible," Olivia said sternly. "Besides, I have to either be the photographer or the caterer. I can't do both."

"I know that. So you'll be the photographer. I can hire someone to help in the kitchen. This is too important. Katia wants you to take her engagement pictures, the formal wedding pictures, rehearsal dinner, showers if there are any and all the candid shots of the ceremony and reception. We'll need a videographer, too."

"That's a lot of work."

"Commensurate with the fee she's paying." Julia smiled.

"She really wants me this much?"

"They both do."

Olivia was flattered, and the praise and acceptance created a warm feeling inside her. It had been months since anyone had acknowledged her talent professionally. Her girlfriends were always very sweet about the Christmas pictures she shared with them or the group shots at birthday parties. Julia was right. Austin and Katia could hire a photographer from Chicago or even New York if they wanted. But they didn't. They wanted her.

"Let me see what I can do about a videographer. I know a good one out of New Buffalo, and if he's booked there's that guy from Indianapolis that Sarah hired," she offered. "You're right, Mom. Wedding photographs last a lifetime. Even generations. These have to be so special."

"Isn't it exciting? Can you imagine what

you could do with her photographs? I mean if this invitation is a preview of what Katia expects this wedding to look like, your photos could be spectacular. Maybe you could send them to one of these bridal magazines. Who knows, sweetheart? Maybe they would hire you."

"Oh, Mom. That's such a long shot."

"Life is a long shot, sweetie pie. How do you know if you don't try?"

Try. Yes. She needed to get her act together. She needed to try. Maybe her mom was right. Katia's wedding would give her an opportunity she hadn't had before. Already she envisioned how she would pose gorgeous Katia and handsome Austin, dressed in their wedding ensembles and standing in a summer garden or next to one of his fantastic antique cars.

"I don't suppose she's talked about the wedding party. Attendants?"

"Actually, yes. Liz is the maid of honor. The baby isn't due until late July or early August, and Katia was adamant that Liz stand up for her. They've become quite close, I understand. Then Sarah and Luke's kids—Annie will be flower girl and Timmy the ring bearer," Julia said, looking down at her pad. "Oh, and Rafe is best man."

Olivia's hand froze, and slowly she put her pen down. It made sense. Rafe was Austin's best friend. Before Katia came to town, one of the only people Olivia ever saw Austin with was Rafe.

Olivia put her hand to her cheek as her face grew hot. It was hard enough to take Rafe dressed in jeans and boots. In a tux, he'd kill her. She'd have to wear armor to deflect his charm…except for the fact that he terrified her nearly as much as he magnetized her. Well, she just had to make sure that armor was extra-strong. She had vowed never to get involved with anyone in horse racing. She didn't need to relive that kind of heartbreak.

In any case, the way he'd acted last night proved that whatever connection they might have made had been severed. There was even a chance they could meet at Austin and Katia's wedding as photographer and guest. Professional. No emotion.

Yeah, right.

"What's wrong?" Julia asked.

"Nothing. Why?"

"You haven't taken a breath since I mentioned Rafe Barzonni."

"We, uh, we had a slight altercation," Olivia admitted sheepishly. She twirled her finger around in a circle on the pad, the way she'd done since she was a child whenever she was trying to think up an excuse.

"How slight are we talking?" Julia probed cautiously.

"Okay, not a fender bender, but not legally actionable, either."

"Oh, for heaven's sake, Olivia, what did you do?"

Olivia peered up at her mother, wishing she didn't feel so small and ashamed. Surely, there would come a day when she would handle her life with more confidence. But obviously she wasn't there yet. "After you left the funeral dinner, Gina asked me to take a plate of food down to the horse trainer, Curt, in the stable where he was working…"

"Yes, I saw the stable. Go on."

Olivia wished her mother wasn't so anxious for this confession. Olivia folded her hands in her lap to stop herself from squirming as she explained about the photo shoot with Rowan and the social media debacle.

"Why would he be mad about that?" Julia asked, her eyebrows knitted together in confusion.

Olivia heaved a deep sigh. "Because he specifically asked me not to let anyone see them."

Julia dropped her forehead to her palm. "You didn't."

"I did. Well, not on purpose. I forgot about the promise. Spending time with Rowan made me think about how I first fell in love with horses, and I wanted to thank Sarah for all those times she took me to her dressage class."

"I so wished I could have afforded classes for you, too," Julia said despondently.

Olivia reached out to her. "It's not that, Mom. I never felt bad about it. I didn't care about riding. I cared that I was there. I got to touch the horses and talk to them. I took pictures of them on those disposable cameras I bought with my allowance."

Julia gave Olivia's hand a little squeeze. "And Sarah, being your number one fan, posted the photo. I'm sure it was phenomenal."

"One of my best," Olivia admitted. "Sarah alone has had over a hundred likes on it. People I don't know are Tweeting it and sharing it. It's been a nightmare." She didn't want her mom to know she was also enjoying the attention.

Julia was quiet for a long moment before she said, "It'll blow over. Things like this always do."

"I'm not so sure. Rafe wants to race Rowan professionally. He said that he didn't want people who might also be judges or reporters to see photos of Rowan before he was ready to be presented publicly. Rafe and his father had talked about trying to get Rowan into the trials for the Kentucky Derby, at the very least."

Julia's mouth fell open. "You left that part out."

"Pretty bad, huh?" Olivia asked glumly. "He's going to hate me forever."

"And so what if he does? You take some photographs of him at the rehearsal dinner and the wedding and—" Julia brushed her palms against each other "—pffft. You never see him again. Frankly, I don't remember ever seeing him in the deli. As far as you're concerned, he's out of your life."

What Julia said was true. Rafe could be out of her life forever. But if she was honest with herself, that wasn't what Olivia wanted.

Despite the accusations he'd hurled at her

the night before, she would never forget the feel of his arms around her when he'd pulled her back from Rowan's stall. When they'd spoken in the stable, she'd never felt quite so alive. The air had seemed electric and yet the conversation had been easy and comfortable. She'd felt as if she could talk to him forever about horses, photography—anything.

Olivia didn't want a couple of photo shoots to be all there was between her and Rafe. She wanted more.

A great deal more.

And that terrified her.

CHAPTER TEN

WHEN MADDIE CAME into the deli a few days later with an armful of posters for the Indian Lake Horse Race Fundraiser, Olivia agreed to post them in the front window. She was wary about associating the deli with the sport that had almost ruined her and her mother, but the fundraiser was for the hospital. Olivia and Julia had always volunteered their time and talent to the hospital's foundation; it was one of Indian Lake's largest employers, and the doctors and nurses often treated people in need at no charge.

"I knew I could count on you," Maddie told Olivia. Maddie served on the fundraising committee. "I figure that between your deli and my café we can get the word out to half the town. Oh! And Nate told me to thank you for your help." Maddie handed her the Art Deco–style posters that Isabelle Hawks had designed.

Olivia studied the watercolor illustration

of jockeys on Thoroughbreds crossing a finish line. "It's not much. These are beautiful."

"They are, aren't they?" Maddie agreed. "Makes me want to take up horseback riding."

A chill snaked down Olivia's spine, and her ears filled with her father's curses and screams when his horse lost at the track.

Will this pain never go away?

Olivia struggled through the mire to focus on her friend. "Is there anything else I can do to help?"

Maddie was thoughtful for a moment and then put her hand on Olivia's shoulder. "As a matter of fact, there is. We need you and your camera in the tower."

"The tower?"

"On the day of the race. They've built a new judges' tower at the fairgrounds just for this race. The professional photographer quoted us over five hundred dollars for a two-minute race. Can you believe that? But…well, could you do it, Olivia? I know horse races, in particular, must be…rough for you, but it would be so great if you would."

Olivia didn't know how to turn down a friend. Maddie had done so many things for her. Sticking up for her in grade school, teaching her how to scull, championing her photography... The list was endless. Surely she could put away her hurt and fear to help. This was the closest Olivia had been to a racetrack since those days with her father. Could she do this? Her stomach roiled, and she swallowed hard as she looked at the anticipation in Maddie's eyes.

"I've never shot a race before, but I could study up on the particulars," she said slowly. Olivia wasn't quite sure what she'd gotten herself into, but she was confident she had the technical skill to pull it off. Suddenly, she wondered if Rafe would be there with Rowan. He hadn't mentioned the race, but why would he pass up that kind of opportunity for his prize horse?

It seemed that no matter what she did to avoid Rafe, he kept coming back into her life like a rogue wave. Unexpected and all-consuming.

"I'll get you all the details," Maddie said. She hugged Olivia. "Thanks for doing this for us. You're the best." She made her way toward the door and waved. "I'll see you at the races if not before."

"Yes," Olivia replied solemnly. "At the races."

BY THE TIME race day arrived, Olivia had passed out so many brochures for the hospital fundraiser that she felt personally responsible for the enormous turnout at the fairgrounds. According to the announcer, the grandstand was packed with over fifteen hundred people. Olivia made her way up the midway beside the track, where food vendors were selling everything from caramel apples and popcorn to fish sandwiches, corn dogs and elephant ears. To the west of the midway were two neon-lit Ferris wheels, a Tilt-A-Whirl and bumper cars. An old-fashioned calliope played carnival tunes.

The April air was shot with festive spirit as Olivia searched the crowds for her friends. She had promised to meet Maddie, Liz, Sarah and Katia across from the horse barn. During the annual county fair, the barn housed prize cows and pigs that the 4-H kids had raised. Today some of the finest racing horses in Indiana stood only yards away from her.

Olivia tried desperately to control her emotions. Half of her was terrified to even come near the fairgrounds because this entire event reminded her far too caustically of her father. One minute her stomach churned with bile, the next minute she thought about see-

ing Rafe again and her heart tripped over it-
self. Maddie had confirmed to her that he
was racing Rowan today.

She wished she could put her unpleasant
memories in a balloon and let them float
away, but it didn't work like that.

She didn't know Rafe well enough to di-
vulge her phobia about horse racing to him.
At this point she figured she was nothing
more to him than a thorn in his side.

"There she is. Olivia! Olivia!" Maddie
shouted loud enough that Olivia heard her
name over the whirring of the cotton candy
machine beside her.

Olivia had two cameras on sliding straps
around her neck, and her shoulder bag held
her best lenses, including a high-powered
zoom lens that could capture the hairs in
Rowan's nostrils from the grandstands. Not
that she was thinking about Rowan in particular.

Nor should she be thinking about Rafe.

"Hi, guys," Olivia said, plastering a bright
smile on her face as Maddie rushed up and
hugged her.

"Don't you look adorable," Maddie said,
taking in Olivia's white poet's coat, skinny

jeans and sneakers. "I see you're cocked and loaded."

Sarah kissed Olivia's cheek. "Let me guess who you hope will win today."

Olivia shot Sarah a quelling look. "I told the judges that I'm simply a second pair of eyes."

Liz grabbed Olivia's arm. "Wait a minute. I'm behind here. What are you doing with the judges?"

Sarah rushed to explain why Olivia had volunteered to be a finish-line photographer.

"Yeah," Maddie said. "Saved the committee five hundred bucks. And that was the pro's reduced fee."

Olivia blushed. "It was the least I could do. I can't claim to be a pro, but I'm going to rig up one of my cameras to a laptop for the judges. That will be the real photo-finish criteria. I'll be right there with them and snap as many shots as I can get as all the horses come across the line."

"This is really exciting, Olivia," Liz gushed. "I've never been to a horse race, so it's all new to me. Although Gabe is really nervous for Rafe."

"He should be," Olivia blurted. *I know I am.* It was one thing to volunteer to help, but now that the moment was here, Olivia could only think of excuses to leave. Everything about this day set her teeth on edge. Including the fact that she'd obviously told Sarah too much about her confusing feelings for Rafe.

Maddie's eyes swept back to Olivia. "Why do you say that?"

Sarah grinned mischievously. "Olivia knows quite a bit about Rowan and Rafe's plans for this race, don't you, Olivia?"

"Not so much," Olivia groaned. *Even my friends are part of this nightmare. Why did I promise to do this? Oh, yeah—loyalty. More like stupidity.*

"Don't kid us. Gabe told me all about that photo that Sarah posted of Rowan." She glanced accusingly at Sarah then laughed. "I also know no harm was really done. Gabe said Rowan has trained really well recently, and he and Rafe both think he'll win. Especially because Rafe found a new jockey from downstate who's been working out with Rowan for the past week."

"No kidding?" Olivia beamed.

"Yeah, a girl!" Liz continued. "All the better jockeys are off to Florida or California for the Graded Stakes competitions for the Kentucky Derby. There's just nobody available.

But Gabe said Rafe was determined to find somebody who could put Rowan through his paces."

Olivia tried to squash the jealousy that reared up inside her without warning. What did it matter that Rafe had hired a female jockey?

Suddenly, Olivia couldn't wait to see Rowan. She'd promised herself she wouldn't bother Rafe before the race, but there was still an hour and a half until Rowan's big event. Her gaze lingered on the horse barn.

"Hey," Olivia interrupted Liz and Maddie, who were still talking about the jockey. "I have to get this camera to the judges and get them set up. Where should I meet you all for lunch?"

"Nate said there's a great pulled-pork sandwich stand near the Tilt-A-Whirl. We'll meet you there." She looked at her watch. "How about one o'clock?"

"Great," Olivia said. "I'll see you then."

When Olivia was halfway to the horse barn, she turned back to see her friends duck into the bingo tent. She smiled to herself, hoping Sarah was just meeting Mrs. Beabots. Olivia didn't want to think all her married friends were into playing boring bingo for recreation.

Olivia entered the barn expecting to see Rafe, Gabe, Nate, Mica or all four. Owners and trainers were leading horses toward the back door, which led to an exercise track, but there was no sign of any Barzonnis.

She went down the aisle, admiring the Thoroughbreds. Though she wasn't a horse expert, she'd seen enough races with her father to know that these horses were older than three or four years. She passed a beautiful chestnut horse with a black mane who was young and every bit as muscular as Rowan. Instantly, she realized this was the horse to beat.

The thought had barely crossed her mind when she heard a familiar whinny. Two stalls down was Rowan. He was leaning over the door, trying to get her attention.

She rushed toward him. "You remembered me!" she said enthusiastically, and as always, with no thought to consequences, she threw her arms around his neck, put her cheek against his face and hugged him. "I can't believe how much I missed you."

Rowan curled his neck around her, bringing her closer to his chest.

Olivia was stunned when tears stung her eyes. How was it possible that Rowan remembered her after only one encounter? She knew she would never forget him, and not just because his photo had caused Rafe so much frustration. Though human and horse, their hearts had touched.

She stroked his snout. "You look amazing. Rafe was right. He saw the potential in you before you'd reached it. He's really good for you." She kissed his nose. "I'd tell you that I wish you luck, but I don't think you need luck. You're a winner. I guess I saw that in your eyes that first time we met. The thing is, I've always been afraid of races. Well, not actually the part you do. But the way racing affects human beings." She didn't know why she was confessing all of this to an animal, but she couldn't stop the words from spilling out. "Not all humans are good people. Sad to say, I knew one who was just about the worst you could imagine."

She pulled back and held his head in both her hands. "But you don't need to hear any of that right now. All you need to do is think about running like the wind. I would love to see you running across those fields out there. Not just on a racetrack."

She stroked his neck and hugged him again. "This will be my first time seeing you run, and I'm looking forward to that. When you win, everyone will be taking your picture. This time Rafe can't yell at me for doing what a thousand people out here will be doing, too."

"You're right, I can't," Rafe said.

Olivia nearly jumped out of her skin. "Darn it, Rafe, you did it again!" She whirled on him. "I swear I am going to get a cowbell to put on you."

He laughed. "Sorry. I learned how to do that when I was a kid. How else was I supposed to steal Mom's cookies and biscotti?"

"Are you trying to scare me? Is that how you get your kicks?"

"No. But I confess to eavesdropping."

"Oh."

"Look, Olivia. I owe *you* an apology this time. I was pretty rough on you, and I shouldn't have been. This has all…" His voice faltered.

Olivia reached out and touched his arm. "You don't have to say it. I know. It's okay. I'm sorry, too."

He swallowed hard. "Forgiven, then?"

"Yes."

"And we can move on?"

She hesitated. Move on to what? Did he

want more from her? His apology told her that he had been thinking about her over the past weeks. He hadn't forgotten her. That was something. "Move on. Yes." She smiled.

"Good," he said, taking her hand and holding it gently. He placed both their palms on Rowan's neck. "I think he missed you, too."

Too?

Had Rafe actually said that? She had to be hearing things. She'd convinced herself that Rafe considered her a pest, if he even thought of her at all. But he'd said *too*. Suddenly, she felt lighter and happier than she'd felt in weeks.

"So," Rafe said. "You see how lean he looks? He's really come into his own these past weeks. Curt has been working him constantly and it's paid off."

"I heard you got a jockey."

"Who told you that?"

"Uh, Liz said you hired someone from downstate. A woman."

Rafe threw his head back and laughed. "Jenny is sixteen. She's a junior jockey and all I could get. But she's only eighty-nine pounds and has been riding since she was two. She's not good enough for a Graded

Stakes races, but for this—" he gestured in the direction of the track "—she'll do fine."

Sixteen. What was the matter with her? How could Olivia feel jealous or threatened when she and Rafe barely had any relationship at all?

Olivia feigned humor the best she could, smiling too broadly and laughing a bit too loud. "Ha! Just goes to show how rumors get started. Especially in a small town."

"Rumors are like that anywhere, Olivia. Especially with the internet."

Olivia winced. Point taken.

Rafe put his hand on her shoulder. "I'm sorry. I didn't mean that how it sounded. Please don't take it personally. I meant it when I said we should move on."

Olivia's stomach knotted in confusion and anxiety, but Rafe's hand on her shoulder felt warm and protective. As he pressed a little deeper, he searched her face for her reaction. Apparently, she had struck some emotional chord in him. He didn't want to stay mad at her, and he needed her to acknowledge that they were adult enough to forgive and forget. Was he asking her to be friends?

His eyes were the color of the bluest spring sky, filled with unspoken promises. At that moment Olivia realized she was lost in him. Did he know she would give anything to feel his lips against hers? Could he sense her heart thrumming in her chest? Why wasn't he saying anything? And why was his hand moving so achingly slowly from her shoulder to the nape of her neck?

"Wish me luck," he said with his mouth so close, his breath warmed her nose.

The pressure of his lips on hers was ever so slight. Just as he started to pull away, Olivia thrust her arms around his neck and pulled him in. She kissed him back tentatively at first, savoring the satiny texture of his lips. The swell of emotion in her heart nearly overwhelmed her. As strange and foreign as her feelings were, she welcomed them. Rafe cupped the back of her head, holding her as if he didn't want to let go.

When Rafe finally pulled back, he released her slowly, his hand lingering in her hair.

"Will you?" he asked.

Olivia was spellbound. Her pleasure and joy had vanished as quickly as it came. Suddenly, she felt alone in a way she never had before. She didn't understand any of it. "What?"

"Wish me luck."

"Good luck," she managed.

He smiled softly and his eyes were filled with sincerity. Had that earnestness always been there? How had she missed it? She was the photographer. She caught emotions in people—even animals—each time she set up a shot. But for some reason Rafe's feelings eluded her. Perhaps his grief had overshadowed everything else—until now. Was this the real Rafe? And if it was, had she been the one to cut through his sorrow? Why her?

He leaned down and kissed her on the tip of her nose. "If you'll root for us, I know we'll win."

With a jolt, Olivia remembered where she was. She was at the fairgrounds and a horse race was about to begin. She was back in hell. Back in the kind of place where her father had gambled away her future. This was the epicenter of betrayal, and it was Rafe's element.

"Yes, Rafe. I'll cheer for you," she lied.

CHAPTER ELEVEN

THE JUDGES' TOWER was four stories high with a 360° view of the racetrack from the roofed enclosure that was large enough for a dozen people. Luke Bosworth's construction crew had built it as their donation to the hospital fundraiser. The pine structure felt solid as Olivia climbed the staircase, noticing that the struts, stilts, stairs and crooked, knotty natural pine railings had been sanded to a smooth finish. The shutters and side walls were painted a dark pine green that blended in with the surrounding forest. The rustic details told Olivia that Sarah must have helped her husband design the tower. Sarah had contributed her talents to Maddie and Nate's lake house, and this tower had that same Sarah Jensen Bosworth aesthetic.

Inside, Olivia was pleasantly surprised to find battered, tin ceiling fixtures, stained cedar floors and plenty of outlets and surge protectors.

Her friends hadn't shared many details about the construction project, and it had clearly been a much larger undertaking than Olivia had imagined. Sarah and Luke had built this tower to last a lifetime. Maybe longer.

Olivia had assumed this was a onetime fundraiser. Did Sarah know something she didn't? Sarah and Maddie were as close as sisters, and Nate Barzonni was a heart surgeon at the hospital. If there were plans to make the horse race an annual event, they would have heard about them.

Olivia's heart tripped. Stalled. Her fear of horse races and gambling clutched her chest and impeded her breathing. She wiped her palm across her clammy forehead. Maybe she needed to see a therapist. It had been a long time since she'd reacted this strongly to her past. But then, she hadn't been confronted with her phobias for years.

Olivia understood with resounding clarity that the hospital foundation or someone in Indian Lake expected horse races to become a fixture in the community. That thought terrified her, but it was out of her control. She had a job to do today, and then she could avoid the fairgrounds for the foreseeable future.

As her breathing and heart rate returned to normal, she peered out onto the track. From this vantage point, her camera would be able to capture the critical sequence of events at the finish line.

Just below the south-facing opening was a long wooden table surrounded by folding chairs where the judges would sit and watch the race. There was a telescope on a tripod stand with no recording device attached to it. Curious, she thought, that one of the judges believed his eye was so impeccable, he didn't need any technological backup.

She shrugged. *Works for baseball umpires.*

She had just removed one of her cameras from around her neck when she heard a gravelly voice behind her. "You must be the camera lady."

"Photojournalist," she corrected as she took in the tall, lanky and handsome man with sharp gray eyes so intense they looked silver. She guessed he was in his early seventies. He wore a white straw cowboy hat over a mass of coarse gray hair, and his blue Western-style shirt was belted into a pair of faded jeans with an enormous gold-and-silver buckle imprinted with a man on a horse and the word *Champion.*

"Howard Stillman," he said, grabbing both her hands in his, though she still held her camera. He pumped both her hands and the camera up and down. "Nice to meecha."

"Mr. Stillman."

"Judge Stillman." He leaned very close with a flirtatious gleam in his eye. "But you can call me Howard."

Then he released her hands, slapped her on the shoulder and moved around the table. "Let's see what we got here." He rubbed his hands together and opened his laptop.

As he waited for it to boot up, Howard jabbered on about himself. He explained that he was a "traveling judge" and worked the independent race circuit across the US. He was quick to relate his repertoire of personal statistics, though Olivia hadn't asked. In fact, she had a difficult time replying to anything he said given his rapid-fire delivery. Howard confirmed that he was indeed in his early seventies. "Though," he said, hitching his chin up haughtily, "people say I don't look a day over sixty."

"I'm sure they do," Olivia agreed, though she'd pegged him from the first glance. Then again, she was a photographer. She saw the world in a higher resolution than most.

For example, though he was lean and muscular—from constantly riding and tending horses, he mentioned in one of his rambling monologues—Olivia's sharp eye caught a slight arthritic gait as he rose from the folding chair and then sat back down.

Howard's constant chatter was wearing on her, but she saw through his bluster to his disappointment that his life and career had brought him here to this little town to judge a charity horse race. Compassion for Howard found its way from her heart to her hands as her fingers slipped around her Sony NEX-5R and she quickly slapped off a dozen shots of Howard as he worked on his laptop. Then to cover her true motives, she spun around the tower and took shots of the tower interior and then readjusted her lens for some long-range shots into the grandstand and down onto the track.

Through her camera's eye she saw Curt Wheeling leading Rowan out of the horse barn. Rafe beamed at his mother, who walked beside him, her arm around his waist.

Gina would be saying all the encouraging words her son needed at a time like this. Olivia adjusted the lens again and zoomed in on Rafe's face.

She was over a hundred yards away, but she caught every nuance in his eyes as he gazed lovingly at his mother. He nodded and smiled so brightly, Olivia had to close her eyes for a second. The image would stay in her mind forever. She knew that kind of unbreakable bond because that was what she had with her own mother.

She had shared furtive, painful glances with her mother when they'd been at racetracks with her father. Even as a child, Olivia believed she could read her mother's mind. Her father's gambling had also cemented the bond between mother and daughter. Perhaps it was true that out of all pain came a measure of joy.

"Olivia?" Howard said behind her.

Olivia hadn't noticed herself tuning him out the moment her lens found Rafe. Her face grew hot, and when she turned to face the older man, she realized she'd also failed to notice the tower filling up with people. Nearly a dozen men and women sporting binoculars, iPhones and cameras had gathered in anticipation of the race.

"Yes, Howard?"

He wiggled his finger, motioning for her to join him. "What cameras did you bring?

I was at a race outside Lexington for a private corporation last week. They loaned the judges a Phantom Flex."

Olivia swallowed hard. "That's a fifty-thousand dollar camera."

Howard's eyes twinkled. "It was shock and awe on my part, I gotta tell you."

"Well," she replied, unable to hide her embarrassment, "I thought I'd give you my Sony. I also brought a Casio ZR200 that can do slow-motion video. If we have any trouble naming a winner with those, I've learned some tricks with Twixtor we can use once I get the footage downloaded to my computer."

Howard took the Sony, put it to his eye and adjusted the lens for the finish line. He handed the camera back to her.

"Have you ever shot a race before?"

"No," she admitted.

"I was afraid of that. This being a volunteer effort." He shoved his hands into his pockets. "This is more than precise, detailed work—it has to be infinitesimally precise. A nanosecond can make a winner." He shrugged. "It doesn't matter if these horses are bred for vanity or as a hobby, or entered in this race on a whim. Trust me—once they get to that starting gate, all bets are off. Sud-

denly, everyone catches the fever. The jockeys, the owners, the trainers…and certainly
the horses."

"The fever," Olivia repeated. She felt as if
she was talking underwater. The people in
the tower dissolved from her field of vision
as if she'd put too much acid in her develop-
ing solution. Everything faded out…

*She was eight years old with her father at
the races in Arlington, watching the horses
round the final turn and head to the finish
line. Her father's thick, dark hair glistened
in the sunlight, and his sharp jaw lifted as he
shouted excitedly. In his left hand he held a
racing form and receipts that showed the bets
he'd placed. Olivia reached out to touch his
white knuckles, wondering why those pieces
of paper were so important to him.*

*Then she looked up at her father and saw
joy fill his face.*

"I won! Olivia, I won!"

*He lifted her in his strong arms and cov-
ered her face with dozens of kisses. "I won!
Now I can buy your mom that washer and
dryer she needs. I knew I could do it!" He
bounced her up and down. "I had a feeling
it was my day. My day!"*

Then he hoisted Olivia up and onto his

shoulder. "Come on, pretty girl. I want to take you down to the paddock so you can see the horses."

"Can I ride one?" she asked.

"No. They won't let you ride them. These are special horses. They make kings out of men."

"They do?" Olivia wondered why all these men who rode the horses weren't wearing crowns.

By the time her father had picked up his winnings and chatted with some "friends" he knew at the "cages," most of the horses were being led into the horse trailers down at the paddocks. Others were being brushed and put in the stables.

Only one horse was still on display. Dozens of people clamored around the horse, his owners and the jockey with cameras and microphones.

"That's American Dream," her father whispered reverently, pointing at the chestnut Thoroughbred. "I have a brochure with all his statistics for you to keep, so you'll remember him. You should always remember the winners, Olivia. They give us inspiration."

Olivia nodded. "Can I take a picture of

*you next to the horse, Daddy?" She pulled
her pink plastic camera out of the white pat-
ent leather purse her mother had given her
for Easter.*

*"I don't know if they'll let us," he said
sheepishly. "Maybe we should just go."*

*"No," she'd insisted. "I have to get a pic-
ture of the winner."*

*Her father grabbed Olivia by the waist and
held her up so she could get an overhead shot
of the jockey sitting on the horse. Then he put
her down and instructed her to take one of
him standing near the rail.*

*"When we get them developed, we'll glue
them together and it will look like I'm in the
winner's circle with them."*

*"Okay!" Olivia replied, delight coursing
through her body...*

Olivia shook herself back into the present.
She'd felt like a winner that day, and she'd
thought she'd understood her father.

Jake Melton had caught the *fever* all right.
And it had burned them all.

"Olivia?"

Howard was talking to her again.

Olivia felt as if she was swimming in deep
waters; she was in danger of drowning in the
past. She fought the current that pulled her

under and tried to focus on the man in front of her. "I'm sorry, you were saying?"

"I said I won't be using any camera at all. I'm somewhat old-school. I have a telescope I've used for years. On the other hand, I have a new Marathon Adanac digital stopwatch to clock the time. Time is history and can make or break a horse's future. I'll be announcing the race. I tested the sound system earlier this morning—it's pretty darn good." He barely took a breath as he spoke.

Olivia was thankful Howard didn't appear to need another person in order to have a conversation. At the moment she was still clearing the water out of her ears. "I'll put the Casio on a tripod and set it up for video, then use the Sony to take as many shots as possible."

"Great," he said. "I want the count at the first quarter mile. Try to capture the back field, as well. Then at the second turn, get the middle field, though the front runners will be key. In these amateur races, the winner usually comes from those front three runners unless there's a strategic runner in the back. Once they hit the last turn, right up to the finish line, each second is important—each nanosecond, even."

"I'll get it all for you," Olivia replied confidently. And she believed it. Though she'd never been hired to photograph a professional sporting event, she had spent hundreds of hours documenting football games, basketball games and baseball championships at Indian Lake High School.

"Sounds like a plan." Howard handed her a sheet of paper. "Here's the roster of horses, their numbers and the names of the jockeys and owners. I included their colors because that's how I memorize them. This race is easy because there are only eight horses running."

Olivia studied the list. Rowan was number four. She looked up at Howard. "Who's the favorite?"

"Mr. Blue." He pointed to the sheet. "Red and white. Watch him. I saw him run yesterday." Howard shook his head. "That horse should be in the Derby trials, he's that good."

"Really?" Olivia scanned the list. Other than Mr. Blue and Rowan, there was Old Man River, Sensation, Silver Lining, Swept Away, Mama's Boy and Dark Knight. Howard's tip to memorize their colors helped enormously.

"Now, I suppose you know most of these people," he said, motioning toward the staircases.

Olivia glanced over to see Sarah, Luke, Annie and Timmy walk in. Sarah was dressed in pink jeans, a floral blouse and pink sneakers, and Annie's outfit was almost identical. Olivia smiled. Sarah and Luke had obviously blended their lives quite well. Olivia had admired Sarah's courage to love a man who'd been so deeply in love with his first wife that after her death, he'd nearly lost himself to grief.

Sounds like someone else I know.

Tamping down her thoughts of Rafe, Oliva hugged her friends and greeted the kids. "I can't believe what a fantastic job you did on the tower," she gushed. "Neither of you said a word during the construction. I feel like I should have helped. I can wield a mean paintbrush."

Luke put his hand on her shoulder. "We were inundated with volunteers. It actually went much faster than we'd thought. Two weeks."

"No way." Olivia turned to Sarah.

"It's true. It was like one of those Amish barn raisings where they finish the whole structure in a day. Luke and Jerry and his crew did most of the staircase in sections. We hired a roofer for the shingles, and everything was painted before we set it up here."

Luke grinned. "Yeah. It took longer for the cement pilings to dry than it did to get the walls and shutters up." He stopped and shared a glance with Sarah. "Well, almost. But you know what I'm saying."

"I do," Olivia said. "And I know everyone on the foundation is very appreciative."

Sarah nodded happily. "Nate and Maddie are taking us out for a steak dinner to thank us."

"Yes, and Timmy and I get to come, too," Annie said, slipping her hand into Sarah's.

"I'm getting a burger and a chocolate sundae at the Louise House after," Timmy interjected as he rocked triumphantly on his heels.

Just then, they heard the blast of trumpets over the loudspeaker. "Ladies and gentlemen. Friends and fans. We of the Indian Lake Hospital Foundation welcome you to the first annual Indian Lake Hospital Horse Race."

The grandstand roared with applause, and Olivia scanned the crowds with her camera, taking pictures. Sweeping over the excited faces, Olivia paused when she saw Mrs. Beabots dressed in a black-and-white knit suit and a small black straw hat with a band of white ribbon around the crown and hanging down the back. The older woman held a pair of binoculars to her face, and with her nearly platinum hair cut in a chin-length bob, she was the picture of 1960s sophistication. If Olivia used a diffused filter and airbrushed Mrs. Beabots's lines and wrinkles, the result would resemble a snapshot from her older friend's past. Next to her sat Maddie and Nate, who were poring over their brochures and pointing to the parade of horses as they met the "Call to the Post" from the announcer. Liz and Gabe, Austin and Katia, and Cate Sullivan, Isabelle Hawks and Mica Barzonni completed the row.

As Olivia swung her lens toward the paddock, Howard turned away from the telescope and glanced at her. "Somebody around here has some pull."

"What do you mean?"

"The portable starting gate." He pointed to the track, where a huge John Deere tractor was unloading an eight-stall starting gate. It was a smaller version of the electromagnetic twenty-stall rigs she'd seen in the past, but for Indian Lake's purposes, it was perfect.

She adjusted her telephoto lens so that she could watch the action.

"There they go," Howard said, gesturing toward the people leading the horses to the gate. "The cowboys of horse racing. That's what we call the assistant and head starters. It's bad enough that claustrophobic Thoroughbreds are confined to ten-by-twelve stalls in the horse barn. But put one of those high-strung horses in a two-and-a-half-foot by eight-foot gate stall, and they can go ape. I've seen one kick a man nearly to death down in Texas, and once I saw a two-year-old kill herself trying to jump out. There—see? Those assistant starters have to get the horse to the stall, keep it calm and then shut the back end gate, hold it closed and hope the horse doesn't spook and kick him in the head. It's one of the most dangerous jobs in sports."

Olivia gaped at him. "I had no idea." As a child, she hadn't paid attention to anyone on the track except the horses. She barely even registered they were ridden by jockeys. Olivia loved the animals, and her dreams as a little girl revolved around visions of riding a classic stallion like Black Beauty or a pure white horse like Pegasus. She understood too well the dangers of gambling at the track, but she hadn't really considered how certain jobs in horse racing put people at risk, too.

"Most folks don't. They think this is all about a single lap around a track."

Frowning, Olivia realized she was just such a *folk*. She'd focused so long on her fears that she hadn't investigated the intricacies of horse racing enough. Quickly, she took a couple dozen shots of the horses walking to the starting gate with the assistant starters. Olivia had been tasked to chronicle as much of the event for the hospital archives as possible. The Hospital Foundation also wanted photographs they could post in the hospital lobby.

Though this was an amateur race, the jockeys wore brightly colored silks that matched the colors on the horses' bibs.

She spotted Rafe, Rowan and their jockey heading toward the gate. Jenny was red-haired with freckles all over her face and neck. Tiny and short, she wore royal-blue-and-gold silks, racing goggles and shiny black boots. She didn't look a day over ten. Olivia felt foolish for being jealous of the young girl. As Olivia snapped shot after shot of the three of them, a prickle of apprehension ran down her back.

Rafe was acting as his own assistant starter. After what Howard had just explained, she couldn't help but worry about Rafe's safety. Even if Rowan didn't freak out, what if another horse tried to jump its stall?

Olivia lowered her camera and put her palm over her thrumming heart. She was afraid for Rafe. Perspiration broke across her forehead and upper lip. She wished she could be down there on the track with him; help him. But what could she do? This was his game. He'd chosen it.

Reason returned to her as Irwin Levine, the announcer, introduced each horse and its owner. The crowd cheered. She heard Rafe's name and she was filled with excitement.

Her heart thrummed even faster as she remembered his kiss. Her cheeks flushed with warmth that spiraled to her core. Her legs wobbled, but she held on to the window ledge.

Something had happened today between her and Rafe. It was more than a kiss for luck. Something had opened in her heart and ushered in a new season. Deep emotions caused her to fill with pride and anticipation as she watched Rafe through her camera's eye. What was happening to her?

CHAPTER TWELVE

AN EARSPLITTING HORN blast began the race. Eight Thoroughbreds sprang into action with a burst of applause and cheering from the crowd. Next to Olivia, Howard peered through his telescope at the race. Olivia's fingers couldn't move fast enough. For the first time ever, she was glad she had her slow-motion video grabbing every nanosecond of the action.

"Coming around the first turn, it's Mr. Blue in the lead position, Black Knight and Rowan on the outside. Mr. Blue is looking like this is a walk in the park for him," the announcer nearly shouted into the microphone, his own enthusiasm dialed up high. "In fourth and fifth it's Swept Away and Old Man River. Oh, wow. Rowan is slipping to fourth as Swept Away pours it on."

Olivia was shocked that Rowan wasn't running better. From the way Rafe had talked up his horse's talent, she'd been prepared for Rowan to walk away with the trophy. She found herself pulling for Rowan, though she knew she shouldn't be. She was there as a journalist. It wasn't her place to have a favorite. Besides, wasn't that the spark that fed gamblers? Picking a favorite, betting everything you had on something you *hoped* would make you a winner?

As she clicked another set of photos, she realized she'd angled in on Rowan. From what she could see, he was barely panting. Was Rowan taking this race seriously? Didn't he know what this win would mean to Rafe? Did she, really?

Olivia snapped a close-up of all the jockeys' faces as they drew up to the second turn. Jenny's expression changed the moment they rounded the turn. Instantly, her composure altered to fierce determination and she shouted to Rowan, cracking her crop just above his flank.

Rowan leaped ahead of Old Man River and in less than fifteen seconds was a half length ahead of Swept Away. Pouring on the steam from the outside lane, Jenny moved Rowan to the middle lane and squeezed between Mr. Blue and Black Knight.

"Coming around the third bend, it's Mr. Blue in the lead. Rowan in second. Rowan has left Black Knight in the show position," Irwin called.

Olivia snapped dozens of photos, silently cheering on Rowan.

The rest of the pack seemed to drop away as if they'd lost steam, but of course, they hadn't. Both Mr. Blue and Rowan had soared out in front and put so much distance between them and the pack that it almost looked like two different races. This was the difference between amateurs and professionals. Losers and winners.

Feeling her blood ignite with exhilaration, Olivia had to force her body to remain as calm as possible. She needed steady hands to take the shots, and the most important one was coming up.

"Clearing the third bend, it's Mr. Blue in the lead by a nose. Rowan still pouring it on. Black Knight is dropping to fourth, and Swept Away is now coming in third," the announcer bellowed into his microphone. As he continued a second-by-second narrative of the race, Olivia followed Rowan and Mr. Blue as they neared the finish line.

"Go, Rowan," Olivia finally said aloud, though no one could hear her. Everyone in the tower was screaming and yelling for their favorite horse. "Rowan! You can do it, boy! I believe in you. Come—on! Row—an!"

Just as Olivia shouted the horse's name, the two front-runners crossed the finish line, and she snapped the final photo. "Oh, no." She exhaled all the energy that had been building inside her. Mr. Blue had just won. Rafe would be crushed. She envisioned the disappointment in his eyes. He'd been so happy…

"And it's Rowan by a half a nose!" Irwin exclaimed loudly. "Yes, Rowan is our winner! Mr. Blue places and Swept Away takes show! Congratulations to all our horses and jockeys. Gentlemen and lady, an excellent race."

The people in the grandstand exploded in cheers and applause. Olivia heard the thundering of feet as they banged their approval— or disapproval—on the metal grandstand flooring.

Olivia stared blankly at Irwin Levine and then at Howard.

Howard smiled. "A hometown winner. Isn't that great?"

Olivia blinked. She must have fallen asleep and woken in another dimension. It wasn't possible. She knew she'd seen Rowan lose, not win. She'd captured the moment on her camera.

"My camera—" Olivia quickly pulled up the six most recent shots. This would set the record straight.

Howard took the microphone and gave a long congratulatory speech to the hospital foundation and all the volunteers. He read off a long litany of hospital administrators who had sponsored various aspects of the event.

Olivia was engrossed by her photos. They all showed that Rowan had won. Yet she could have sworn she'd seen Mr. Blue cross the line first. She should have been happy, even ecstatic, but something nagged at her. Her eyes had never failed her before. She'd looked down the nose at a grasshopper via her macro lens, but she'd seen the grasshopper from ten, maybe fifteen yards away before zooming in. Her vision was better than twenty/twenty.

"Howard, are you sure? About Rowan?"

"Absolutely. Why? Do you see something different on your camera?" He looked down at the Sony in her hand.

"I thought I saw Mr. Blue cross the finish line first, but my pictures confirm your call. You should check it out."

Howard took the camera from her and scrolled through the final shots. "Yes, they confirm my judgment. Still…" He rubbed his chin and handed the camera back. "This is the disadvantage of where you were standing."

"But I was right next to you."

He shook his head. "Not quite the same. My telescope was right on the line. Exact. The tripod is even a bit to the right of the finish line. I never would have guessed this race would be so close. Frankly, I haven't seen one this close since 1989, when Park Avenue and Probe finished in a dead heat at the Hambletonian Stakes. Next year, when we set things up, I want a camera smack-dab on that finish line." Howard pointed to his telescope. "If I'd known there were horses here that were this good, I would have insisted on a professional race photographer."

Olivia felt the slight and frowned. "Howard, I believe I was well-suited for the job."

He threw his head back. "Oh, no! It's not you I'm talking about. We should have been more precise in our camera placement. Perhaps we should have mounted one from the ceiling here so it would point directly on that vertical line. In the end, though, the most important thing is this." He held up his stopwatch. "The minute hand was stopped at two minutes and the second hand registered only a few seconds more.

"I don't understand," Olivia said.

"Rowan finished in just over two minutes. It's always been said that the Kentucky Derby is the fastest two minutes in sports. There have only been two horses in history to ever finish under two minutes. That's Secretariat in 1973 and Monarchos in 2001. Rowan finished in two minutes and one second even. That, my friend, has only been accomplished twice in history, if I recall correctly. Yessiree. That Barzonni has got himself a special horse."

"And Mr. Blue?"

"A half second different. Which is also uncanny. Both those horses could bring in millions."

"Yes," she replied quietly, thinking of Rafe and how his life might change because of this race. This phenomenal win.

"Shouldn't you be getting down to the winner's circle to take more photographs?"

Her eyes widened as she realized she'd promised not just the foundation, but Rafe, that she would take plenty of photos for posterity. "You're right." She stuck out her hand. "It was nice meeting you, Howard. Thank you for the quick education. Next year I'll be more prepared. I promise."

"I'll count on it, Olivia," he replied.

Olivia packed up her two cameras then gathered her satchel and the rest of her gear. When she got home, she'd play back the footage. If she needed to, she could use Twixtor to slow the motion to ten thousand frames per second and enhance the shots. Despite all of Howard's explanations, Olivia wasn't completely convinced of Rowan's win. This was her first time in the judges' stand. She didn't know squat about finish lines and photo finishes. She was clearly no expert, but her gut told her something was wrong. Always a stickler for the truth, Olivia promised herself that once she saw the video and was assured that Rowan had won, she'd put the matter to rest.

If he wasn't the winner? Then what, Olivia?

What would she do with the information? Tell the judges? Have the trophy recanted? How would she tell Rafe? How could she come down on him with news like that? And what would he do? It would cause him embarrassment and disappointment. What would it mean to Rowan's chances of another race? Maybe it didn't matter. Rowan had run an exceedingly fast race. Howard had even said he was one of the fastest horses he'd ever seen. Rowan was a natural for racing whether he was the winner at the silly Indian Lake track or not.

Olivia's head ached with tension, all of which she'd caused herself. If she was smart, she'd put the camera away and never look at it. Let it lie. Be done with it. Move on.

Was she so bent on destroying Rafe's joy? And why? Was she jealous that he didn't have fears about gambling or racing? Was she so self-centered that she would hurt another person just to make herself feel righteous?

Putting her fingers to her temple, she massaged the pain away. "You really are your own worst enemy, Olivia," she grumbled to herself.

She slung her satchel over her shoulder and turned to leave.

Most of the spectators in the tower had left, but Sarah and Luke were waiting for her. They each held the hand of one of the children.

"We thought we'd walk down with you," Sarah said, taking Olivia's arm as they neared the stairs. Then she leaned over and whispered, "What are the chances of you talking Rafe into letting Timmy sit on Rowan for a photograph? As of today, he's decided he wants to be a jockey and own a horse." Sarah laughed.

"I don't know the protocol for this kind of thing, but I should think that after the formal shots are taken, Rafe wouldn't mind."

"You're so sweet, Olivia. It would mean the world to Timmy."

As they descended the stairs, Olivia said, "It's a hard life being a jockey."

"I'm not worried. Are you kidding? Timmy's the spitting image of Luke. He'll be over six feet and—"

"Made of twisted steel?"

Sarah grinned at Olivia. "I've always said you had the sharpest eyes in town." She turned to Luke and Timmy. "C'mon. Let's go see Rowan."

The winner's circle was nothing more formal than the area next to the gate that led to the horse barn. Olivia saw Jenny sitting on Rowan, holding a bouquet of long-stemmed red roses tied with a bright blue-and-gold ribbon. The Barzonni family was posing next to Rowan, and Maddie and Mrs. Beabots stood nearby taking photos with their iPhones.

Annie broke away from Sarah and rushed

up to Liz, hugging her. Then she barraged Liz with questions about the new baby. Since Liz was in her fifth month, her "bump" was visible in the spring-green linen dress she wore.

Rafe was talking to Gabe, both men smiling and slapping each other on the back. Gina called out Olivia's name.

Rafe froze and lowered his arm as he scanned the group. When his eyes came to rest on Olivia, his face burst into a luminous smile. He excused himself from his brother and made his way toward her.

"Olivia! Can you believe it?" He grabbed her by the shoulders and held her. How was it possible for her to see so many colors in one person's eyes? And each had a name. Happiness. Joy. Sincerity. Hope. Elation.

"You saw it all, right?"

"Yes, I did. Through my camera and—"

He pulled her close for a hug and whispered, "I knew that kiss would bring me luck."

His breath brushed against her skin like a feather: tickling, soft and teasing. When his lips skimmed her neck, she thought it was a mistake. That he didn't really want to kiss her in front of his family and all her friends. But then he lingered there, and the pressure of his lips against her skin sent chills to the top of her scalp and down her spine. If they'd been anyplace else she would have grasped his face in her hands and brought his mouth to hers once more.

He broke away and turned to his family. "Okay, everybody. Olivia's here, so let's take these photographs with Rowan quickly. He needs his rubdown."

Olivia fumbled with her Sony. Her fingers were numb; probably because there wasn't a nerve ending in her body that hadn't been incinerated by the penetrating look in Rafe's eyes. Not to mention the heat from his lips. She swiped the back of her hand over her forehead, pretending she was shielding her eyes from the sun.

She was getting her bearings. Rowan had run a race in two minutes. In less than twenty seconds, Rafe had turned her to dust with a simple kiss and a smile she would remember till the day she died. No man had ever looked at Olivia as if she were the only woman in the world.

What was happening with Rafe? Was it too soon to ask him what exactly his kiss had meant? One part of her understood that their kiss could have been just what he'd asked for—luck—but the other part of her heart ached for him in a way she'd never felt before. Maybe if she told him she had these feelings, he would clear up his intentions. Or would her confession shove him right back to his paddock, never to be seen again? She was conflicted and confused. Fearful, apprehensive and exhilarated. Perhaps the best plan was to understand herself better before she tried to figure out Rafe.

All she knew right now was that as Rafe left her side to hustle up to Nate and Maddie and position them next to Rowan, she felt alone. Again.

This was the second, maybe third time she'd felt like this. Why did that keep happening? There was no explanation for the void she felt when she wasn't with him.

You've lost your mind, Olivia. That's what's going on.

"Olivia? Hellooo." Rafe was waving at her.

"Sorry? Did you ask me something? I was setting the light."

"Is this okay? Nate and I on this side?"

"We can do one like that, but I want one with you on Rowan's right and both Maddie and Nate on the left. We'll do the same with Gabe and Liz, then Sarah and Luke. By the way…" She walked forward up to Rafe. "I forgot to ask. Timmy wants to sit on Rowan's back. He thinks he wants to be a jockey now."

Rafe placed his hand on Olivia's cheek. "Absolutely. You'll make it a memento he'll cherish all his life."

"What a lovely thing to say."

"That's what you do, Olivia. You capture memories. You lock them up in your camera and hold them hostage." His eyes burned into hers then focused in on her lips.

No mistaking what he was thinking. She was thinking the same thing.

"Listen," he said. "My mom is throwing an impromptu barbecue at the house tonight to celebrate. Please come."

"And bring my camera?" *Or my apron?* She had to ask. After all, the Barzonnis didn't ask Olivia or her mother to be guests. They were staff. Olivia held her breath, and her lungs burned as she waited for him to deliver the devastating blow.

"No camera. Just you. I want you to share in my victory."

"You want me to be there?"

"Yes. All my friends will be there, too. You could ride out with Austin and Katia. Do you want me to ask them for you?"

"No, thanks. I can drive myself. It's not a problem. Thanks for inviting me."

"Thank you for accepting," he replied, his dark-lashed lids lowering as he peered at her mouth again. "Six o'clock."

"Sure."

Olivia swallowed hard, smiled and had to consciously make herself walk away from his compelling eyes and tender voice. She had to get back to work. Her friends were counting on her.

So was Rafe.

CHAPTER THIRTEEN

RAFE CLEANED OUT Rowan's stall and helped Curt with bathing, rinsing and brushing the exhausted horse before heading inside to get ready for the evening guests. By the time he had showered, shaved again and put on clean jeans and a blue-and-white cotton shirt, he was pacing. Rolling up his sleeves, he put on his watch and looked out his bedroom window for the fifth time in half an hour.

Olivia had said she'd come to the barbecue. He should have made her promise. Did he tell her the time? He couldn't remember. He should have put his number in her cell so that she could call him. He should have told her how cute she looked today.

He probably shouldn't have kissed her in the horse barn. But there was something about Olivia that reminded him of a fragile butterfly, and that comparison uncapped a riot of protective emotions. He knew these feelings well because they were also behind his defensiveness of Rowan when he'd thought Olivia had made those photos go viral on purpose.

Impulsive. Rafe, you need to think first and then react. How many times has Mom said that?

Well, he'd been nothing but impulsive with Olivia. Leaped before he looked. He couldn't believe how much she'd filled his thoughts since they'd met at his father's funeral. He'd been tied to the farm and training Rowan, but there wasn't an hour that went by that he didn't see her face in his mind's eye.

No woman has ever captured me like that.

His worry was that his impulsiveness might have scared her. When he was with her, he sensed her trembling, as if she wanted to fly as far away from him as possible. Then she'd look at him with those soft brown eyes and he lost all reason.

He glanced out the window. Still no Olivia.

Yeah, he'd screwed up. He shouldn't have grazed her neck with a kiss in front of everyone, either. That might have been too much, too soon. But she'd smelled so good, like spring hyacinths or lilies or roses. He couldn't resist.

He groaned. Could he be any more wired?

The excitement of the race and then the thrill of the win had caught him off guard. Rafe thought he'd been prepared for all possible outcomes, but he couldn't have anticipated this feeling. In retrospect, Rafe realized that the only thing he'd prepared himself for was failure.

Deep down, he'd never actually believed that he would own a horse as talented as Rowan, much less race him. They'd never had a horse good enough to win. Winning had been his father's dream, so Angelo had high standards. Even when Rowan showed promising results, Angelo had held back his praise. Rafe had recognized how special Rowan was from the day they'd brought him home. But he'd never let himself fully believe what a winner they had on their hands until now.

Horses had bonded Rafe to his father in a way that simply being a son, an heir to the farm, never could. Rafe had devoted his life to realizing his father's dream, and today he'd finally done just that.

Rafe's grief had transformed to joy. When he was standing in the winner's circle with his brothers and mother and his fingers curled around that huge silver trophy, Rafe could have sworn on a stack of bibles that his father was standing beside him. In that instant he remembered hundreds of things his father had said. Memories of his father saddling up horses, racing over the fields, jumping across the creek, riding through damp autumn leaves and wintery, snow-covered hills filled his mind. Rafe felt his father's presence so intensely he nearly burst with emotion.

He'd tried to hold it together, but he'd been watching Olivia's expressions as she snapped the photographs with the family. At the instant he felt what he thought was his father's hand on his shoulder, Rafe had shivered. His smile must have faltered because Olivia had immediately dropped the camera and caught his eye. He'd frozen, hoping the imaginary pressure on his shoulder would not lessen.

Olivia had quickly adjusted her lens, and he realized he was in the crosshairs of her next photos.

She knew. She saw. She was in the moment with him.

Since then, Rafe had felt as if he'd crossed into a new world. He was exhilarated, filled with a freedom he hadn't known existed. He felt powerful and accomplished. He realized a lot of it was adrenaline. Chemicals. Endorphins. All of which had nothing to do with reality. But he was going to enjoy this while it lasted.

Today he'd thrown off the crushing shroud of his father's death. He'd been carrying remorse over never having given his father this win. Even as a kid, he'd wanted to show his father he could ride faster, jump higher and excel in just about anything involving horses and racing. Childish as it was, he'd always wanted to be his father's favorite, so he'd hitched his dreams to horses. With Rowan's win, he'd achieved what Angelo had always wanted. Now it was up to Rafe to decide how far he wanted to take his dream.

Rafe rubbed his chin. That was a scary question to consider. He didn't have an answer. His brief moment in the sun, hearing the applause, listening to the accolades from his family and friends and smiling for dozens of website and newspaper reporters had been thrilling. He could see how that kind of fame could become a narcotic. But was that what he wanted?

He honestly didn't know.

What he did know without a doubt was that he liked looking up and seeing Olivia watching him. He liked her gentle voice and her deep brown eyes, but what intrigued him more than he wanted to admit was her ability to look right into him and see something that made her eyes sparkle and her lips part into a beguiling smile. He wondered if she realized she did that each time she saw him.

Suddenly, a memory came to him. It was last fall, in Austin's kitchen after a tennis match. Olivia had been delivering food from the deli. He'd practically bumped into her, being distracted by the intense game and the fact that he'd been late to pick up his mother from an appointment. He'd excused himself, and he remembered that Olivia didn't respond with a rude comment, as he expected and probably deserved. She was polite, and he'd glanced back at her. Her brown eyes had gleamed with an inner smile. She'd been very busy and went back to her work right away.

He hadn't noticed much else about her at the time, and he'd completely forgotten the encounter until just now.

When she'd catered his father's funeral, he'd noticed her genuine compassion and empathy. Most of the guests had offered clipped words laced with fear. Fear of their own deaths. They'd avoided direct eye contact for the most part. He understood that they likely just didn't want to make the family cry more than they already had.

But not Olivia. She was different.

Until today, Rafe had tried to convince himself that what he'd felt when he was with Olivia was transference or displaced grief. Or some psychological coping skill.

Mourning his father would take a long time, but now he knew his grief had nothing to do with his reaction to Olivia. Though they'd gotten off on the wrong foot about Rowan's photograph going viral, he believed that it was an accident—of sorts. Either way, it was in the past.

All Rafe wanted to think about was the future because suddenly, everything seemed brighter. Happier.

He stopped pacing and looked out the window again. He could see all the way down the long drive. His eyes grew wide as Olivia's delivery van turned into the entrance.

"Happy. Is that what you are, Rafe?"

He wasn't quite sure. He definitely wasn't as sad as he had been, which made sense given the race win—and Olivia's kiss. But genuine happiness? What was that, exactly? He'd had a happy childhood. His home was safe. They lived on a farm and never went hungry. He'd never had to endure any major family dramas. But he had always had the sense that there should be more to life than backbreaking work in the sun. He would live and die on this farm. He was thirty years old and he'd never met anyone he wanted to spend a long weekend with, much less a lifetime. His last long-term girlfriend had been in junior high school. For the most part, the women he met didn't understand the responsibilities, heartbreaks and pressures of being a farmer. Gabe had experienced the same thing, until Liz. But then again, Liz was essentially a farmer.

He peered through the white wooden slatted blinds as Olivia parked. Rafe felt his smile spring from some forgotten labyrinth in his heart. Warmth coursed through his body, and he couldn't get to the door fast enough. He flung it open, shot across the parking area and reached Olivia just as she was locking her vehicle door.

"Hi," he said breathlessly. "You're here."

"I am," she replied, looking into his eyes but not smiling back at him. "I had a lot of work to do—"

He grabbed her hands. "But you came, anyway. I'm really glad."

"You are?" A lovely smile transformed her pretty mouth, and it was all he could do not to steal a kiss.

"Yes," he said and then pointed toward the pool and terrace. "See? Everyone is here already."

He tugged her hand to lead her toward the party.

She shook her head. "Maybe I should see if your mother needs any help in the kitchen. I could—"

"No," he interrupted again. "Not tonight. No working tonight. I even told you not to bring your camera. Remember?"

"Yes, Rafe. I remember." She searched his face. "What is it? You seem different tonight. You're acting different."

"You can see that?"

Her smile drifted away and she squeezed his hand. "Is it because of the win?"

How could he answer her when he himself was clueless about everything going on in his life right now? Standing here, holding her hand, nearly made the entire world feel right. But what did that mean?

"Not all of it," he finally said, wondering why he was holding his breath.

"That would be enough for most people." She chuckled good-naturedly.

It's because of you.

How idiotic would he sound if he said that to her? They hadn't known each other a full month. Yet her kiss had been like no other. Sweet. Lingering. Mind-blowing in its heartfelt desire. Rafe found himself thinking far too often about how long he'd have to wait for another kiss. She was like the beautiful princess holding the key to his desires. Suddenly, he wanted to be the guy who made her dreams come true. But it was too soon for that, wasn't it?

"I guess I'm guilty of thinking big," he said.

"Lofty goals. I can tell. Rowan in the Kentucky Derby would be just about the biggest race I could think of."

"Actually, there's the World Cup in Dubai."

"Arab Emirates. I've heard of that race."

"Really? I'm surprised."

"Why? Because I'm just a waitress? A caterer?" Her reply came with an attitude and a boulder-size chip on her shoulder. Something wasn't right; he saw it in her guarded expression. The surprising sting of her words put him on the defensive.

"Did I say that?" he asked in a demanding tone, his own anger rising much too quickly.

"Sorry," she replied softly. "I don't know why I said that."

"I do."

"Really? Why do you think?"

"Because at Austin's house last fall I ignored you. Or at least you thought I did."

"I'm always invisible to people around here," she said, lowering her head.

He slipped his finger under her chin and lifted it until her eyes met his. "That's not true. Most of the people here tonight are your girlfriends. My brothers. You know them all very well. You just don't know me, that's all. And I'd like to change that."

She swallowed hard. "You would?"

"Yes, Olivia. I would like that very much." He leaned down to kiss her. Just as his lips brushed hers, she pulled back.

"Rafe, I came here tonight because I need to talk to you."

"I thought that's what we were doing." Her eyes had lost the soft brown lights that seemed to sparkle just for him. Instead, he saw determination and something else in her gaze. Distance? "What is it?"

She twisted her hands together, and tears welled in her eyes.

"Olivia?"

"Rafe, I don't know how to tell you this or even if I should tell you this, but…"

"Please, go ahead."

She inhaled deeply. "Rafe, Rowan didn't win the race. He lost."

CHAPTER FOURTEEN

SINCE THE SECOND Rowan crossed the finish line, Olivia had gone back and forth between what her eyes told her and what her camera had captured so many times that her head was pounding. She hadn't had time to inspect every single photograph but she'd uploaded the most important ones to her computer and reviewed the slow-motion footage before coming to the barbecue. And she'd seen the proof.

To make the situation even graver, in two days she would have to present copies of all her photographs of the race to the officials. They had hired her. The photographs would be examined by both amateur and eventually professional race judges. They could even be published, Howard had told her. Mr. Blue's owners had the right to demand a retraction if they found evidence that supported his win. At that time, it would officially go on the books that Rowan had lost.

Olivia couldn't imagine how devastated Rafe would be. The last thing she wanted was for him to find out from an investigative board or a published article that his victory was being rescinded.

She raised her eyes to his crestfallen face.

"What are you talking about?" he demanded.

Olivia's mouth had gone dry, but the tears that had welled in her eyes burned like acid. "I saw it from the judge's tower." The rest of her explanation died on her lips. She swallowed hard and tried to wet her lips. Looking into Rafe's confused eyes, she saw a new pain there: betrayal.

Olivia knew now she'd made the wrong decision. She shouldn't have come here, and she should have never brought the truth to Rafe's attention.

She strove daily to prove she was not her father's child. She would never keep the truth from anyone she loved. Though she didn't believe she was in love with Rafe, she cared about him. Maybe it was infatuation. Maybe it was friendship. But if she wanted any kind of a relationship with Rafe in the future— which she did, with all her heart—then they had to start with honesty. At least, that was what she'd convinced herself until the words *Rowan didn't win the race* crossed her lips.

In the end, I'm just like my father. Destroying lives. Killing dreams.

"It doesn't matter what you think you saw. The judge declared him a winner. Besides, I thought you were supplying the camera that took the pictures to prove it."

"I…I did. Two of them. My digital camera showed he won. That's the one that Howard checked."

"Then it's settled. It was the official call."

She nailed him with a penetrating gaze. "That's what I'm trying to tell you. I brought two cameras. The second one was a slow-motion digital that I could amp up to nearly ten thousand frames per second. He never saw those shots because— Well, he just didn't. After I left the fairgrounds, I went over it all at home. It's only by half a nose, but Mr. Blue was the winner."

Rafe stared at her. She could tell he was processing the information. He was as still as stone. She wished he'd say something, but instead, the sparkle she usually saw in his eyes dulled, reminding her of misty, gray, late-winter mornings when the earth wasn't quite awake with spring, yet wasn't deep in winter slumber, either.

"What are you going to do with it?" he asked.

"Do?"

"Are you going to show your pictures to the judge?"

He'd caught her off guard. She hadn't figured that out yet. "I don't know. I wanted to tell you—"

"Oh, so am I supposed to go rat out my own horse to the officials, then? You want me to do the dirty work?" His voice rose with each word. His back stiffened. He looked a foot taller. He lifted his chin imperiously.

"I have to give them to the judges," Olivia said. "They expect them in a few days. I wanted you to know first." She felt her own power rising slowly within her. "You do what you think is right."

"Right?" he bellowed. "You think it's right that I take this win away from my father's horse? You think it's *right* to tell my mother that her husband's horse failed? Did you see her face today? Did you see my brothers? All they talked about was how happy they knew our dad would be watching Rowan win. You think it's right to ruin that memory, Olivia?"

She didn't realize she'd balled her fists until she flexed her nearly numb fingers. How could she answer him? No, she didn't think it was right to rob the Barzonnis of Angelo's legacy. She didn't think it was right to impugn Rowan's reputation. But she didn't think it was right to keep the information to herself, either…not that she really had a choice. She supposed she could keep the slow-motion footage and give the judges the half-truth. Only she and Rafe would ever know that Rowan hadn't won.

On the other hand, if she handed in everything and the judges saw how accurate her work had been, that it could affect the outcome of the race, she would be applauded. It would be a huge step toward the photojournalism career she'd always wanted. But her dream would come at a price. A big one.

"No, it's not right," she said finally. When all was said and done, she couldn't hurt Rafe like that.

He peered at her. "You must think I'm stupid."

"What are you talking about?"

"You're ambitious, Olivia, and that's a good thing, but somehow me and my horse have gotten caught in your net. You're using

Rowan for your own gain. It's selfish, really. If those pictures show Mr. Blue won, you'll be famous."

"Famous? That's ridiculous."

"Is it? The whole world loves racing. It's thrilling. It's sport and competition. And the animals are gorgeous. A hometown story like this hits the internet, and believe me, reporters will be at your door—and mine." He folded his arms across his chest.

She had to admit that the idea of her photos garnering attention, making a difference, was enticing. She'd just been considering that option herself. She couldn't think of a response.

"The problem here, Olivia, is that you don't understand the first thing about Rowan or me or what any of this means to my family."

She nodded, not taking her eyes off his. "Well, I know I have a special connection with Rowan, too. I love him already." She cut off her next thought. Had she really said that out loud? Did she mean the horse or the man? How deep had she burrowed in here? Rafe was right. She didn't know him or his family very well, but she wanted to. She wanted to know everything. She wanted to know how far his dreams of racing went, even though it terrified her. Did he like working the farm?

Or did he want to escape like Nate and Gabe? What kept him here? Was it loyalty to his father? Love, respect or responsibility to his mother? Or all three?

At this moment Olivia despised her need to always tell the truth. Sometimes, it could be a serious flaw. Her mother had told her once that she had to be careful with the truth. Julia had explained that truth-telling could lead to losing friends. Olivia countered that if her friends didn't want the truth, then they weren't her friends. Julia had pointed out the difference between simply stating facts and building a relationship.

No relationship could be built on lies, but often, strategic timing when it came to delivering the truth was the glue that kept the relationship together.

Olivia realized she was absolutely guilty of bad timing.

"You do have a connection with him," Rafe agreed. "But you're not part of his life."

"I'd like to be."

Rafe's eyebrow hitched up, and he fixed her with a steely blue gaze. "But something is holding you back. I've seen it, Olivia. There's a wall around you that even Rowan couldn't get through. I know I can't. You've got your shields up."

"So do you."

"I should," he countered. "You want to hurt me. And my family."

"I don't *want* to hurt anybody. I was just telling you the truth."

"Fine. So, are you going to tell me the whole truth?"

"I don't know what—"

He uncrossed his arms and put his hands on her shoulders, leaning in close. "I see your fear when I talk about racing. It's not there when we're just talking about Rowan or the other horses. It's not the animals that frighten you. It's the racing. Isn't it?"

The air in Olivia's lungs burned like an inferno. She felt as if she'd burst into flames on the spot. If only she could. Then she wouldn't have to tell him the whole truth. If he was so angry, why didn't he just send her away? He could dismiss her and that would be the end of it. She'd figure out a way to get over these feelings. Surely there was some kind of anti-emotional wrecking ball she could use to tear them all down. She wondered how many years it would take to forget his kisses. To forget him.

She'd told Rafe one truth and it had crushed him. She was amazed he was still talking to her. Why did he want to know her deepest fears? Why did he care? What difference would it make to him?

She had hurt him. Devastated him. The whole truth would drive him away for good. Instead, she wanted to mend the rift she'd already caused. She wanted to see those flashes in his eyes that he seemed to reserve for her alone. She didn't know how he appeared to shut out the entire world except for her when they were together. She couldn't do that. In fact, when she was with him she was hypersensitive to everything going on around them. Right now, for example: the cool evening breeze that ruffled his dark hair and the spring grass that had yet to be cut; the setting sun's golden rays; the buds of the weeping cherry tree beside the kitchen door and the half-moon rising in the east. She heard the sound of Rafe's breathing, and she saw the shadow in his eyes as he waited for her to answer him.

She had always considered herself a keen observer of nature and her surroundings, but the truth was she saw more, felt more, when she was with Rafe.

She must be falling in love with him. And that made it even harder to tell the truth about her father.

"Racing is dangerous. Not just for Rowan, but for you, too, Rafe."

"How so?"

"I saw you out there. You were acting as the starter assistant. What if Rowan bolted or kicked? What if you got really hurt?"

Rafe flung his head back and dropped his hands to his sides in exasperation. He took a deep breath. "This is what I am, Olivia. And Rowan was bred to run. He's a Thoroughbred and though most of them bite and nip and can be really cantankerous, he's not. You've seen that."

"It was his first time in that tiny little pen at the starting gate. Howard told me that Thoroughbreds can go crazy—"

"But he didn't," Rafe countered. "I won't deny that I was nervous, but that's why I wanted to be out there with him. I knew if he saw me, he had a better chance of staying calm. He was always calm around my dad, but—"

Rafe opened his palms and then closed them. He stared at the ground.

"He's not here," she finished for him. "I'm so sorry he wasn't."

"Me, too. And that's what I need to explain to you. Racing was the thing that gave my dad joy. The farm and its success drove him. He was an ambitious man. There are still people around Indian Lake who say he was a tyrant, even a thief, when it came to how he acquired his land. But I only know his side of the story."

"What did he tell you?"

"That he spent his youth on the streets in Sicily and was hungry nearly all his life. He swore he would find a way to get to America, and he did. He went to New York first and found it just as gang-infested and brutal as Italy. But he got a job and saved his money. He heard about the farms here in Indian Lake from a tourist in the restaurant where he worked. He heard the land was cheap. He came out here and bought this first parcel. He said he knew how to grow tomatoes and started with that. When he learned of other farms going up for sale, he offered to buy them, rather than allow corporate farms to come in. At the time, his neighbors were willing to sell to him. He never stole anything from anybody. At least not in this country.

He was proud to be an American. Proud that he learned the English language and proud to work the land."

"And the horses came later?"

"Not really. He had a workhorse from the beginning. My mother liked to ride, so he bought a horse for her for twenty dollars. By the time I showed interest in horses, he'd already been looking at Thoroughbreds. He knew they could also make a lot of money if they won."

Olivia struggled with her vow to listen and not judge. Not react. Beating back her fear, she tried to open her mind to what Rafe was sharing with her. "Did he like to gamble?"

Rafe chuckled. "You're so funny."

"Funny? How?"

"My father's entire life was a gamble. Living on the streets means you have no roof over your head. You live in cardboard boxes, under bridges—whatever you can find. Waking up every day was a gamble, Olivia. Working a cargo boat to get to the United States was a gamble. Then trying to work a farm when he wasn't a farmer—that was a gamble. If anything, I'd say my dad was driven by fear of the *known* all his life. He'd known too much poverty to ever go back. He had no family. My mother said that was why he wanted so many children. He would have been happy if there had been twelve sons." He laughed.

She touched his hand. "You really loved him," she whispered, her heart swelling.

"More than I could ever tell him."

"But you're telling him now. With this win."

"I am."

"I think I understand now." Her eyes plumbed his. "Thank you for telling me all this, Rafe. I didn't know."

"So you see, Olivia, this little hometown race was a very big deal for this family. It was like—well, my father coming back to us. Even if just for two minutes. He was there today with all of us. Cheering us on. Sharing in the winner's circle."

She gasped and her hand flew to her heart. "Rafe. I saw it. That moment. I caught it on my camera. You really did feel his presence, didn't you?"

"Yes, Olivia. I did." He choked out the reply. "So you see? This wasn't just a race. It was a gift to my dad."

"I understand."

Cocking his head slightly, he studied her.

"So what are you going to do? Are you going to talk to the judges? Take this away from us?"

Olivia realized that despite the fact she'd laid the burden at Rafe's feet, he was not taking up the gauntlet. He would not do anything about the slow-motion pictures or what she'd seen. She wasn't the official judge or the person in charge. She had no authority in this matter.

"The reality is, Rafe, that Rowan ran a stellar race. If it had been a Graded Stakes race, with another win or two, Rowan could run in the Kentucky Derby. He's that good. Mr. Blue was just as fast, so he's a contender, as well. In the end, their times are the only criteria that will matter to the racing world. I'm not going to do anything, Rafe. I have the photos if you ever want them, but for now, they'll stay on my hard drive."

"You'd do that?"

"For you—and for Rowan, I'll do it."

"Thank you for being a real friend, Olivia," Rafe said and put his arms around her.

She leaned her cheek against his hard chest. He smelled of spice and soap, but not the leather she'd picked up when he'd kissed her today in the fairgrounds' horse barn. He hadn't been to see Rowan since his shower, she guessed.

She was glad he'd opened up to her even though she'd been less than forthcoming about her own past. His respect and love for his father radiated out from him with every word. She knew Rowan's win today had gone a long way toward easing Rafe's guilt and grief.

If she'd brought up her fears, which were in complete conflict with Rafe's motivations, they might have walked away from each other and never known this moment. Holding and comforting each other.

She could feel his heartbeat against her temple. It was in perfect sync with hers.

She'd done the right thing. She'd keep the truth locked away in the past where it couldn't hurt her again.

CHAPTER FIFTEEN

OLIVIA WAS GLAD she'd worn a jacket to the barbecue. Now that the sun had set, it was downright chilly. Fortunately, Gabe and Nate had built a huge fire in the pit at the edge of the terrace. Everyone had grouped their chairs around the fire, and now they were munching on the chips and guacamole that Maddie had made.

Gina had set up a buffet of hamburgers and all the fixings, a huge Italian romaine salad with parmesan cheese and olive oil dressing, and cannoli for dessert.

Olivia watched Rafe build an enormous hamburger with two charcoal-broiled patties, slices of Swiss cheese, dill pickles and tomato. Olivia wasn't quite sure how he was going to get his mouth around the monster burger, but he did. He grabbed a beer and waited patiently while Olivia filled her plate with salad and placed a plain burger sans bun on the side. She smiled up at him as she selected a bottle of water.

Rafe frowned at her plate. "You'll starve if you eat like that."

"I'm saving my calories for the cannoli."

"Can't argue with that. Mom makes the best." He paused. "Neck and neck with your *macarons*."

She smiled, happy that he remembered her cookies. She remembered he'd called her the cookie girl.

"I'll make some extras for Liz's baby shower and slip them into the refrigerator for you."

"Better mark the box with my name, otherwise Mica will eat them all."

"Good tip." Olivia laughed as they walked over to the fire and joined the rest of the family.

"Olivia, come sit next to me," Maddie said, patting the faux wicker chair next to hers. "The fire is really warm."

Rafe put his plate on a small folding table and moved it next to Olivia. Then he pulled up a chair beside her. To his left was Gabe, who sat with Liz on a chaise, rubbing her shoulders while she warmed her hands near the fire. On another chaise, Austin and Katia chatted with each other. Olivia greeted Sarah and Luke, who were zipping Timmy and Annie into windbreakers. Isabelle Hawks sat in a folding chair next to Cate Sullivan and Mrs. Beabots, and though they gave Olivia a wave, it was clear they were deep in discussion and didn't wish to be disturbed at the moment.

"So, little bro," Gabe said with a wide grin. "Has the thrill of victory worn off yet?"

Rafe shook his head. "Absolutely not. I figure this day lasts till midnight. I've got hours to bask in it. Tomorrow it's back to real life."

"Good for you," Nate added. "You should squeeze this for all it's worth."

Gina sat on a chaise across from Rafe with a black shawl shot with silver threads wrapped around her. Over her legs she'd placed a summer blanket. Sam Crenshaw sipped a glass of red wine in an Adirondack rocking chair beside her, his gaze distant. *"Bella luna,"* Sam mumbled, pointing at the rising moon.

Gina patted his hand, and Sam lowered his head and smiled at her. Noticing that Olivia was watching, Gina focused her attention on Rafe. "I think they should schedule the Indian Lake race in June next year when it's warmer. This early in April is practically winter. We were lucky the snow had melted off the track."

Rafe wiped his mouth with a paper napkin. "There's a reason for that."

"And that is?" Gabe asked.

"It may be a charity race and for most people it's just for fun, but a couple of the horses, like Swept Away and Mr. Blue, can use their times to get into the competition at real tracks like Hawthorne Racecourse in Cicero. Or Arlington. Possibly a Graded Stakes race like Delta Downs in Louisiana."

"So you're telling me that there's no such thing as a friendly horse race?" Nate asked, sipping on a margarita.

"Not to a Thoroughbred owner. Every horse in that race came from a racer. Sire or mare. They were all bred to run. Just like Rowan. Every owner has dreams. Big, small. Doesn't matter. It's my guess that every one of those owners thought their horse was going to win today. Even the slowest one. He wouldn't have been there if the owner didn't think he had a chance. None of the horses had run before, or if they had, Curt and I hadn't heard of it. Now three of them, Rowan, Mr. Blue and Swept Away, are primed for the circuits for next year's Derby."

"What about this year's Kentucky Derby?" Olivia asked.

Rafe put his plate down on the table. "It's too late for this year. Next year they'll all be three years old, and the better horses like Mr. Blue and Swept Away will have tested themselves at Gulfstream Park or Golden Gate Field. It will be a year of crisscrossing the country to gain the points they need to enter the Kentucky Derby."

"Points?" Nate interjected. "I thought all a horse had to do was win two hundred and fifty thousand, give or take ten or twenty grand, and he was in. That's what Dad always said. I've heard about some of these horses that win a race in April before the Derby, and boom! Like Delta Downs. Six hundred thousand to the winner. That's it. He's in."

"You're behind the times, bro. Two years ago the qualifying process changed drastically. The days when any Graded Stakes races would count toward a horse making his way to the Derby are over. Now it's much tougher."

"How so?" Gabe asked.

"It's all based on points now. Each horse has to earn thirty-six points in Graded Stakes races and he has to finish in the top four in every race. And those races have to be Kentucky Derby Prep races, specifically."

"Scam!" Nate yelled.

"Conspiracy!" Gabe concurred. "That's un-American."

Olivia realized she'd been shoveling salad into her mouth as she tried to block out the litany of racetracks that turned her blood to ice. On her last bite, her hand was shaking so much, the salad fell off the fork. She put the utensil down and wrapped her hands around the plastic water bottle to steady them.

How was it possible that she had locked away the pain her father had caused her for nearly half her life but suddenly, in the past month, she was revisiting memories of him and his gambling at every turn?

She couldn't ignore the fact that her inner turmoil had started when she'd met Rowan and Rafe.

Rafe was immersed in the racing world. He'd just told her that winning races was the only dream that brought his father joy. Olivia realized that Rafe had also been drawing her a very clear picture of who he was and what he wanted to do with his life.

The Indian Lake Hospital Foundation Horse Race wasn't just a single event for Rafe or Rowan. It was a beginning. It was a test. Much like the other owners, Rafe had wanted to see which horse was king of the field. Olivia had photographs to prove that Mr. Blue had won this race, but that didn't change the fact that Rowan was a trophy-winning horse.

As Rafe told everyone about the intricacies of qualifying for the most prestigious horse race in the United States, Olivia felt as if she was falling down a tunnel, getting farther and farther away from the real world and the people around her.

Thirty minutes ago she'd been proud of herself for keeping her fears hidden, but she'd only fooled herself. Nothing had been solved.

And it was her responsibility to deal with it all.

Here she sat in the middle of a discussion about the astronomical sums of money it took for a horse to win a place in a prestigious race, which offered even more money. With each word her friends said, Olivia's blood pressure rose until she heard the thrumming of her heart in her temples. She felt lightheaded. Thank goodness she'd only grabbed water to drink. Even the caffeine in iced tea would have set her heart tripping like a faulty metronome.

Get a grip, Olivia.

Earlier, she'd felt as if she was falling in love with Rafe. Yet, how could she be?

His love, his dream, was her fear.

He'd proven to his father's ghost that Rowan was all that Angelo had hoped he would be.

But it was far from enough.

Looming in the back of her mind was the disquieting shadow of racetrack gambling. She hadn't seen any evidence of Rafe succumbing to that vice, but there was always the chance that he could. Being around the tracks could be hypnotic and lure even the most resolute people. And if they were together? Her deepest fear was that she would succumb to the betting cages, put her savings on the line and slip into addiction. She was her father's daughter, after all. She would be no better than the man who betrayed her and broke her mother's heart. How could she even consider being with someone whose lifestyle could put her on that path?

Olivia looked over at Rafe as he talked with his brothers. Mica had joined the discussion about Rafe taking Rowan to the Illinois Derby in two weeks. Gabe and Nate were urging Rafe to try his wings in a professional setting.

Every bit of the conversation made Olivia nervous. It wasn't just the racing, though. Their encouragement reminded her of lectures she'd given herself, too many times to count, about her own dreams of a photojournalism career.

Olivia chewed her bottom lip anxiously. Why couldn't they talk about something else?

"Raphael," Gina said, leaning forward and pulling her shawl up around her neck. Maybe she would be the voice of reason. "I'm behind you one hundred percent. If you want to enter Rowan in Illinois, I'll give you any money you need to do it. Your father would want me to."

Olivia sank back in her chair. Gina was no help.

"Thanks, Mom, but I think I've got this." Rafe smiled. "I'll have to talk to Curt and see what he thinks. It's in two weeks, but I think we could get in."

Mica lowered the beer he'd raised to his lips. "Two weeks?"

"Yeah," Rafe replied. "Why?"

Mica's tone was concerned. "You can't be serious, Rafe."

"Of course I'm serious."

"We're planting corn and soybeans till the end of this month. The first of May I've got six guys hired to help us with the machines to plant the tomatoes. You know it takes six of us to run the tomato plants down that conveyor. I've only got four guys from last year. Two are new. They'll need some training. Not a lot, but some. You and I agreed we're doing three hundred acres in tomato plants this year."

"I know," Rafe replied, lowering his gaze.

Olivia heard the disappointment in Rafe's voice. From the tension in Mica's voice, it sounded as if this was not a brand-new topic.

"We talked about this last spring," Mica said with painstaking emphasis on each word. "Our planting season overlaps with your horse-racing season. What's worse is that the second round of trials for the Derby are in the fall when we're harvesting. Those are our two busiest times of the year. I need you here, Rafe."

"Did I say I was taking off? I'm only going over to Chicago!"

Mica stood up, taking his plate and his beer. "You know what? I don't care. You do what you want. You always have. Dad always let you do what you wanted, when you wanted. I'll take care of the farm. You go play with your ponies."

Mica stomped across the terrace and toward the house.

"I didn't say that!" Rafe bellowed.

Gina whipped off the blanket she'd put over her legs. She squeezed Sam's hand. "I'll go." She rose and followed Mica.

Sam nodded and looked at Gabe and Liz. "How long has Mica felt this way?"

"Forever," Nate and Gabe said in unison.

Rafe stood up. "Honestly? I never knew." He stared after his brother and mother as they met at the door and then went inside.

Rafe looked down at Olivia. "Sorry."

Mrs. Beabots stood up and said, "I believe the Barzonni family needs to be left alone, ladies." She turned to Isabelle and Cate. "Why don't you both get your things and take me home? I'll make us some tea. Olivia? Do you have a ride back to town?"

Mrs. Beabots obviously considered her an outsider to the Barzonnis. But then, the older woman didn't know about Rafe's kisses. Or their arguments.

"I drove myself," she replied. "I should help clean up."

"It's okay, Olivia," Maddie said. "Thanks for offering. Nate and I can handle it."

"I'll help, too," Gabe volunteered.

Luke looked at Sarah. "We should get the kids home, as well."

Sarah nodded. "You're right. They have to get up early—Annie has voice lessons and Timmy's got swimming at the YMCA. "

Everyone gathered their plates and placed them on the big trays that Gina had provided.

Olivia walked over to Rafe. "Thanks for inviting me."

"Sure," he said. "This isn't how I expected it to go."

"Yeah, you're supposed to have several more hours of limelight to enjoy."

"Fat chance," he replied glumly. "But listen, if I can swing it somehow and can register for the Illinois Derby, will you come?"

Olivia stared at him. She hadn't expected an invitation to another race. In fact, she hadn't expected anything from Rafe ever again. She'd convinced herself that she shouldn't see him or even be acquainted with him. They weren't good for each other. They were completely at odds.

Only, he didn't know that.

"To be your photographer, you mean?"

"Yeah. For Rowan."

"For Rowan," she repeated.

But not as your date.

At least Olivia knew now for certain: they were still at square one.

CHAPTER SIXTEEN

"DID YOU SEE the lake last night, Olivia?" Maddie asked as she zipped up her black-and-fluorescent-green wet-suit jacket. "The sky was totally pink, and so was the water. Nate and I were standing on our deck and I felt like I was living inside an opalescent bubble of light," she continued as she took her position behind Olivia and prepared to hoist the sculling boat on her shoulders.

"Okay, everybody," Sarah shouted. "Heave!"

Olivia groaned as she worked in unison with Sarah, Maddie and Isabelle to lift their sculling boat off the racks while Liz held the doors open.

It was the first row of the spring. These mornings were some of Olivia's most cherished times with her friends. Skimming over the placid waters, she was always able to forget her worries and concentrate on the rowing and how every muscle in her body had to work in perfect synchronicity with the other women. They were a unit, striving for one end—this blend of nature and human physical exertion. Time stood still for Olivia when they rowed, sometimes moving so fast she was shocked they'd circled the lake so quickly. They were often the only people out on the water. Because they rowed near dawn, there were seldom any swimmers about, and speedboats and skiers were not allowed until ten. Today two fishermen in a rowboat bobbed behind the cattails and reeds along the shore. Those with bigger, fancier fishing boats didn't fish on Indian Lake.

Olivia knew she'd missed a thousand photographs over the years, but that was the point of sculling. She had to stay focused. Here she was only a cog in the human machinery that gave flight to their vessel.

"Are you sure it's safe for you and the baby to be rowing, Liz?" Olivia asked. "Should I even ask that? You're not offended, are you?"

Liz laughed as they made their way from the boathouse down to the shore. "I'm fine. My doctor says I'm the healthiest expectant mother he's ever seen. Apparently, all the years of physical work in the vineyard have helped."

"Good," Sarah said, "because you'll need

a lot of biceps power lifting kids, trikes and monstrously full laundry baskets."

"Are we grousing, Sarah?" Maddie teased as they put the boat in the water.

"Not really. I wouldn't give up any of my new life with Annie and Timmy for even a millisecond of my past. What I'm saying is I don't know how Luke did it alone for two years. How does anybody take care of kids and hold down a full-time job? It takes both of us and Mrs. Milse to keep up with the house, the groceries, Beau, the trips to the vet, the dentist and the doctor for checkups."

Olivia was the first in the boat and picked up her paddle. "It sounds foreign to me," she said as they rowed away from shore and swept out to the middle of the still lake.

"Not to me," Isabelle put in. "I spent my entire childhood taking care of my younger brothers and sisters. My mom had to work, and being the oldest, all the chores and baby-sitting fell to me. I hated it. While they went out and played, I did the laundry. I don't want any part of diapers and midnight feedings." She shivered. "Gives me the willies to think of being chained to one kind of life. One option." She shook her head. "Not for me."

Liz laughed to herself as Sarah stepped up the speed with her shouts of "Pull! Pull!"

"That's because you haven't met the right guy yet, Isabelle," Liz said. "I never thought much about it before I met Gabe. Then everything in my life changed."

Olivia stared at the morning sun as it rose behind a band of mottled clouds and sent striations of pink, red and lavender across the glassy water. The sight was magnificent and spellbinding. She wished she had her camera so she could capture the glory of the colors. Then she'd show it to Rafe.

Rafe.

Olivia froze midmotion and had to scramble to get back in sync.

"Olivia. You okay?" Liz asked behind her.

"Fine." Olivia picked up the pace. "Sorry."

"I've never seen you miss a beat like that," Liz said. "Weird."

No, it wasn't weird. It was Rafe. Olivia hadn't been able to get him out of her head since last night at the barbecue. In fact, she'd barely slept at all.

Yesterday had been like riding an emotional bullet train straight across uncharted country. She'd gone from trepidation verging on fear about the horse race to insecurity about her ability to photograph the race, to an argument with the judge about the outcome. To say nothing of what had happened with Rafe.

Closing her eyes, she could still feel the gentle pressure of Rafe's lips against hers. Olivia had been kissed plenty of times, but never like that. Olivia was a practical woman. Even in her craft, she tried to present things as they were. Raw. Truthful. So it was more than a little difficult for her to explain what happened to her when Rafe kissed her. After spending an entire night dissecting yesterday's events, Olivia knew the only truth was that her life would never be the same.

For years she'd heard patronizing comments from her mother's friends and even simplistic explanations from her own girlfriends that when the right man came along, things would change. She would change.

But Olivia didn't want to change. At least, not like that.

She wanted to *make* some changes. That was certain. She'd told herself she simply hadn't had the time to do so. Her catering schedule was packed. They'd had a busy month at the deli. She had events to plan, including a wedding.

She stopped herself cold. She was doing it again. Cramming her hours and days with everything that wasn't the one thing she wanted. Her photography. If she was too busy to try, she couldn't fail. If she was honest with herself, though, her hectic schedule was an excuse she'd been hiding behind for years. Deep down, she was afraid of taking a chance on herself. Because that was exactly what it was: a chance. A gamble. Was she a risk taker like her father? And if she went the distance, would she become addicted to the hunt like he had? Would she hurt her mother? What if she had to move away? Julia didn't deserve to be abandoned twice in her life by the people she loved.

"Pull!" Sarah shouted as they rowed over lily pads on the north side of the lake near the lodge.

Sarah's instructions shook Olivia out of her daydreams.

"You guys with me?"

"Yea, Captain!" they yelled back.

Olivia wiped the sweat from her forehead with the sleeve of her sky-blue-and-black wet suit, pulling with all her might. The pink of dawn had faded into a brilliant blue. Spring trees were only beginning to bud, but

the forsythia and rhododendrons that dec-
orated the gardens of the lake houses had
burst into color over the weekend. Soon the
long branches of the maples and oaks would
spread out over the water's edge and shade
the piers and beaches. The sandhill cranes
would come back, and the seagulls that dot-
ted the skies over Lake Michigan would nest
along Indian Lake, as well.

On clear summer evenings, Olivia would
close up the deli and she'd come out to the
lake and comb the dense, grassy inlets for
muskrats. Maybe this year she'd find the ea-
gle's nest that one of her deli patrons had re-
ported a week ago.

This summer she would be audacious.
She would put herself, her life and her talent
to the test. Rafe had told her that she could
photograph Rowan whenever she wanted.
Although Rafe could be possessive of his
prize-winning Thoroughbred, somehow
Olivia had the feeling that Rowan was the
key to taking the next step in her career. Despite all the complicated emotions between
them, the invitation was there.

"Bring her in slow, ladies!" Sarah called
as they headed in toward the boathouse.

Olivia looked up. They were finished?

How was that possible? She felt as if they'd just gotten out on the water. "I thought we were going to make three passes," Olivia said as Sarah gave the command to lift their oars.

"We made four, silly." Maddie chuckled over her shoulder. "Boy, you really have been in Neverland today, haven't you?"

"Huh?"

Isabelle scoffed, "Usually, I'm the one who's off in the clouds. I don't think you heard a word we said today, Olivia."

The boat hit the sandy shore and halted. They all hopped out and walked the boat up to the beach.

Sarah led her crew as they hoisted the boat onto their shoulders.

"I'll take the key up to Captain Redbeard," Isabelle said when they'd placed it back on the rack.

"I'll put the oars away," Maddie offered. "So are we all set for next Sunday? Weather permitting?"

They all agreed, and once everything was put away, they began the walk up the hill to the parking lot. Olivia's van was closest to the pathway. She unlocked her door, looked up and saw Sarah, Maddie and Liz standing in a semicircle next to her with concerned expressions on their faces.

"Are you okay, Olivia?" Liz asked sweetly.

Maddie put her hand on Olivia's arm. "Something's up. What is it?"

"I don't know what you're talking about." *How could they tell I'm upset? All we did was row—just like always.*

Sarah took a step forward with her hands on her hips. "Olivia Melton. We've been friends since we were kids. You haven't been yourself for weeks. I asked you four different questions out there on the lake and you never answered me. I can tell when your mind is someplace else. It happens all the time when you're taking pictures. But this is different. Are you sick and you don't want to tell us? Is it your mom?"

Olivia exhaled so deeply her chin sank to her chest. "It's not my mom and I'm not sick." She looked up at her girlfriends. She wasn't going to escape without telling them the truth. But what was the truth?

"Fine," Sarah said. "Look, we want to help, but if you don't want our help, we'll butt out."

Olivia reached out and took her hand. "It's not that, Sarah. It's…well…something *is* different." She hesitated. "I just don't know what it is."

Maddie leaned in. "When did this start, exactly? Maybe we can nail it down for you."

Olivia rolled her eyes, unsure if she'd chosen the wisest course of action. Maybe this was one of those times when selective truth might come in handy.

No, that just wasn't her style. "I think it started…when those photographs of Rowan went viral."

Sarah groaned. "Oh, no! I'm so sorry, Olivia."

"I know. I forgive you. It's Rafe who was so angry."

Sarah nodded. "I should apologize to him, too."

"It's not necessary. He actually wound up apologizing to me after he stormed into the deli that night."

Liz's jaw dropped. "When was this?"

"Two weeks ago," Sarah and Olivia said in unison.

Sarah turned back to Olivia. "But he's okay with it now, right? We're all Kumbaya and holding hands?"

Olivia lowered her eyes sheepishly. "Yes." She fiddled with her car keys. Without thinking it through, she blurted, "I kissed him. No. I mean, actually, he kissed me. I didn't see it coming. I'm pretty messed up over it all."

Liz clamped her mouth shut, her eyes wide, while Maddie gasped and brought her hand to her mouth. "Rafe? Where?"

"On the lips, of course." Olivia glared at Maddie.

"I meant, where were you when this happened?"

"In the horse barn at the fairgrounds yesterday before the race."

Sarah inhaled. "Before the race and not after?"

"Well, then, too. Why?"

Maddie stepped in front of Sarah, put her hands on Olivia's shoulders and said, "Olivia. Rafe is a Barzonni. You can ask Liz. Barzonni brothers don't ask. They take, conquer and claim." She turned to Liz. "Am I right or am I right?"

Liz's eyebrow shot up and she folded her arms across her belly. "Right as rain."

Olivia felt the blush spread from her scalp to her toes. "Well, he sure can kiss."

"They all can." Maddie chuckled. "And neither Liz nor I would have it any other way.

I also know Rafe pretty well. He's not the kind of guy who goes around dispensing random kisses. He's always been very serious. If Rafe kissed you two times in one day, I'd say there's a lot of thought behind it."

"Do you really think so?"

"I'd bank on it," Maddie replied. "If he'd kissed you only the one time after the race, I'd say that was probably enthusiasm. You know, glee over winning. But the one before that? Hmm. That's another thing altogether."

"That's kinda what I've been thinking. I know that Rafe and I got off on the wrong foot with the viral media thing. But he apologized to me before I could say anything to him. I know he's—" she paused as her eyes tracked from Maddie to Liz "—they're all going through a rough time since their dad's death. I think it's harder on Rafe than any of his brothers, though I don't know for sure."

Liz nodded thoughtfully. "Gabe said he was worried about Rafe because of how wrapped up he was in pleasing his father."

"Nate said the same," Maddie added.

"Yeah… I'm wondering if what he feels for me isn't just some kind of transference or grief novocaine," Olivia continued. "Like, to kill the pain. That's the worst part. I can't let myself hope for anything more because he's in an unstable place right now." She couldn't stop tears from welling in her eyes. "That's all it is. I'm part of his bereavement."

Sarah, Maddie and Liz flung their arms around Olivia.

"That's not true!" Maddie exclaimed.

"How can you tell?" Olivia sniffed and wiped her tears. This was worse than she'd thought. Now she was shaking and crying over Rafe. She hadn't wanted to face it, but the truth was right in front of her eyes.

Olivia's friends didn't answer right away, and she knew exactly what they were doing. They were scrambling for compliments about her character and her talent. How honorable she was and that she was a good friend. They weren't answering her because secretly, they thought Olivia might be right. There was a very good chance that Rafe, a decent, caring and intelligent guy, was lost in his grief. He was a sensible man. Not the kind of guy who normally went around falling in love in a matter of weeks.

Olivia's heart felt like a stone in her chest. How ironic. She who always argued for truth, claiming it was the best option in all situations, was facing a truth she didn't like one bit.

Olivia was in love with Rafe. She'd never felt so miserable in all her life.

CHAPTER SEVENTEEN

COURAGE STRUCK OLIVIA like a thunderbolt. At least, that was the excuse she gave herself for staying up past midnight at her computer, scrutinizing her photographs with the critical eyes of a jeweler. Too often, she'd looked at her work with nostalgia or to boost her ego as she frittered away another evening alone. But not tonight.

The minutes flew by as she selected her best shots of friends, strangers, landscapes, insects, flowers, animals, sunsets, boats, lighthouses, sky, earth and water.

This was her fifth pass tonight and though she was tired, she was determined to send every subpar photograph to her trash bin.

By one o'clock, she'd discarded nearly a thousand shots. To her surprise, she still had over five hundred color and black-and-white images in her "keep" folder. They were the winners.

Well over a year ago, Olivia had compiled

a list of magazines and online publications that she believed would be a good fit for her talents. She'd tucked it into her desk drawer, and for a long time it was just something she pushed aside when pulling out her checkbook to pay her rent or her cell phone bill.

Tonight she'd gone over the list as if she'd never seen it before. She crossed off the *New York Times* and the *Washington Post* as well as *National Geographic*. Olivia was serious about going for her dream, but she also believed that applying to places that didn't take newcomers would only result in a pile of rejection letters that would depress her terribly.

She had beautiful interior photographs of Mrs. Beabots's parlors and dining room that could be well-suited for *Veranda* and *Victoria* magazines.

There were action sequences of her friends as they rowed across idyllic Indian Lake, which were perfect for *Vermont Sports Magazine* or the *Outdoorsman*.

And of course, there were wedding photographs. She'd take the plunge and submit them to *Bride's Magazine*, but she knew it was a long shot. Still, nothing ventured...

The most surprising revelation had been the volume of animal shots. She had five times as many animal photographs as any other category. From tree frogs to lop-eared rabbits, Olivia zoomed in on animals. She'd always been drawn to the natural world, but this was ridiculous.

It took close to an hour to get through the insects alone, but it was when she counted up the horses that she sat back and took a deep breath.

She'd been capturing horses on film since she'd accompanied Sarah to her dressage classes. It was no wonder she felt a strong bond with Rowan, Pegasus and the rest of Rafe's horses. Olivia remembered often stopping along a country road and shooting photographs of horses romping in springtime pastures or lazing with their foals. It was a wonder she ever reached any of her destinations for all these moments she caught on film.

Yet, she had not a single photo of herself on a horse—or any riders, really. The horses were always running free across fields or woods.

Her shots of the Indian Lake Hospital Race were the exception. In two short minutes she had taken over a hundred photographs of Rowan with Jenny, along with all the other horses and jockeys. Each photo was sharp and astoundingly lifelike, as if the runners would come right out of the screen.

Putting her elbows on the desk, she dropped her face into her palms. "I gotta get a handle on this thing," she chided herself. When it came to taking pictures of horses, her trigger finger was out of control.

She raised her head as an idea brightened her thoughts. *Maybe this is a sign telling me I'm on the right track. Maybe this means I'm supposed to be a horse photographer.*

Olivia knew she'd have to be extraordinarily talented to compete with professionals. She went back to the computer and scrolled through her Rowan file.

Twenty minutes later she was staring wide-eyed at the screen. These were the photos. These images just might get her somewhere.

It was an honest assessment. If anything, she was ultracritical of her work, which was one reason she'd never ventured out into the marketplace. If she kept telling herself she could get better, work on her skills, buy more advanced equipment, then she'd never have to enter the race. Never have to risk failure.

She leaned closer to the screen and stared into Rowan's huge brown eyes. When she'd taken this shot, she'd sensed that she'd found something unique in Rafe's horse. There were a great many people who didn't believe that animals had souls, but Olivia wasn't one of them. In Rowan, she'd recognized everything from intelligence to determination. There was nothing ordinary about him. Now he'd proven that to the world.

It didn't matter that he had lost by a nose. It was the running time that would define Rowan. His power on the track. The people in the racing world would be talking about him for many years to come. He would be coveted. His progeny would bring a great deal of money to Rafe, if he decided to breed him.

One afternoon, one race, and Rowan and Rafe's future had been rewritten. And now Olivia realized hers had, too.

She liked to think she was the master of her own fate, though her past had certainly given her reason to believe otherwise. But now fate had given her an opportunity, and she had to make the decision to seize it.

Olivia filled out applications for a few online magazines and uploaded appropriate samples of her work. With each submission, she grew bolder. She sent Mrs. Beabots's elegant Thanksgiving dining room table setting to *Veranda* and emailed a dozen photographs of Annie and Timmy with Beau to *Golden Retriever Weekly*.

She saved the best for last. To *Louisville Magazine*, she submitted the action shots of Rowan's race. The still photographs of Rowan, Pegasus, Rocky, Misty and Merlot she sent to *Horse Illustrated*.

It was nearly dawn by the time she finished filling out the applications and writing cover letters. Oddly, she wasn't the least bit tired.

Seeing her reflection in the computer screen as day lit the earth outside her window, Olivia stared at her inbox, hoping it would soon hold the message that would change her life. Or maybe it wouldn't. Maybe no one would want her work.

If that happened, she would have to face the fact that she'd tried and lost. All these years she'd leaned on the excuse that her career was yet to come, that she wasn't quite ready for it.

But now she had no more excuses.

In her head, she heard the blaring sound of the horn that had signaled the start of Rowan's race. He'd bolted out of the starting gate because being held back was the worst feeling in the world to him. Olivia had been mired at the starting gate for so many years, its confines had become comfortable.

Taking those first few steps was terrifying, but it was what she needed to do.

As she stood to make coffee, she remembered her promise to Rafe.

"What have I done?" she moaned as she opened up her sent folder.

Quickly, she opened up the application from *Horse Illustrated* and reread the fine print. It clearly stated that any work submitted would not be reprinted without consent of the photographer. The *Louisville Magazine* submission had the same stipulation.

She leaned back in her chair and blew out a deep sigh. "I'm okay. Everything's okay."

Olivia smiled. She'd taken the biggest step of her life. She wondered why she still felt the same. She'd expected to feel empowered and fearless after all she'd done. Instead, it was just another day, and if she didn't hurry, she'd be late for the morning crowd at the deli.

CHAPTER EIGHTEEN

OLIVIA ADDED HALF a cup of mayonnaise and three beaten eggs to the white sauce in a deep-lipped skillet before throwing in a huge pod of oven-roasted garlic, still warm and squeezed from its skin, of course. After adding two cups of steamed broccoli florets, she poured the mixture into the buttered soufflé dish that her mother had used when she was a little girl. It still made the best broccoli soufflé on the planet. She put it in a water bath and slid it into the oven.

She washed her hands and then consulted the menu that Gina Barzonni had given her for Liz's baby shower that evening. Cold smoked Atlantic salmon with lemon dill sauce. Check. Italian bread with flower butter molds. Check. Field greens, walnuts, feta cheese and strawberry salad with strawberry vinaigrette. Check.

Maddie was bringing an antique wicker tram filled with her exclusive lemon-curd-filled lemon cupcakes. Knowing Maddie, they would be spectacular.

In addition to Liz's friends, Gina had invited a dozen or more women from her Catholic Church Sodality. Gina had explained that since this was her first grandchild, her friends were looking forward to this baby almost as much as she was.

While the soufflé baked, Olivia went to her closet to pick out something to wear. Gina had told her not to wear anything that resembled a uniform because she was both the caterer and a guest. Of course, she could use one of Gina's pretty aprons while putting the food out, but that was all. Gina had hired two servers who would clean up so that Olivia was only responsible for making the food and organizing the buffet table.

Olivia frowned as she flipped through her wardrobe of chef's jackets, black slacks for formal catering and white slacks for summer events. She had more than a dozen full-length aprons fresh from the Indian Lake Laundry, bleached, pressed and hung on hangers. There were tunics, shirtdresses jeans, cargo pants and T-shirts she wore when photographing, but no pretty dresses or skirts to wear on dates or to parties. Her closet revealed the life she led.

Pulling out her large clip, she let her hair tumble down her back. There was a very good chance that she'd see Rafe today. Surely, he knew about the shower with all the fuss Gina had been making about it.

She didn't have time to run down to Judee's and buy a dress, and though Katia and Sarah lived only a few blocks away, both of them were several inches taller than she was. Borrowing from them was out of the question.

There was only one woman who was about the same height as Olivia. She looked at her watch. She only had two hours till she had to leave for the shower. She pulled her cell phone out of her jeans and dialed. The call was picked up after the first ring. "Oh, Mrs. Beabots! You're home. I need a favor."

STEPPING INTO MRS. BEABOTS'S closet was like taking a trip back in time to a world of Parisian elegance Olivia had only read about.

"What is all this?" Olivia asked.

"Chanel, mostly," Mrs. Beabots said as she pulled Olivia deeper into the enormous walk-in.

"This is the size of my bedroom." Olivia gasped as she took in the double racks, built-in drawers, glass-enclosed cabinets that held purses and hats, and an entire wall of shoes.

"It was a bedroom once. A nursery, to be exact," Mrs. Beabots explained. "Frankly, it was a jumble until Luke came to live here before he and Sarah got married. He revamped the whole thing, putting in these double rows so I can hang the blouses on top and the skirts on the bottom. Then on this side, as you can see, are all my dresses, coats and gowns."

Olivia studied the dozens of ball gowns encrusted with pearls and sequins, bugle beads and jet beads. "Where in Indian Lake would you wear something like that?"

"I didn't wear them here," Mrs. Beabots replied in the clipped manner she sometimes used to cut off an inquisition once she felt the questions were getting too personal.

Mrs. Beabots had many secrets. She never talked about her life before she and her husband, Raymond, moved to Indian Lake. They had owned the Rose Street Grocery for a time and then sold it to Louise Railton, who turned it into the ice cream and candy shop. Standing in this closet, Olivia realized just how much she didn't know about her octogenarian friend. She wondered if Mrs. Beabots would ever share her past.

Mrs. Beabots walked past a swathe of black-and-white blouses and skirts, considered the pearl-gray section, then continued to a group of pink, coral and sky-blue blouses and spring floral skirts. She stopped and pulled out a soft apricot silk blouse with long sleeves and a ruffled collar. Then she matched it with a full, black cotton skirt. "Do you think this blouse is too dated? The color would be lovely with your brown eyes and dark hair," Mrs. Beabots said, holding the pieces up to Olivia's body and assessing them with a very critical eye. "You'll need earrings."

Mrs. Beabots went to a drawer built into the far end of the closet. Above it were several shelves filled with ornate Art Deco and Art Nouveau perfume bottles. Olivia recognized them instantly as collectors' items. Below these were current perfumes. She peered at the labels. Shalimar. Boucheron. Chanel No. 5. Coco. They were all French.

Mrs. Beabots twirled around. "These!" She held up a pair of dangle earrings fashioned of coral stones and crystal.

Olivia smiled and shook her head. "Too flirty. Not really my style."

"Hmm. That's right." She raised her index finger, and her eyes widened. "I have it!" She turned back to the drawer and withdrew a red jewelry box, which she handed to Olivia. "These will be perfect for you."

Olivia opened the box and stared at two glimmering, white pearl studs. "What are these?"

"Mikimotos. Raymond gave them to me for Christmas one year. I don't remember when. You should have them, Olivia. They're understated. Simple. Elegant." She reached out and held Olivia's chin between her forefinger and thumb. "That's what you are. A pearl. Hidden in her shell."

Olivia sighed and dropped her shoulders. "You're right. I've just begun to see that." Emotions she'd never acknowledged but which had been buried in her psyche for years, perhaps all her life, were threatening to overtake her. "For so long, I've just been making ends meet. And I was happy enough helping my mom, putting in another day at the deli. Even planning events was exciting—for a while. Now it's not enough. Nothing is. I feel like I'm between worlds. I'm filled with anxiety. I feel like I don't have enough time and yet when I have time to myself, I don't know what to do with it. I daydream about things—er, people—I shouldn't. I have no idea what's happening to me."

"I do," Mrs. Beabots replied calmly. "You're coming into your own."

"My own?"

"Your real self is breaking out of its cocoon. I can relate. I was twenty-four when it happened."

"Twenty-four. I'm twenty-seven."

"My observations have been that most people hit that pinnacle of illumination about your age. Thirty-two is average." She leaned forward and winked. "I like to keep track of things like that. Makes me feel like I've learned something in all these years I've spent on earth."

"So you think what I'm going through is normal?"

Mrs. Beabots folded her arms across her chest and gave Olivia a stern look. "Only if you've done the one thing you should have done by now. Have you sent your photographs out to magazines?"

"Funny you should ask because just last night, I did. I've been putting together a digital portfolio forever, but I haven't had the courage to actually send it out. I figured it was worth a try, though they probably won't get the emails, anyway."

"I'm curious, Olivia. What is it that terrifies you so much about going after your dream?"

She shrugged. "Failing. Not being good enough. As long as no one sees my work, they can't criticize me. Then I won't have to deal with rejection. And these days it's everywhere, from everyone. We have a website for the deli and our catering and for the most part, our customers are complimentary. A couple of times we were understaffed and didn't have enough ingredients to fulfill an order, and that criticism was so awful that I've never forgotten it. Once I send my work out there—" she made a sweeping gesture with her arm "—every person who sees it can go online somewhere and tear me down. It doesn't matter if they have an educated, trained eye or not. Their voice today is as loud as a New York photography judging panel was back when you were wearing all these Chanel suits."

"My goodness, I had no idea. I don't play on the internet, so I don't know about all these things." Mrs. Beabots gave Olivia a soft smile. "What I will tell you is that even back in the sixties, photographers were exposed to derision in their own way, as well. If their photos didn't sell to the nondiscerning masses, they didn't keep their jobs, either. Francesco Scavullo may have been the top fashion photographer back then, but he had to get started just like you must do. He had to take that first step."

"I know, but—"

"You've already taken the first step, Olivia. Your heart is leading you to do the right thing. Now you have to keep at it. Send a hundred inquiries, if you must, until someone hires you or buys your photographs. Don't leave a single stone unturned. You're not a whole person until you explore all the facets of your talent. You're just beginning to understand the depth of your courage. Just how far will you go to reach your dream? Take chances and see what happens. If you fall or fail, get back up on that horse and ride it. That's what life is about—taking chances and making mistakes, and hopefully, you will learn from those errors."

Olivia looked down at the pretty blouse and skirt. "You know, I used to have pretty things like this in my closet. In high school, you know? But ever since then, I mean, after my father left, there hasn't been any money for nice things for either me or my mom. I was thinking that if I could sell some of my photographs, maybe I could help her out a little more. We could even take a trip to Florida like she wants."

Mrs. Beabots put her hand on Olivia's shoulder. "So thoughtful and giving. That's what I've always seen in you, Olivia. Your generosity. It spills out of every pore. Sarah is like that, too. All my girls have that quality, and that's why I don't mind doing extra little things for them when they need it. You keep the blouse and skirt. I won't wear them again. Too young."

"Are you really sure?"

"Of course, my dear." She smiled. "And the pearls. I'd rather you have them now than after I'm dead."

"Don't talk like that!" Olivia gasped. "You're the youngest person I know, in spirit."

"I believe in biting off a huge hunk of life every day. Spend your hours wisely, Olivia, no matter what your age. You can't get them back."

"I'll remember that. Thank you for all this." She followed Mrs. Beabots out of the big closet and into her enormous silver, gray and pink bedroom, complete with Art Deco daybed and two matching club chairs around a white marble-faced fireplace. She checked her watch. "I'd better get going. I still have to change and get my soufflé out of the oven."

Mrs. Beabots led the way to the front door and as she opened it she asked, "Olivia, when were you going to tell me about Rafe?"

Olivia drew up short, her eyes wide. "Who told you? Sarah? Maddie?"

"Why, no one's said a word, dear," Mrs. Beabots answered sincerely.

"So you were guessing that there's something between us?"

"Not exactly." Mrs. Beabots smiled compassionately and said, "I saw you at the race with him. In the winner's circle, remember? When he kissed you, you closed your eyes as if you were drinking in every nuance of the moment. That wasn't the first time he kissed you, was it?"

"Oh, no. You could tell that, too?"

"Actually, that *was* a guess. I purposely used that horse-riding metaphor earlier to test you. You smiled ever so slightly when I said that. That's when I knew. So, you like him?"

Olivia nodded. "I know I shouldn't."

"Why on earth not?" Astonishment filled her eyes. "He's from a good family, and from what I know of him, he seems pretty level-headed. I know he's a hard worker and takes his responsibilities seriously. These days, that's saying a lot."

"It's all too fast. I feel like I've been hit by lightning or something. I think about him all the time. I've never been like that about a guy. I'm hoping I'll see him this evening, but I'm not sure. And if I don't, I'll be very disappointed."

"So it's the same fear that has kept you from contacting publishers for your photographs? You're afraid you won't measure up."

"Is that it?"

Mrs. Beabots kissed Olivia on the cheek. "It was until you hit Send on your computer. In your heart is where you'll find courage, Olivia."

CHAPTER NINETEEN

ALL THE SHOWER guests except Liz and Olivia had left the party before the sun started to set. What little food was left over, Olivia packed up in plastic containers and left in Gina's refrigerator. She filled an insulated canvas tote with the last of her serving pieces and recounted the coffee cups in the sectioned cardboard storage box.

"Hi," Rafe said, walking into the kitchen. The navy cotton shirt he wore accentuated his eyes, which blazed across the room and took her breath away.

"Hi," she managed to say, although her mouth had gone dry and her nerves were on high alert.

She hadn't seen him at all today and wondered if anyone had noticed how many times she'd glanced out the living room window toward the stable and the training track. Finally, she'd figured he must not be home. She hadn't seen Mica, either, and Liz and Maddie had told her Gabe and Nate were back at their respective houses. Olivia could only assume that the two Barzonni men who still lived on the farm had gone somewhere else for supper.

"Is the coast clear?" Rafe asked. The sound of his boot heels against the ceramic tile floor sounded so sure. Steady.

Olivia couldn't have moved if her life depended on it. She clutched the straps of the tote so he wouldn't see that she was shaking. Was he going to kiss her? Apparently, he liked to pick odd times and locations for kisses. Horse barns and winners' circles. A kitchen was closer to normalcy. She had to give him that. "Everyone is gone," she said eventually.

"Even my mother?" He moved closer.

Olivia could smell the spice and leather she remembered, and warmth seemed to radiate off him. She wished he wouldn't stand this close to her unless he was going to take her in his arms. Another minute or two of being this near to him, enduring this kind of anticipation, would surely cause a stroke.

Oh, great. I'm perspiring. That must be really attractive.

She could feel droplets forming at her temples. "Uh, your mom is having a glass of champagne with Liz. Well, I mean, Liz has ice water…" His mouth was curling into a mischievous grin.

"I was thinking," he whispered, taking another step toward her.

She dropped her eyes to his lips, already feeling them on her mouth. "What?"

"I thought I'd make one of your dreams come true."

How could he know what she was dreaming about? Was she that transparent? Her eyes flew up to his as he broke into a huge smile. "And that would be—"

He reached for the tote and took the straps out of her hand. "Come on. I'll help you pack this stuff up and then you're mine for the rest of the night."

"Um, Rafe?" She hesitated. What had he meant by *the rest of the night*? She furrowed her brows in bewilderment.

He laughed again. "You're so much fun, Olivia. You should see your face. I'm not going to hurt you. Where's your sense of adventure?"

Was he insinuating she was a coward? She squared her shoulders. "I'm not going anywhere until you tell me what this is about."

"Killjoy." He chuckled. "We're going to the stable."

"Oh."

"My surprise involves Rowan."

"Oh!" she said brightly, grabbing her purse off the kitchen counter. "Let's load the van, then."

RAFE LED ROWAN out of his stall and put a Western riding saddle on his back. He placed the bit in the horse's mouth and straightened the leather bridle strap around Rowan's ears.

"What are you doing?" she asked as Rafe straightened the saddle over the saddle blanket. Her stomach fluttered with anticipation.

"What does it look like? I thought we'd go for a ride."

Now her stomach was doing backflips. She took three steps back toward the door. "No. I can't. Rafe, you don't understand. I've never been on a horse in my life."

Rafe kept working and without looking at her he said, "What's that got to do with anything?"

"But I don't know the first thing about—" She flapped her hands at the reins and bridle. "About that stuff."

"You'll be fine. I'm with you," he said,

going to Pegasus's stall. She was already saddled, so he led her out with the reins.

Olivia couldn't believe Rafe wasn't taking any of her objections seriously. He acted as if she was going to get up on Rowan's back and ride him. The idea was ludicrous. Not even when she used to go to Sarah's dressage classes had she ever climbed up on horseback.

"So," Rafe said. "I'll be riding Pegasus. Rowan is all yours."

Olivia shook her head back and forth while giving Rafe a diffident smile. "Oh, no, I'm not. Rowan is a highly trained sportsman-animal-horse...whatever. He's used to expert jockeys, not neophytes," Olivia babbled. "I can't—"

Rafe circled around Olivia and knelt down, one hand on the stirrup and the other hand on her bare ankle. "You have to do this. Through your camera you experience animals in a way most humans can't dream of, but you can't truly understand horses till you've been on one. And having a rider is natural for Rowan. Allow me to do this for you," he said with such earnest sincerity that Olivia nearly melted on the spot. But it wasn't enough to quell the terrifying scenarios whirling around in her mind. She could fall off Rowan's back, or he could break a leg...and Rafe would be forced to shoot his prize horse. She closed her eyes. She had to calm her overactive imagination. What she needed was a reasonable, acceptable excuse not to ride.

"Rafe, I'm not dressed for riding," she tried. "I didn't bring any riding clothes. And I'm wearing a skirt!"

"You've got tights on, though, right? That'll work."

"I can't do this."

"Sure you can. Rowan loves you. I'll keep it to a trot. No racing or even galloping, but I want you to know what it's like to be part of him. You can't know Rowan unless you ride him."

Olivia placed her hand on Rafe's forearm and felt the strength of his taut muscles. "I'm scared."

"I'll show you the way." He looked at the stirrup. "Just slide your foot in here. I'll hoist you up. Then swing your right leg over the back of the saddle. Nothing to it."

Olivia did just as he instructed and in one swift and all-too-simple movement, she was sitting on Rowan's back. She'd expected her fear to roil in her stomach forever, but once she was in the saddle, her nerves eased. Oddly, everything felt natural. Safe.

As Rafe handed her the reins, their fingers touched, causing a thrill to shoot straight to Olivia's heart.

He gazed at her with such confidence that he put the last of her trepidation to death.

"Put the right rein in your right hand and the left one in your left. He's so smart you don't even have to tell him anything. But basically, you steer him like you would a sled. You do the same thing with your thighs. Gentle pressure from either thigh helps him know which way to go. Pull back and he stops. That's enough instruction for now."

Olivia drew assurance from Rafe's even tone and realized that Rowan hadn't bucked her off. He was peaceful with Olivia. Perhaps their heartfelt bond went even deeper than she'd thought. "I'm really going to do this."

"Uh-huh." Rafe looked at her quizzically and then asked, "Do you think you'll be warm enough? Why don't I get a couple sweatshirts out of the tack room."

"Thanks," she said as Rowan snorted and jerked his head up. He took a couple steps backward, and suddenly she didn't know how to control him. Her heart pounded. She gripped the reins tightly, but still he seemed to squirm. Rafe kept walking away as if nothing was happening.

"Rafe?" Olivia called.

"Be right back!" He waved and continued through the door to the tack room.

Olivia's fears ignited like a brush fire. What if she fell off? What if Rowan got spooked by a snake or critter out there in the woods and bolted? What if she was responsible for Rowan taking chances he shouldn't take and then he got hurt because of her inexperience?

To her relief, Rafe returned a moment later with two hooded sweatshirts, which he tucked into a roll and strapped onto Pegasus's saddle.

"Maybe I shouldn't do this, after all," she said. "I hope you'll understand."

Rafe came over and put his hand on the saddle horn. "See this? It's like a handrail on a staircase. Well, almost. Hang on to it until you get used to the sway of the ride. You'll be fine."

"What if he bolts and then when he's running he breaks his leg and can never race again? It would be all my fault and you'd never forgive me and then I'd feel guilty and heartbroken and—"

Rafe put his hand on her knee and squeezed. "Olivia! Stop. That's not going to happen. No wonder you're a photographer. You have such an imagination."

"I never use my imagination in my photos. I shoot the real thing," she corrected him.

"Great. Well, if you ever need a second career, you could write stories to go with your photographs. Probably make a fortune," he said, putting his hand on Rowan's snout and leading him out of the stable.

Olivia hung on to the horn with white fingers while she waited for Rafe to bring Pegasus out to join them. He moved ahead of Olivia and signaled to Rowan with a cluck of his tongue.

"I thought we'd just ride down to the fields," Rafe said. "Mica and I planted all the corn and pickles this week. We're still ten days or so away from planting the tomatoes."

Rafe rode right beside her, which gave her a huge measure of comfort and security. Olivia was astounded at how far off the ground she felt. All these years, she'd despised the idea of horse racing because of the gambling that her father had been addicted to and what agony he'd brought down on her mother. She realized she feared riding because it put her one notch closer to becoming just like him. But now her perspective began to alter.

Rafe leaned over and stroked Rowan's neck. "He's really terrific, isn't he?"

"Yes," she replied. She was still holding the horn, the reins bunched up under her stiff hands.

"Do you feel confident enough to let go of the horn and just hold the reins?"

"Not really." She chuckled nervously. "But I will."

"He knows you're nervous, so he'll be understanding."

"Rafe, he's a racehorse. He's a champion and he's going to want to run and his genes precondition him to being as nervous as I am and—"

Rafe laughed again. "Boy, you sure do ramble, don't you? This isn't an ordinary horse, Olivia. This horse knows you probably better than I do."

"I wouldn't say that," she countered.

"I would. He knows your soul in a way I can only hope to."

Olivia was speechless. Rowan was Rafe's pride and at this point in his life, she'd guess, his reason for being. His passion. Yet, he was admitting that she had a special place in Rowan's heart that Rafe didn't own. Was that true? And how could he tell? Just from the way the horse greeted her and tried to put his head around her? Was that it? Or something more? Perhaps Rowan was being extra cautious with her on his back because he loved her. Was this peacefulness that Olivia felt unusual for Rowan? She couldn't stop the smile that crept onto her lips as confidence settled over her shoulders and spine.

"Let go of the horn and trust," Rafe said gently, reaching over and placing his hand on hers. They rode a few steps farther. "You'll be fine."

His voice was calm and reassuring. She'd told herself since the beginning of spring that this was a new season for her. This year she would be bold. That was what Rafe wanted from her now. He had faith in her. She needed to have faith in herself.

Olivia let loose of the horn in one quick motion. She held the reins just as he instructed.

"Now feel the pressure of your thighs. Don't dig into him because that's his signal to run. Just flex them a bit so you feel the difference. There, that's good. Keep your back straight. Yes. Like that. Now, Olivia, I want you to do something else for me."

"What?" she asked nervously. There was so much to remember and it all felt foreign.

"Enjoy the scenery." He smiled and pointed to the east. "See the full moon rising over there? The sun will set in a bit, and if we're lucky we'll get a wonderful sunset."

"Maddie said there was a gorgeous one the other night at the lake. Everything was pink. The sky. The water. It must have been amazing."

"A sunset reflected in water is very beautiful," he mused. "That gives me an idea. Use your reins to turn Rowan to the right down that little dirt path where we run the tractors to the next field. I want to show you something."

Olivia followed Rafe and Pegasus down the narrow dirt road. Up ahead, she saw a thick grove of trees that were beginning to leaf out. There were three huge weeping willows and a cluster of spreading maples. As they drew near, she spied a large pond and around the water's edge, fat Canadian geese sat in the spring grass. The scene was idyllic and reminded her of an Impressionist painting.

"Rafe, this is so beautiful."

"This is my secret place," he said as they brought the horses up to the trees. Rafe dismounted and dropped his reins. Then he came over to Olivia and held up his arms. "Put your hands on my shoulders. I'll help you down. We'll learn dismounting when we go back. Then your lessons will be complete for the day."

"You're a very good instructor, Rafe. Have you ever thought of teaching?"

"You know, I actually have. I get a kick out of seeing young kids ride their first time. Uh, and some adults, too." He winked at her. "But my dad always wanted to race."

"I understand all about obligations to our parents," she said under her breath as she placed her hands on Rafe's strong shoulders.

The instant Olivia was on the ground, she put her arms around Rowan's neck and hugged him. With her cheek next to his cheek, she closed her eyes. For a long moment she didn't say a word, immersing herself in the exchange of energies she felt from Rowan. She couldn't be sure, but she believed he was sad she was no longer on his back. She stroked his snout and kissed him. "Thank you for being my friend."

Rowan nickered.

Olivia laughed and gave him another quick hug. She turned to Rafe. "He's such a joy."

"I know," Rafe replied quietly, taking her hand. "Come on."

Rafe led her over to the pond. The sun was finally slipping below the horizon. Crimson streaks shot across the sky, and an amber glow flooded the earth. The water reflected the pallette of colors. "It's wonderful," Olivia gushed. "I wish I had my camera."

"Where's your phone?"

"Ah! In my pocket." She'd forgotten she had it. It was hard to think of anything else but Rafe when they were together.

"Quick, now. Before it's gone," Rafe said, pointing to the reflection in the water.

She tapped off a few dozen shots. Then the colors turned indigo and violet. The moon rose in the eastern heavens—enormous and mesmerizing.

"So beautiful," she said, wishing her phone camera was adequate for capturing the moon.

"I was thinking the same thing myself," he said, standing behind her. Placing his hands on her waist, he turned her around to face him and without another word, he kissed her.

For days Olivia had thought about little

else other than Rafe and his kiss. Now that his lips were on hers, she was mindless. She couldn't think of a single thing. All she could do was feel the intense heat that started in her chest and filled her entire body. Yet at the same time, his lips were cool. So was his skin. She placed her hand on his cheek and felt the strong cut to his jaw. She lowered her hand to his neck, feeling the hard muscles where his shoulders began.

He pulled her close to his chest, and she could feel the pounding of his heart. She wondered if he could feel hers, too.

His lips went from gentle to possessive in an instant. She didn't know where her breath started and his took over. She had never felt these enormous, heady, intoxicating emotions about anyone ever before.

Rowan whinnied. Pegasus snorted.

Rafe pulled away and chuckled. "I think we're being summoned." He didn't release her.

Olivia realized that she didn't know which she liked more: being kissed by Rafe or being held by him. Both were delicious and incomparable.

"Chaperones. Who would have guessed?" She laughed.

"Not me, I assure you," he whispered, kissing the tip of her nose. "I'll help you back up."

"Before we go, I just wanted to say..."

"What is it?"

"You said this was your secret place. I never had anything like that."

"No? Where did you go with all your secrets? To think about things? To figure things out?"

She shrugged. "I always talked to my mom. Sometimes my friends, I guess."

He hitched his chin back. "Yeah. I guess girls would do that."

"You didn't talk to your brothers or Austin?"

"Not really."

"What about your dad? You said you two were very close."

"We were as close as he allowed us to be." He looked down at their hands, which were entwined. "He didn't share much, even with my mother. Each of us boys—well, we all kind of did our work and our own thing when we needed solace or comfort. I came here."

"But you loved horses and so did your father. Would you have loved them if your dad hadn't?"

He peered at her for a very long moment. "I never thought of it quite like that. I think I would. I know I sure love these two horses."

"I understand. But the racing—"

"Yes," he said slowly, though Olivia got the distinct impression he wasn't quite sure of his answer. It was one thing to love horses. She wanted to know if the racing was just because of Angelo.

Rafe picked up Rowan's reins. "I want Rowan to be all that he can be. He's an exceptional racer. If we didn't have to plant... if I weren't tied to the farm—" He stopped himself and cleared his throat. "Well, there's no end to what he could do if he had real opportunities."

Olivia heard the regret in Rafe's voice and she knew she had her answer. Racing was paramount to him. Rafe would never be happy with a life that didn't include racing horses.

Racing might be in Rowan's genes, but it was in Rafe's heart. "This race that's coming up in Illinois...is it important?"

"Not as much as it would have been if Rowan could have been a Kentucky Derby contender. To make that happen, I would have had to enter him in races all winter and spring, and a lot of those races were in California. I could never have gotten away from the farm for even a fraction of the time that would've required. Now that I look back, I can see how little my dad was doing around here. Once Gabe left, the workload was very difficult. Mica has been talking about hiring another permanent hand. Even a comanager to take Gabe's place. Frankly, until the Indian Lake race, Curt and I didn't exactly know what Rowan was capable of accomplishing."

She put her hand on his cheek. "There's been a great deal for you to consider, hasn't there?"

"Yes," he replied with a somber expression that touched her heart. "I'm excited for Illinois, though, and I'm glad you're going to be there." He tilted his head and regarded her tenderly.

"Me? Why?"

A smile broke across his handsome face. "Haven't you figured that out? I think Rowan won the last race to impress you. Like I said, your kisses are lucky."

Then he kissed her lightly, took her hand and helped her up into the saddle before getting back on Pegasus.

For the rest of their return to the villa, Olivia wondered what it would be like to ride beside the man she loved for the rest of her life.

CHAPTER TWENTY

IT WAS NEARLY closing time at the deli and though Olivia hadn't seen a customer for half an hour, she kept the open sign lit until the very last minute. She'd learned over the years that her patrons from the surrounding offices would often dash to the deli and buy up the last of the cookies and brownies for late-afternoon meetings. If there were any *macarons* or chocolate-chip cookies left, she kept the door unlocked while she cleaned the kitchen and dining area. Every penny in the restaurant business counted.

Olivia cleaned off the grill with a charcoal block, scraped off the residue and then wiped the surface until it glimmered. She'd already washed all her pots, pans, dishes and utensils, and put them in their proper places for tomorrow's breakfast and lunch crowds.

She'd just picked up the broom to make the final sweep through the kitchen area when she heard her name.

"Olivia! Good. You're still here." Katia rushed into the deli with a wide smile.

"Hi, Katia." Olivia glanced at the grill she'd just broken a sweat to clean. "Are you here for one of Austin's grilled beef sandwiches?"

Katia followed Olivia's gaze and chuckled. "Not after you're all shut down." She eyed the pastry display case. "But I will take those German chocolate brownies."

"How many?"

"All of them. Everyone at the office loves them. Especially my boss, Jack. He never makes dessert for himself. Frankly, I think the only recipes he knows are for smoothies and his vegetable juice concoctions."

Olivia grinned. "Very healthy. And admirable."

"But no fun." Katia laughed.

Olivia took out a bakery box and filled it with the seven remaining brownies. Katia reached into her purse for her wallet.

"The real reason I'm here, Olivia, is to find out if you play tennis."

Olivia paused as she reached for Katia's credit card. "Tennis? Not since high school."

"But you were good, though, right?"

"How do you know that?" Olivia asked, swiping the card.

"Sarah told me. Mrs. Beabots confirmed it." Katia's smile shone with just a bit too much intrigue for Olivia's comfort.

"No secret is safe in Indian Lake with those two living next door to each other."

"Ah! So it's true. Mrs. Beabots said you were city champ."

"No big deal. It's not like I went to State or anything."

"Sarah said you're very athletic and that you were more than amazing on the courts until you broke your ankle." The transaction rang through and Katia put her credit card back in her wallet.

Olivia rolled her eyes as she closed the box. "It was a long time ago. I haven't played much since then." She shrugged. "I haven't had the time. This place, plus planning weddings for certain friends I know..."

Olivia studied that certain friend as she handed her the brownies. Katia had an ulterior motive, judging by the too-broad smile and the overly bright gleam in her eyes. "Out with it, Katia. You want to change the wedding venue? You're flying to Italy and getting married there, instead?"

"Actually, we *are* going to Italy—and France—for our honeymoon, but this has nothing to do with our wedding plans. I love all your ideas. I came to ask if you'd like to play tennis with me and Austin on Sunday evening. I'm making salmon afterward."

Olivia cocked her head to the right and peered at Katia suspiciously. "Three for tennis?"

"Rafe makes it doubles," Katia nearly squealed.

Olivia gaped at her. "Rafe. Hmm. So, whose idea was this?"

"Rafe's. He's going to call you."

Olivia's cell phone rang in her jeans pocket.

Katia's eyes lit up. "That's him!"

Olivia glared at her friend. "I need to have a very serious talk with you, Katia. After this call."

"Sure. Fine." She pointed at the cell phone. "Answer it. Say yes!"

Olivia picked up. "Hi, Rafe. How are you?"

She never took her eyes off Katia as she spoke with Rafe. Olivia had only known Katia for seven months or so, since she moved back to Indian Lake. Katia was a few years older than Olivia, so they'd never been acquaintances in school. Katia's mother had been the McCrearys' housekeeper, and from what Mrs. Beabots had told Olivia, Katia had been very much in love with Austin before her mother abruptly moved them to Chicago when Katia was sixteen. Austin had been devastated when she left and had developed a bit of a reputation as a recluse over the next decade. His only close friend was Rafe. Now that Katia had returned, she and Austin had rekindled their love for each other. It was a very romantic story. Olivia wondered if it was as romantic as the story she was building with Rafe.

He was shouting at her over some kind of heavy equipment.

"Rafe, where on earth are you?"

"In the field on my tractor," he said. "I'll make this short. Austin and Katia want us to play tennis on Sunday. Are you free?"

"Yes, I'm free. But I don't own a racket anymore, or shoes, and I—"

He cut her off. "I have a racket for you. Katia said you can borrow shoes from her. I think it would be fun and I really want to see you again. We'll be working late every night, but Sunday evenings are mine. Say you can make it."

"Yes, Rafe. But I'm very rusty with my game."

"No worries. I'll teach you. After all, I'm your riding coach now. Why not add tennis? See you at six."

"Six," she confirmed and then he hung up.

Olivia looked at Katia. "So was it really Rafe's idea, or did you and Austin decide to invite us to play tennis together? Hmm. I'm just wondering, Katia, what made you think that Rafe and I would be suitable partners?"

Katia stared at her with faux innocence. "You wouldn't accuse me of matchmaking, would you?"

"Sure I would. Spill."

"Okay, Mrs. Beabots said that there might be something going on between you two, and Austin and I are so deliriously happy that we thought we could fan the flames a little. Rafe is always so busy and between you and me, he's got some of that hermit thing going on…like Austin did until I came back. One of my priorities is to get Austin more involved outside his company and his new start-up in Scottsdale. Honestly, there is so much expansion at the plant that if I didn't make plans for him, he'd sleep there."

"I doubt that, Katia."

"It's true! That's why I'm making him take two weeks in Europe with me. I wanted three, but it's out of the question. The plant reorganization should be done around the time of the wedding. He'll need a vacation by then."

"Sounds like it."

"In the meantime," Katia continued, "I need to get you some tennis shoes and a tennis outfit."

"I think I have an outfit somewhere in the back of my closet. I might even have shoes, and if I don't, I'll run down to the sporting goods store and get some." She paused as she thought about the commitment she'd just made. Not only was she going to see Rafe again, but this was the first time they would be attending a social function as a couple, too. *A couple.* Olivia had to get used to that. She had never dated anyone long enough to be considered a couple, at least not since her freshman year, when she'd gone to a Christmas dance and then a spring formal with Don Shelly. She hadn't thought about him in over a decade. She'd barely thought about tennis in that long, either.

Olivia wasn't sure if it was coincidence, but she had a narrow streak of the recluse in her, as well. The struggle of building the clientele at the deli and the even more difficult task of amassing catering customers had consumed her life. What little spare time she had, she devoted to photography. Olivia wasn't certain if she was a workaholic, but the state of her social life suggested she might be becoming one.

She hoped she was good for Rafe because she was beginning to see he was very good for her.

Austin's housekeeper, Daisy, opened the door and greeted Olivia. "How nice to see you," she said. "Everyone is out on the terrace. I was just making lemonade."

"I'll help you," Olivia said reflexively. This was the first time she'd entered Austin's home as a guest, not a caterer.

"You won't be doing any such thing," Daisy said, shutting the door as she stepped inside. "Katia has dinner under control and after your tennis match, your only job is to enjoy." Daisy smiled as she led the way down the long hall, past the soaring staircase and into the kitchen that led to the backyard, the pool and the tennis courts.

Austin's home was one of the few old mansions in town that hadn't been converted into apartments. It sat at the end of elegant Maple Avenue, still Olivia's favorite street in town, on two immaculately landscaped acres. Austin's family had come to Indian Lake not long after WWI, a working-class family in the burgeoning auto industry. Three generations later, Austin was redefining the family business again with his high-tech, waterproof cell phone and tablet screens, which had already been picked up by two major smartphone manufacturers. Olivia believed, along with a great many people in Indian Lake, that Austin's new business would bring a new workforce to Indian Lake. It would also ensure that the lovely McCreary mansion would be maintained for another generation.

Just as Olivia reached the kitchen, Rafe came through the back door, flinging it wide and flashing a smile at her. "I was just coming in to see if you'd arrived." He rushed over to hug her. "Wow, you look cute."

"Thanks," she said, glancing down at her white tennis skirt, navy V-neck sweater and her brand-new high-impact sport sneakers. She hadn't worn the tennis outfit since her senior year. Shockingly, it was too big in the waist and she'd had to pin it to hold it up. Olivia hadn't paid much attention to her weight over the years, but she figured that replacing her high school diet of hamburgers and French fries with veggie salads and low-fat recipes had resulted in a smaller frame. Olivia had tied her long hair back to keep it away from her face while delivering—she hoped—a mean backhand.

He took her hand and slid her arm through his. "I was really happy to learn that you played tennis. You didn't tell me."

"It didn't come up. I sold my racket years ago."

"I bet that was tough."

"It was a fundraiser for a little boy who had leukemia. It was a good cause and he's doing well now."

Rafe squeezed her hand. "Admirable."

They walked out the kitchen door to find Katia and Austin volleying a ball back and forth. Katia heard their voices and stopped to wave at Olivia just after she'd lobbed the ball back to Austin, who smashed it across the court and would have won a point.

"Katia!" Austin groaned. "The ball!"

Katia glanced at the bouncing ball and then smiled at Austin. "Come on, Olivia's here." She raced across the court and hugged Olivia.

"I'm so glad you could come. You'll save me from being annihilated."

Austin walked up, took Olivia's hand and air-kissed her cheek. "Don't mind her. She'll do anything to get off playing with me. I taught her to play when we were kids, but she never really took to it."

Katia shook her head. "Listen, this is going to be a disaster. All three of you play like champions, and I'm just a novice. But I do love the sport," she confessed.

Olivia splayed her hands apologetically. "I'm not sure I'm going to be any good at this. I haven't played in years. I don't have my old racket…"

"Oh!" Rafe strode over to the outdoor table, which was strewn with towels, cans of tennis balls and several rackets in zippered cases. Rafe picked up three rackets and jogged back to Olivia. "You can have your pick. Depending."

"What are my choices?"

"I figured a Wilson juicer since we're just playing doubles and it's only for fun. No real competition going on here. It's a shorter handle and since we're playing doubles, most likely you won't be shooting from the baseline or hitting a lot of powerful ground strokes."

Olivia looked at the familiar rackets. She reached for the Wilson racket in his right hand. "This is a Burn. I used to use a racket like this because I *am* a baseline player." She peered at him suspiciously. "How did you know that?"

Rafe glanced at the racket sheepishly. "I looked you up online after Mrs. Beabots told Katia that you could have gone to State."

Olivia turned to Austin. "You didn't tell him? So that means you didn't know, either?"

"After I went to New York for prep school, I didn't keep up on much of anything going on in Indian Lake. By the time I went to college, my tennis competition days were over."

Olivia nodded. "I truly get that. I was the same way. As far as I was concerned it was just a part of my teen years."

Rafe handed Olivia the Burn. "Let's volley for a few minutes and work out the kinks. Just you and me. How's that?"

"Good idea," Olivia said.

Katia nudged Austin, "We'll get some lemonade. Then we'll play."

Olivia walked toward the clay court. "I've

never played on clay. This is the real deal, isn't it?"

"Nothing like it, if you ask me. I joke with Austin all the time that the main reason he's my friend is because of his clay courts." Rafe laughed as he bounced a tennis ball off the face of his racket. "Try that racket and let me know if you like it. You can use mine if you don't."

Olivia spun the racket and checked its balance. The grip was perfect and the leather grabbed her fingers in just the right grooves. She swung it with a wide downward stroke and then pivoted and took a practice backhand. "This racket is brand-new," she said as she went to meet him at the net. "You didn't buy it just for…?"

He twirled his racket in his hand. "I had a feeling we might want to play more than once. A lot, maybe."

Olivia couldn't stop the smile that burst from her heart and found its home on her lips. "Oh, you did?"

"Yeah, that's what I was thinking." Rafe took his stance and readied to serve the ball to Olivia. "You ready?"

"Sure," she answered, leaning forward, feeling her calf muscles tense as she lifted each foot, making sure she was ready to pounce in whatever direction he sent the ball.

Rafe's serve was perfect. When Olivia swung, the ball hit the edge of her racket and fell straight in front of her as if it had deflated. "Rats," she groaned and picked up the ball. "I told you I was rusty."

"It's okay. You serve it back to me. You'll get your sea legs back."

"I hope so, for your sake," she joked as she stepped behind the baseline. Olivia threw the ball up in the air a couple of times before she got the feel of the racket, the ball and the clay court under her feet. Everything about it felt familiar, yet foreign at the same time. The ball seemed to descend in slow motion. She waited for it to drop to the precise point it needed to occupy for her to hit it with her racket's sweet spot. The muscles in her biceps tensed with determination, and she swung at the ball, delivering one of the most textbook-accurate serves of her life.

As Rafe lobbed the ball over the net, every subtlety of the game came back to her. She remembered the sound of her high school tennis coach's voice. She remembered that she had a tendency to pull short when she should follow through with her swing. She hit the ball back to Rafe. He volleyed back to her.

Olivia dashed to the left side of the court, where Rafe was trying to make a point, but she shot low from near the baseline and scooped the ball back to him, short and just over the net, where he almost fell to catch her return.

Rafe missed the shot.

Victory jolted through Olivia like lightning. Raising both arms in the air, she jumped and shouted with glee.

Austin and Katia applauded her from the corner of the terrace. Rafe stuck his racket under his arm and did the same.

"Great going, Olivia!" Rafe came around the net to where she was standing. Without any warning, he put his right arm around her waist and pulled her close.

"That's my girl," he said proudly and kissed her soundly. With a wide smile and his arm still around her waist, he turned to Austin and Katia. "Want to wager who's going to win this match?"

Olivia went stiff in Rafe's arm. His comment was a simple, ordinary social witticism. She knew he had no hidden agenda. He didn't intend to bet his life savings on this tennis match; he probably didn't even mean it literally. She should take a vote of confidence from his comment. She should realize that he was impressed with her skills. Instead, she'd let her fear take over.

Olivia beat back her phobia as if she was delivering a smash serve to her opponent. She softened her shoulders and allowed herself to feel the comfort of Rafe's strong hand as he massaged the back of her neck. She smiled at him and when he looked at her, she brightened with the wink he gave her.

He seemed so at ease with her. How she envied that. Whenever she was around him, she felt like a bottle rocket about to blow. Rafe was conscientious, a hard worker and loyal to his family and friends. She liked to think she possessed these qualities, as well.

The difference was that Rafe was born into a strong family unit, or at least as strong as one could be. Olivia's life had been exactly like Rafe's until her father had betrayed them. The schism in her family had scarred her deeply.

Her growing feelings for Rafe made her realize she had to find a way to confront her past, conquer and bury it. Olivia didn't want to spend even one more day of her life bracing against an invisible foe whose only purpose was to kill her joy. No matter how reassuring and kind Rafe was, Olivia alone was responsible for her own happiness.

CHAPTER TWENTY-ONE

IT WAS NINE o'clock when Olivia got home, which for most people was an early evening, but they all had work the next day. Olivia put the new racket Rafe had given her in the closet next to her front door. Though she and Rafe had lost the match by a single point, the game had been fun. Olivia thought she'd performed quite well, considering her long absence from tennis. Rafe talked about playing again in the near future, though he hadn't actually set a date.

Of the four of them, Katia seemed the most enthusiastic about Olivia's participation. Olivia chalked it up to the fact that Katia had recently returned to town and was still making new friends.

Olivia took off her tennis clothes, put on a robe and started to run a hot bath. While the tub was filling, she turned on her laptop to quickly check her emails. She was expecting an invoice from a butcher in Three Oaks, Michigan, who made exceptional sausage, which they featured on the deli's breakfast menu.

She scanned several emails from camera stores; they seemed to send three ads a day, each, but she often succumbed to perusing them, especially if there were any deals.

Then she saw the email from *Veranda Magazine*.

Olivia cringed before she opened it. It was far too soon for a reply. This could only mean one thing. Rejection.

She clicked on the message and read the boilerplate refusal note.

We are not accepting submissions at this time.

Olivia checked the time and date of the response. It had been sent in the middle of the night, which likely meant it was a computer-generated response. She seriously doubted that a human being had seen anything other than her cover letter.

Glumly, she rose and walked to the bathroom. Just as she reached the door, she heard the click on her computer signaling another incoming email. It was late on a Sunday night. The only messages she'd be getting would be more advertisements. She shut off the water and untied her robe.

Curiosity forced her fingers to retie the robe. She went back to the computer just as two more emails came in. One was from *Golden Retriever Magazine* and one was from *Lexington Magazine*.

More rejections. *Golden Retriever Magazine* at least sent her an actual reply from a real person who commended her work, but stated they had already filled the position. They would keep her photos and application on file if the need arose.

Olivia dropped her chin to her chest and didn't dare look at the screen as she pressed the key to open the email from the *Lexington Trophy Magazine*.

Dear Ms. Melton,
We were quite impressed with your breathtaking photographs of the horse race you sent. You show an uncanny ability to catch action and emotion in your shots. We would like to interview you for an opening we have.
   Please contact our office on Monday morning to set up an in-person interview here in Louisville.
Best,
Albert Allen Simmons III

Olivia read the email three times before the words sank in. "This isn't for real. It can't be."

She rose from her chair and went to the window that looked out on Lily Avenue. "Can this really be happening? Am I finally being the master of my own fate?"

Her stomach rolled and flipped, and chills shot down her back. She pressed her palm to her forehead and she realized her hand was shaking. "Louisville. An interview. Face-to-face."

Louisville was the center of horse racing for the entire country. The Kentucky Derby was the one race that every Thoroughbred owner, trainer and jockey aspired to run, let alone win. Rafe's father had spent most of his lifetime dreaming of the Kentucky Derby. Rafe knew better than to dream that big. When Angelo died, so had Rafe's goal of going to Louisville.

The irony of it all burned Olivia's heart like battery acid. She had no idea what Albert Allen Simmons III had in mind for her. Would she be a stringer? Would she work out of their offices? Would she have to move to Louisville?

Would she have to leave her life in Indian Lake?

The night sky was clear and awash in stars.

A sliver of a waning moon hung above the newly budding treetops. Olivia had never known any life but what she had in Indian Lake. A lot of it had been a struggle, but a bigger part had been filled with true friends who cared about her and whom she loved back.

And now there was Rafe.

She was falling in love with him and though she sensed that he felt the same about her, he hadn't even told her that he cared for her; they hadn't said the words aloud. Perhaps he also felt that their attraction to each other was happening at warp speed. She didn't expect him to make any declarations yet. In some ways, she was glad he hadn't because she wasn't ready.

Olivia was determined to explore her own goals first. That was what all this was about, wasn't it?

There was no denying the fact that she and Rafe fit comfortably together. Even their tennis game had been executed as if they'd played together for years. He was teaching her how to ride and she'd drawn back the curtains on her world of photography for him. They fell into sync so easily it was almost frightening.

They'd only had one disagreement since they met, about her sharing the photographs of Rowan with Sarah. Now she'd done almost the same thing again, she realized.

He'll never forgive me a second time. This couldn't possibly be any worse.

She raked her fingers through her hair. *I need to calm down. I'm really getting ahead of myself here. First, I have to get the job. Heaven only knows how many people are applying. And Rowan's photographs were just part of my portfolio. That doesn't mean the magazine wants to publish them. And if they do, I can withdraw them and take others. Rafe won't ever have to know that I sent pictures of his horse—er—horses as part of my application.*

Feeling her nerves untangling, she walked back to her computer. She skimmed the email once again to make sure she'd read it correctly.

Then she hit Reply and sent Albert Allen Simmons III an acceptance. She explained that she would have to arrange for a day off to drive to Louisville for the interview. She told him she would await his reply.

She hit Send and sat back and left everything in the hands of fate.

ON WEDNESDAY AFTERNOON Olivia entered the office of the sister publication of the *Lexington Magazine*, the *Lexington Trophy Magazine*.

Olivia had been told the magazine was in its start-up phase, and that much was clear. The building was old but located in a newly renovated part of downtown Lexington. The area was scattered with chic restaurants, bars and offices in old three-story brick buildings that sat next to half-demolished structures that were being made into parking garages.

There was no elevator to the second-floor magazine offices, only a creaking staircase with a shaky handrail in great need of bolts and screws. Inside the offices, Olivia found pandemonium. Telephones rang incessantly. Half the furniture looked as if it had come from a garage sale, the other half was inexpensive, modern-looking chairs, bookcases and desks that came from a chain store.

Olivia introduced herself to the receptionist, whose hair was the color of cherry bark, her nails painted with black-as-an-eight-ball polish.

She smiled broadly, smearing her fire-engine-red lipstick on her teeth, and instantly shot to her feet. "Hello, Olivia. I'm Marcie.

Mr. Simmons is waiting for you." She motioned for Olivia to follow her.

As they threaded their way through a dozen desks and stacks of boxes, Olivia noticed that all the writers and editors were quite young. No one glanced at her as she passed; they were all working intently on their laptops.

Marcie tapped on the door, opened it without waiting for a response and motioned for Olivia to sit in the chair opposite the antique walnut desk scattered with an impossibly disorganized slew of papers, magazines and photographs.

Mr. Simmons held a cell phone to his ear and didn't look up. Olivia sat in the chair and waited for him to finish his call.

Albert Allen Simmons III, the managing editor, was not at all what she'd envisioned. He was tall, scrawny and pale-skinned, with a thatch of medium brown hair that was straight on top and bushy on the sides. He looked like a clown to her. Olivia had always hated clowns; clowns were terrifying, ugly and clearly hiding something sinister. The man made her shiver.

He didn't notice. He ended his call and immediately shuffled through the papers on his desk without a word. Long minutes ensued. Olivia didn't know what to do.

With his elbow on the desk, still looking down, he snapped his fingers. "You brought a portfolio like I asked?"

"Yes." She unzipped her portfolio, opened it and slid it on top of the pile of papers under his nose.

He might have said thanks, but it could have been a cough. Still, it was a reaction.

Olivia didn't know quite what to make of him. She hadn't had many interviews in her life, but she was certain this was odd. He hadn't displayed any sense of social courtesy since she walked in the door. No greeting, smile or handshake. She was amazed anyone had hired *him*, much less appointed him to his elevated position.

"These are exceptional," he mumbled but didn't raise his head, which caused Olivia to stare at his skull and notice he had dandruff.

"Thank you."

With an abrupt jerk, he lifted his head and leveled his large brown eyes at her. His face was completely devoid of expression. "I apologize that my regular HR person isn't here to interview you. We're incredibly understaffed this close to Derby week. Everyone is doing double and triple duty. Including me."

"I understand."

He tapped the portfolio with his forefinger. "Where were these race photos taken? I don't recognize the track."

Even if the man had never smiled in his life, Olivia refused to match his sour demeanor. For years she'd dreamed of what it would be like for professionals to admire her work. Now it was happening. This was real. She wasn't about to tamp down her own enthusiasm. Even if she didn't get the job, she was halfway to the finish line. "This was a charity fundraiser for our hospital in Indian Lake. The track has been used for harness racing in the past. This was the first Thoroughbred race conducted there."

Albert shuffled through several pages of her application. "Yet you say here that the track was the same length as Churchill Downs."

"It is. Apparently, the designers had high aspirations when the fairgrounds was built back in the sixties."

"Interesting that they never pursued horse racing, then," he grumbled. With a cluck of his tongue, he lowered his head again and continued looking at her photographs.

He flipped from page to page, then went back and scrutinized a particular shot and then moved forward again. Forward and back. Olivia wished she could take photographs of him as he worked. He was so strange.

"You stated in your email that you'll be attending the Illinois Derby?"

"Yes." Olivia brightened. "This coming weekend, to be exact."

"Good. I'd like you to cover the Illinois Derby for us. It will be your trial run, in essence. If you do well with that assignment, then we'll move ahead in our discussions. Agreed?"

Elation soared through her. "Yes. Certainly." The moment she'd entered Albert's office, she'd expected to be sent away. She'd expected him to have to think things over. She'd expected that her work wouldn't be good enough.

But the reverse had just happened. She was getting a shot. She had to show them that she was absolutely the right photographer for them.

"I'll be very interested in those photos," he said. "You can email them to me. Can you get access to the winner's circle again?"

Olivia kept her hands clamped together in

her lap. She had no idea what to expect from the race. All she'd thought about up to this point was that she'd be spending the day with Rafe and Rowan. She hadn't had a chance to discuss their travel arrangements beyond what time to meet him at the villa. She knew they'd drive back to Indian Lake after the race. As for the winner's circle...she was going out on a limb to make any promises at all, but wasn't that what career professionals did? Take risks?

"I'll do my best."

"Make sure you get those for us. If they're good enough, we may use one for our cover," he said sternly.

With a loud bang, Albert slammed the portfolio shut. "If you give me what I need from the Illinois Derby, I'll expect you to begin working for us right away."

"May I ask how soon that would be?"

"Ten days at most. Like I said, we're incredibly understaffed. I intend to hire someone very soon. You or someone else..." His voice drifted off.

Olivia knew that jobs like this didn't come along every day. She was lucky that her timing was in sync with their needs. Still, it was up to her to pull off her trial assignment and bring back what needed to be the best work of her life.

Albert continued talking, still staring down at her closed portfolio as if she wasn't in the room. "Work is piling up. I have an assignment in New Mexico that needs to be shot, as well. Mustangs. Desert. Mountains. You should probably talk to Bart, one of our reporters, before you leave. He'll be doing the Illinois piece with you.

"I want to do a piece on the race you shot, as well, which I'll also assign to Bart. You can teleconference from your home. Emails. Texts. We do it all the time."

"The race?" *Rowan's race.* She looked down at her portfolio. "Any shots in particular?"

"I like a lot of them. The finish line, of course. And always the winner's circle. After all, that's what this magazine is all about. The winners."

"Right. Sure. Absolutely," Olivia managed. She extended her hand to Albert Allen Simmons III. "I'll stay in touch."

"Do that," he replied as he dropped her hand and sank slowly into his chair, going back to work without another glance in her direction.

"I'll just let myself out," Olivia whispered.

Albert didn't respond, but Olivia doubted he would have paid any attention if she'd shouted.

She closed the door behind her.

CHAPTER TWENTY-TWO

THE GOOD EARTH of the Barzonni farm rolled black and rich under the blades of Rafe's plow. This was the last of the acreage they would plant in tomatoes for this season. In two weeks the crews that Mica had hired would arrive along with the tomato plants. They would work from dawn till the last vestiges of evening light remained to get the plants from the conveyor belt into the holes.

Because Mica had finalized a new contract with Red Gold Tomatoes, they'd decided to plow this unused acreage to bring their total to over three hundred acres of tomato production. If the crop did well, Rafe and Mica stood to eclipse their father's best contract year by over a ton. Red Gold expressed a need for thirteen tons of tomatoes in order to produce twenty million cans.

Rafe was surprised at how much the challenge excited him. He drove his tractor to the southern border of the precise rows he'd spent all day turning. He switched off the engine and watched the sun as it settled easily below the horizon. Spring birds chirped in the tall windbreak pines to the west. Beneath the pines were ornamental dogwoods and redbuds his mother had planted decades ago from little saplings. Every spring she'd trotted her sons out to this place on the farm, with its rolling slopes and surrounding trees. Over the years, she'd planted apple, peach and pear trees. She'd made jams and preserves when they were young kids, though she didn't have time for much canning these days. In recent years Gina had taken over more and more bookkeeping and ordering as Angelo had slowed down.

Thinking about his father and his stubbornness about never seeing a doctor, Rafe ground his jaw. He tasted grit and dirt he'd no doubt inhaled while plowing. He reached for his bottle of water, rinsed out his mouth and spit.

"Fool," he said darkly, feeling the air leave his body as his eyes traveled to the horizon.

Golden light filtered through the trees, illuminated the white dogwood flowers and caressed the ink-dark ground. He could smell the earth and feel the energy of spring, the growing season coming alive. Butterflies flitted around the flower blossoms on the redbuds. Insects buzzed in whorls.

A breeze gently dried the perspiration that trickled down Rafe's temple. For the first time since his father's death, he didn't feel sad as he reminisced about him. Oddly, Rafe felt assurance that everything was just as it should be. He felt his heart swell with pride at all his father had accomplished in his lifetime. This land. The farm. The horses. His family.

For years Rafe's world had centered on horses and racing. It still did.

Yet something was different. Something was changing. He had changed. He felt as if he was seeing his life through new eyes. He understood Mica's passion for the farm in a way that had been alien to him before.

Rafe felt an urge to get down and kiss the land that had provided his father a sense of place and pride and ensured his sons had a future.

"The future..." Rafe rubbed the dirt from his forearm and placed both hands on the tractor's steering wheel. It wasn't that long ago that Rafe had groused about another planting season. Another long summer and the endless days of harvest. But at this moment he counted his blessings. All things considered, he was a most fortunate man. His birthright had been hard-won by his father, and Rafe was grateful.

He only wished he'd told his dad that when he was still alive.

Noncommunication was definitely one of Rafe's flaws. He didn't have a single problem talking to horses, but when it came to humans, he didn't know how to express his feelings. He supposed half his problem came from imitating his undemonstrative father. The rest was his own fault. It was just easier not to get involved. Easier to keep his mouth shut and let others think whatever they wanted about him. He supposed that was one of the reasons he got along with Austin so well. Of course, Rafe had never known his friend's reclusive tendencies were mostly due to the fact that Austin had been brokenhearted over Katia. Austin had never said.

Naturally. Noncommunicative guys did that.

Rafe had never been in love with anyone and couldn't imagine what it felt like to be hurt by someone he loved. He was glad Austin and Katia had found each other and were now planning their wedding. He wanted his best friend to be happy because—

"I'm happy," he said aloud, surprising himself. He looked over at a dove flying into a spruce tree to nest. "Everyone should be happy."

Rafe smiled, and an image of Olivia filled his mind. He'd been thinking about her all day, wondering what she was doing and how things were at the deli. They hadn't fallen into a pattern of phoning each other at the end of their days to talk, but he wanted to start now. He supposed he could call her once he got back to his apartment to discuss the upcoming trip on Saturday to Cicero, Illinois. She'd accepted his invitation, though he honestly didn't feel that she was excited about the race.

As he'd relaxed into the fact that he was more than a little attracted to Olivia, he'd felt a tingle of apprehension that wouldn't go away. She'd stiffened when he'd invited her to the race. Was she recoiling from him?

He couldn't deny that at other times, she'd looked up at him with those warm brown eyes swimming with affection, if not love. And she'd agreed quite sweetly to go with him to Hawthorne Racecourse. Judging by her very apparent love and care for Rowan, she would want to see him run this important race.

He gnawed at the inside of his cheek thoughtfully. There were times when he wondered if she liked Rowan more than she liked him.

He licked his dry lips. No, she could never have kissed him with such surrender and tenderness if she didn't feel deeply about him.

Still, he knew something was wrong. She was hiding something. But what?

Rafe had wrestled with enough emotions since his father's death to fill a lifetime. He'd gone from guilt and grief to anger and resentment to the flush of victory and the joy of finding a woman he just might want to spend the rest of his life with.

Rafe's heart hammered as the idea settled into his bones. "Olivia and I."

Scanning the golden-hued pasture as a flock of birds flew across the darkening sky, Rafe focused on the memory of him and Olivia riding horses together to his secret place. He was always so fascinated to hear her talk of the way she saw the world. It was if she saw everything and everyone with her heart and not her eyes.

She might be a photographer, but to him she was a visual poet. A painter of the world not filtered through the disappointed and distorted eyes of humans.

She had clear vision and the purest heart he'd ever encountered.

Rafe wasn't quite sure how to ferret out Olivia's true feelings for him. She hadn't said anything to suggest she might care for him, and the word *love* hadn't been spoken. Admittedly, he hadn't pushed her for a declaration, either.

Again, Rafe blamed his consistent, intractable flaw of keeping his thoughts and feelings to himself. It wasn't easy for him to share his inner self with others, but Olivia was making him see that the prospect should not be frightening, but liberating.

Rafe realized there were labyrinths of Olivia he had yet to explore and he was anxious to begin. As dark purple shadows swallowed up the terrain, he turned on the tractor engine. It had been a productive day. He took one last look at the rich earth that would soon be planted and hopefully bear a bumper crop for them this year.

Thinking of Olivia, he realized for the first time in his life he was content. In three days he would be racing Rowan in a Graded Stakes race and he'd be with Olivia all day and evening. They would have plenty of time to talk and even if it took him all day, he would not stop until he discovered the source of the fear he sensed in her.

CHAPTER TWENTY-THREE

OLIVIA SAT IN the passenger seat of Rafe's Ford 350, which pulled the horse trailer behind it. Rafe had assured her that Rowan had settled in for the drive without any bad behavior. Curt Wheeling had already driven to Cicero the previous night with a great deal of the gear as well as Rowan's bridle and saddle. Curt's job was to make certain that all the paperwork, stall accommodations and feed were in order, and that Jenny had arrived and was prepared for the race.

Rafe was in good spirits as they drove through the south side of Chicago on the interstate. Olivia had never been to Cicero and knew little about the town other than that it was on the west side of the city, it was the birthplace of Ernest Hemingway and it had harbored hideouts and bars owned by Al Capone in the 1920s.

Rafe appeared happy, regaling Olivia with stories about Rowan's last run around their home track on Thursday night. Twice, he'd reached over the drink holder and touched her hand. He squeezed her fingers for emphasis occasionally but she didn't know if he was trying to find a reason to touch her or if he just naturally became so enthusiastic while telling stories that he did this kind of thing with everyone.

Was she special or not?

And if she was, how in the world was she going to tell him that she was covering this race for a magazine and that if she did well, she would land a job in Louisville? Albert had made it clear that he needed to hire someone. There was a real possibility that this might be the last time she saw Rafe for a long time to come.

Ever since she'd left the *Lexington Trophy Magazine* offices on Wednesday, she'd felt numb. She'd driven six hours up I-65 and didn't remember a single moment of her trip. All she'd thought about was the fact that she was so close to a finish line of her own. Her dream job was within her grasp.

Mine for the taking.

Conflict reigned supreme in her mind. One minute she wanted to shout over a loudspeaker that her photos—her talent—had been recognized by a major publication. Okay, it was a fledgling magazine, but still—this was her dream.

The next moment she felt her stomach churn and her breath hitch as she thought about leaving her mother and friends. Most of all, she realized, she didn't want to leave Rafe.

Not that she'd told Rafe how much she cared about him. And she had no idea if he had feelings for her. Sure, he might have liked kissing her, but so had Bobby Rudolf in the tenth grade. That wasn't the same as love.

At some point Olivia had to tell Rafe about the assignment and the potential job offer, but she couldn't spoil his enthusiasm about the race. This was an incredible opportunity for Rowan, and it was selfish of her to think of herself right now.

The best thing she could do was wait. She would make time to come clean once they were back in Indian Lake.

Rafe was chuckling about something he'd said, and he reached for her hand again. This time he didn't let go.

"Olivia, can I ask you something? It's pretty personal, but it's important to me." Though he was a conscientious driver and only took his eyes off the road for a brief moment to glance at her, in that fleeting second, she read empathy and concern in his eyes. The slight crease of a smile dusted his lips, just enough for her to know that his intentions were honorable and compassionate.

Was this about her assignment? About the magazine job she hoped to land? How could he know? She hadn't even told her mother. Olivia braced herself. "Uh, sure. What is it?"

He lifted her hand and wiggled her arm. "It's that," he replied. "You just did exactly what I wanted to ask about. You tense up sometimes, when I'm talking about Rowan. This time you went rigid before I had a chance to broach the subject. This can only lead me to believe that I make you nervous. Don't you like being with me?" He released her hand and put both of his on the steering wheel.

She felt shame ignite every vein in her body, searing, branding, burning and making her feel insignificant and helpless. She was losing control. She knew exactly what he was talking about. Explaining the magazine job would have been much easier than relating her past and the monsters in her psyche.

"That's not it," she assured him so quietly she wasn't sure she'd actually spoken out loud. "It's not you. I promise."

He shook his head but kept his eyes on the road. A semi hauling three trailers passed them. Rafe moved to the far right lane. "I think it is. When we were at the farm—at my secret place—you went cold as ice not long after I kissed you. And then at Austin's house, when he made the joke about betting on the game, you were so rigid. Your neck was like steel. I have to ask if it's me. Is my touch so abhorrent to you?"

"Oh, no, Rafe. You've got it wrong." Olivia wrung her hands in her lap. "I like it when you touch me. When we hold hands." He was gripping the steering wheel so tightly his knuckles were pale.

He deserved to hear the truth, all of it, no matter how difficult it was for her to reveal. "But you're right. There is something. I don't share this with many people…" She glanced out the window and watched a sea of billboards fly by.

"I hope I'm not most people."

"You aren't. In fact, Rafe, you're the one person who should know because I care about you and I would never want you to have your feelings hurt because of anything I did," she rambled.

Rafe remained silent, letting her continue, but the soft smile he gave her was encouraging.

"I was nervous. I *am* nervous when we go to the races."

"The races?" Confusion filled his voice. "I thought you loved Rowan."

"I do. Very much. It's not the animals, and I have discovered thanks to you and Rowan that it's not the actual race that frightens me. It's the betting. The gambling. The ticket counters and betting cages terrify me." The more she spoke, the less difficult it was to continue with the explanation. "Rafe, when I was little and my dad was around, he was— well, he was addicted to gambling." Olivia had to say it fast, otherwise she'd never get the dreaded confession out into the open. She was afraid to look at Rafe's face. Terrified of the recrimination she'd find there.

Slowly, she tore her eyes from the lines of traffic in front of them. "It was awful for both me and my mom."

"I'm so sorry, Olivia," he said empathetically. "It would be so hard for a little kid to understand what was going on. Any addiction is."

Before she could respond, he placed his hand on top of both of hers, lifting her left one to his lips. "I'm sorry," he said again and kissed her palm.

The warmth of his sincerity raced up her arm and straight to her heart. His caring words and gestures obliterated her fears. Olivia had never thought much about the power of love—the voltage of that kind of positive energy—but she did now.

She realized that though she'd had friends all her life, she'd never put a single one of them to this kind of test of faith. She'd kept her family shame a secret for so long, she'd come to believe she would never be able to share it.

Here was Rafe, in many ways a stranger to her, and yet he understood. The doors to her heart were wide-open for him.

Rafe glanced at her out of the corner of his eye and turned on his signal. "Cicero is our next exit," he said. "And, Olivia, if this is too hard for you, it's okay. You don't have to go on."

"I want you to know everything, Rafe."

"Only when you're up to it," he said considerately.

Olivia was so impressed that Rafe was comfortable with such a deep level of intimacy that she believed she owed him the truth. "My dad only bet on horses. He never played cards or dice or went to a casino. At least that's what my mother told me. He rationalized that it was tradition, that it was natural for a person to bet on horses that were bred purely for racing. That's what he told himself—and us. I remember going to Arlington with him. The horses were so majestic." She sighed. "I suppose I encouraged him to take me. I didn't understand about the losses he was taking. I just wanted to see the horses."

"But you were just a little kid, right?"

"Yes. But still—"

"How could you know? Olivia, do you see what you've been doing? You've been blaming yourself for something you and your mother, I'm guessing, were powerless over."

Olivia's shoulders softened as relief siphoned away another layer of guilt and fear. "I have been doing that," she whispered as the realization settled into her bones. She stared blankly out the window, but she didn't see the exit ramp they were taking or the traffic light. All she saw was her father's agony when his horse lost another race. His despondency and embarrassment had captured them both. The thrill she'd experienced earlier just watching the beautiful horses being led to the gate had vanished so quickly and been replaced with such overpowering negativity that any elation was erased. Abolished, as if she'd never felt joy in her life.

"He left us one day. No goodbyes. No warning. My mother didn't know the amount of the debt he'd racked up until a few weeks later. I remember her crying herself to sleep. I tried to help her. Say things…" Olivia's voice hitched as emotion erupted in her throat and cut off her words. Tears stung her eyes and fell uncontrollably down her cheeks. She brushed them away with her fingertips, but visions of her mother's despair were so vivid and so biting that she continued to cry.

"Olivia, you did the best you could," he murmured and reached over to put his hand on her shoulder. "No wonder you and your mother are so close."

"We are." She lifted her hand to cover his. She could feel his warmth again; it was as if he was infusing her with strength. She laced her fingers through his, wanting more of his confidence to buoy her up. "Over the years we grew the deli and then the catering business. She paid off all his debts and kept her little house and fixed it up. She's pretty amazing."

"So are you."

The smile she gave him came from her heart, though her eyes were still swimming with tears. "Thank you."

They'd come to a stop just before entering Hawthorne Racecourse grounds.

"So you see, Rafe. It's not you that frightens me—it's the gambling. I know it's my problem and I have to get over my fear. For a long time, I thought I had. Until…"

"Until you met me and Rowan," he offered.

"Yes. Everything about my father and the past has come back to me. Not in a good way." This time she lifted his hand to her lips and kissed the back of it. "It's not you, Rafe. Never you."

Rafe leaned across the seat and kissed her cheek. "The one thing I want you to know, Olivia, is that I want to be more to you than just a friend. I'll be there for you. No matter what. Would you let me be that person for you?"

Olivia eyes still stung from the tears she'd shed over her father. Now a new wave of pain built deep in her heart because she knew she'd finally found the one person she loved enough to confide her deepest shames and fears to—Rafe. And he was going to be the one she would hurt the most when she grabbed the tail of her dream and rode it all the way to Louisville.

CHAPTER TWENTY-FOUR

WHAT OLIVIA'S FATHER had said about horse racing was true. Tradition and history underpinned every aspect of the sport and at Hawthorne Racecourse, Olivia couldn't help but feel the ghost of the original owner, Edward Corrigan, who bought the land and ran the first five-race card in 1891.

As they unloaded Rowan from the trailer and met up with Curt, Rafe explained that the grandstand had burned down twice: once in 1902 and once in 1978. This was the first time Rafe had ever entered a horse at Hawthorne, or in any track in Illinois.

"The track is one mile," Rafe explained, "but the homestretch is the longest in the country. I'm thinking this could be to Rowan's advantage."

Olivia walked alongside Rowan, keeping her hand on his snout and wondering how he perceived the commotion and activity around him.

Dozens of pickups, RVs and tricked-out

SUVs pulled horse trailers up to the stable area. Trainers, owners, jockeys and assistants lugged bridles, saddles, equipment, feed and even coolers across the paddock. Beautiful Thoroughbreds pranced across Olivia's path with an arrogance that could only come from an awareness that they were the best.

None of the animals were shy. None were in the least intimidated by their competition. They were princes and they knew it.

Curt led the way to Rowan's stall. "We've been assigned stall number eight. Jenny should be arriving any minute," he said. "I just got a text from her. Her parents drove her up last night."

"How lucky for us that her parents are supportive," Rafe said, coming up behind Olivia. He lugged the saddle and bridle over his shoulder. "Rowan is comfortable with her and understands her signals. That's important."

"I'm glad," Olivia said as they entered the stable. Half the stalls were occupied and she saw two more horses entering right behind them.

The excitement in the air was as tangible as a fistful of spring pollen. The energy was infectious. Olivia felt her pulse speed up as she looked from Rafe's broad smile to Curt's gleaming, pride-filled eyes.

Rafe led Rowan into the stall and turned him around. "Come give Rowan a hug, Olivia. He'd like that. I have to help Curt for a minute and get the rest of our gear."

She beamed back at him. "My pleasure."

Olivia stood in front of the horse and stroked his nose. His coat was as smooth and velvety as sable. He gleamed like a prize-fighter, and she was aware of how deep her affection for this proud and talented animal ran.

She peered into his eyes and once again, she saw and felt an emotion skimmed with joy emanate from him. "I love you, too."

Rowan nickered and dropped his head. Then he craned his long neck around her shoulders and pulled her into him with a jerk. She flung her arms around him, kissed his cheek and closed her eyes.

She didn't need a camera to catch this moment. It would stay imprinted on her heart forever. This was the first horse she'd ever ridden, and she believed Rowan understood that it wasn't a coincidence that she'd waited all these years to have that special experience with him. Rowan might be Rafe's prize horse, but through her bond with Rowan, Olivia overcome her fear of riding.

"Hey, hey." Rafe chuckled as he walked up to the stall. "You better not be trying to steal my girl."

Olivia locked eyes with Rafe, a sweet smile playing across her lips. "He was trying, but he could never—"

Rafe dropped the load he was carrying, put his arm around her waist and kissed her cheek. "Good. Because you are my girl, you know."

OLIVIA SAT IN the box seats with the other owners and trainers and adjusted her camera lens as the final race of the day, the Graded III Stakes, was announced.

Through her viewfinder, she saw Rafe and Curt as they led Rowan to the starting gate. Jenny looked relaxed; she bent down and patted Rowan's neck and adjusted the reins.

As with the Indian Lake race, everything happened very quickly once the horses went to the post. The horn blasted and the announcer shouted so loudly that Olivia jumped. She missed her shot.

Clicking off photos, she realized what an advantage she'd had being in the judges' tower at Indian Lake. Within two seconds, she didn't have a good angle anymore and had to excuse herself and climb out of her row. She stood on the steps, hoping to get a better shot as the horses rounded the turn. She zoomed in on the leaders and saw Rowan among the front three runners, along with Luv Bandit and I Got It All.

Rafe had told her that Luv Bandit had won the Milwaukee Handicap the weekend before. He was the horse to beat, but already, Rowan was two lengths back. Olivia guessed Jenny didn't want to engage Rowan in a speed duel this early in the race. Saving strength for the "run down the lane" was the kind of expert strategy that could lead to a win.

By midstretch, Rowan had gained a narrow lead over I Got It All. Then Jenny used her lead to send Rowan to the inside, though Luv Bandit came up on the outside and really ground it down. Coming around the third turn and into the homestretch, Rowan's confidence was apparent.

All around her, Olivia heard the crowd cheering his name. She kept her mind on her work, but her heart wanted to scream encouragement.

"Come on, Rowan!" someone screamed beside her.

Olivia's fingers flew as she fired away at the camera. The view she had of the home-stretch was flawless. She zoomed in for a few more shots of Rowan pulling away from Luv Bandit and leaving I Got It All in the show position.

The sun came out from behind a cloud and struck Rowan's flanks, making him look like a gleaming, glittering apparition as he shot over the finish line.

The crowd exploded in cheers and applause. Olivia couldn't help jumping up and down. A rotund, middle-aged man at the end of the aisle thrust his arms in the air and shouted, "I won!"

Olivia stood still and looked at the man. Without thinking she asked, "Did you bet on Rowan?"

"Oh, no. I never bet. But he won! He won! Isn't it exciting?"

Olivia couldn't contain her smile. "Yes! It's so exciting!" She turned around and watched the field as Rafe and Curt raced up to Jenny and Rowan. A man in a black business suit handed Jenny a bouquet of red roses. An-other man came up and handed Rafe a trophy.

Curt placed a shiny satin drape over Rowan's flanks.

With her camera to her face, Olivia clicked off more shots. Then she stopped, feeling an unfamiliar euphoria. She was covered with chills from her head to her knees. This was more than being happy for someone else. This was her own joy.

Gone was the anxiety, the roiling stomach, the caustic fear. The tentacles of anger that had ensnared her for so long over her father's choices, his weaknesses and his demons had vanished.

All she wanted was to share this moment with Rafe and Rowan, even though she was only a bystander.

Or was she?

Rafe had told her earlier that she was more. Her heart believed that to be true, and it had led her to reveal her greatest secret to him. And he'd been completely understanding. He hadn't judged her or disrespected her. He'd accepted her just the way she was.

She turned off her camera, pleased with the shots she'd taken today. Once she was home and had a chance to scrutinize them on her computer, she'd select the best ones and discard the others.

"They ought to make Albert sit up and take notice," she said to herself as she followed the crowd out of the grandstand.

Albert.

Olivia had been so caught up in her confession to Rafe, the tearing down of the last remnants of her damaged psyche and then the exhilaration of the race, that she'd pushed all thoughts of the *Lexington Trophy Magazine* to the back of her mind. This was Rowan's day. Rafe's triumph. She'd concentrated so much on Rafe and his feelings that she'd forgotten about her own ambitions. Her own dreams.

Olivia knew deep in her cells that her photographs would prove to be some of her best work. They had the quality and edge that she believed Albert wanted.

I'll nail that job.

Suddenly, despair swept over Olivia like a disease, trampling her joy. Her smile faltered. Her gait slowed to a trudge as she neared Rafe and Rowan. They were surrounded by a bevy of photographers and fans who took pictures on their smartphones. Curt was being bombarded by questions from other trainers he seemed to know. Men in dress suits and ties shoved business cards into Rafe's hands.

Jenny's parents stood just outside the circle, and even they were being hounded by reporters and photographers.

Remembering Albert's order to get plenty of pictures of the winner's circle, Olivia turned her camera back on. She stood back and followed the angle of the sun as it cut through the clouds and sent a shaft of light down on Rowan. Jenny's red hair glimmered beneath her jockey's cap.

As if he sensed Olivia's presence, Rowan lifted his head, turned slightly and stared directly into the camera. She knew the instant she pressed the button that she had a cover photo.

Albert would be pleased.

Olivia lowered her camera as she realized she had only begun her confessions to Rafe.

CHAPTER TWENTY-FIVE

OLIVIA CAME OUT of the walk-in carrying a roaster with ten pounds of Italian beef that Julia had cooked over the weekend. They would use it to make beef sandwiches all week at the deli.

Olivia placed the roast on the butcher block and dried off the juices with a paper towel, then placed the meat on the slicing machine.

The sound of the buzzing blade helped drown out the self-recrimination on a loop in her head.

I should have told Rafe about the job. I should have explained that I'll have to move away. I should have thanked him for helping me overcome my fear of racing and for being a real friend. I definitely should have kissed him again and told him that I think I'm falling in love with him. I should have...

"Olivia, are you going to slice those crumbs, too?" Julia asked, coming over to the slicer and shutting it off.

"What?" Olivia looked at her mother and then down at the roast, which was now perfectly sliced. "I guess I'm done."

Julia put her fingers under Olivia's chin and lifted her face. "Mind telling me what's going on with you?"

"What makes you think—"

"Olivia. Please. I'm your mother. I haven't seen you this glum since you lost that tennis match in high school."

Olivia placed a piece of butcher paper over the meat and wiped her hands on a towel. "I have a lot to tell you."

"You mean there's more besides the fact that you finally sent your photographs out to magazines?"

Olivia's mouth fell open. "Who told you that?" She frowned. "Let me guess. Mrs. Beabots?"

"She knows, too?"

Olivia felt every ounce of breath leave her body. "I didn't tell anyone but her."

The sides of Julia's mouth turned down. "You didn't tell me. That part I know."

"Please don't be hurt. I didn't want to tell you because if I got rejected, then you'd feel bad and I would feel bad and—"

Julia put her hands on Olivia's shoulders

and stopped her with a maternal smile. "I know, sweetheart. And I appreciate your wanting to protect me."

"Thank goodness. So," Olivia asked, "who was it who told you?"

"Sarah."

"Figures."

"I'm assuming your gloomy mood is because you've had some bad news about that?" Julia offered.

"No, Mom. Actually, I'm being considered for a photojournalism job. It's mine for the taking. I just got the text from the editor in chief this morning."

Julia's eyes narrowed. "What? How did this happen?"

"Last Wednesday when I asked for the day off, I went to Louisville and interviewed for a new magazine. The editor wanted to test me first, so when I went to the Illinois Derby with Rafe, I shot it for the magazine as a trial. Mom, those photos were the best of my life. Can you believe it? It's my dream come true!"

Julia threw her arms around Olivia. "I knew you were more than just good. Exceptional. You just needed to find out for yourself. This is wonderful news." Julia backed away and peered at Olivia. "You should be happy, but all I see is sadness. What's the hitch?"

"He wants me to start on Thursday."

"Thursday? That's…really…fast," Julia said, pressing her palm to her cheek thoughtfully. "Can you even do that? I mean, *how* can you do that?"

"I've found an apartment near the offices there. It's vacant and I can move in as soon as I get there. I thought I'd just take a few things to start with, and later, I can rent a truck. I got a blow-up bed. I'll wing the rest."

"Okay. You've got a handle on that part, I guess. Have you told your friends?"

"No. I wanted to tell you first. Then I'll tell everyone. Except, well, there's a problem."

"And that problem would be Rafe Barzonni?"

Olivia's eyes widened in surprise. "How do you know that?"

"I'm not blind, Olivia. You've been acting differently since the day we catered Angelo's funeral. Plus, I have very good hearing. I hear the sweet undertones in your voice when you talk about him—and his horse. But mostly Rafe."

"I didn't realize I did that."

"Are you in love with him, Olivia?" Julia asked, reaching up to caress Olivia's cheek.

"I'm afraid I am. And that's the problem."

"I'm listening."

"The night of the funeral, Rafe made me promise not to distribute Rowan's picture. Then Sarah put it on social media and it went viral. He was furious. I told him it wouldn't happen again. But my new boss specifically wants shots of Rowan in the winner's circle from Saturday's race."

Julia shrugged. "So, you go to Rafe, explain the situation. He's an understanding kind of guy. It's not like half the world won't see those photos now. The Illinois Derby was televised, wasn't it?"

"No, but it might as well have been. It was streamed on the internet."

"See? There you go. He can't hold you to that promise anymore, sweetheart. As far as I can tell, the issue is moot."

"You really think so, Mom?"

"I do," Julia said confidently.

OLIVIA DIDN'T HAVE to wait long to talk to Rafe. Just after the lunch crowd thinned out that day, he called and asked her to join the family for Monday night lasagna at the farm.

"I'd love to, Rafe," Olivia said. "Can I bring anything? Salad?"

"I don't think so. My mother prides herself on her Italian cooking, as you might have guessed. But if you have any of your *macarons* lying around, I could go for a few. Or a dozen."

"I'll see what I can do," she promised, thanking him for the invitation and agreeing to show up at seven thirty.

Though she didn't have any fresh cookies, she always kept several dozen in the freezer.

After cleaning up and closing the deli for the afternoon, Olivia went home to change.

She stopped by the Indian Lake Nursery on the way to Rafe's farm and bought a pink hydrangea plant for Gina. It was precisely seven thirty when she drove up the long drive and parked behind the villa.

She grabbed the bakery box of *macarons* and the hydrangea and started for the back door. She had the odd thought that of all the times she'd come to this house, she'd never entered through the front door.

Was the back door considered the servants' entrance?

Or the family door?

Same door, different perspective. She admonished herself for dwelling on it and knocked.

From inside, she heard a woman's heels clicking across the ceramic tile floor. "Is that you?" Gina whisked the door open. "Olivia!" Her eyes fell to the massive pink blooms. "Is that for me?"

"It is," Olivia replied, holding the flower out for her. "I know it's one of your favorites. It's forced, so you'll have to be careful we're well past frost before you put it outside."

"How pretty and so sweet of you to remember! Come in," Gina gushed. "I'm just putting the herb-and-garlic bread together."

"Can I help you?" Olivia asked, following her into the kitchen.

Gina shook her head. "The table is set. Mica is getting ready. I sent Rafe to the wine cellar." She smiled secretively. "One of Sam's best bottles. We're celebrating the win. Shh. I'm not supposed to tell you, but Rafe said it was important you be here. He says you're good luck for him and Rowan."

Olivia blushed crimson red. "He said that?"

Rafe walked into the kitchen carrying a bottle of cabernet sauvignon and four red wineglasses. "I most certainly did. Mom wasn't supposed to spill," he said good-naturedly.

He put the bottle and glasses on the granite counter. Then he kissed Olivia's cheek. "Thanks for coming. It wouldn't be the same without you."

"I don't know about that." Olivia lowered her eyes, feeling guilty standing in their spotlight of affection. She hadn't expected Rafe to give her any credit for Rowan's victory. On the way over, she'd convinced herself that she had to tell him about Louisville tonight. She hadn't realized it was a special occasion, and the celebratory mood made her falter. It was bad enough that she had to explain she was moving out of state and that she'd used her photos of Rowan to land the position. But to do so when they had invited her over specifically to toast Rafe and Rowan's success? Olivia's stomach twisted with anxiety.

Gina tore romaine lettuce leaves and threw them in a big glass bowl. She added sliced Bermuda onion, fresh mushrooms, crisp bacon, hard-boiled eggs and shredded Parmesan cheese.

Mica walked into the kitchen wearing what Olivia privately considered the Barzonni dress code: blue jeans, pale blue cotton button-down shirt and cowboy boots. Although Mica was a year younger and an inch shorter than Rafe, the two looked like twins. Mica, however, didn't beam quite as brightly as Rafe. He was probably exhausted from a long day in the field.

"Hi, Mica." Olivia smiled. "Can I pour you a glass of wine?"

"No," Mica said, holding out his arm. "You're our guest tonight. Remember? I'll pour *you* some wine."

Rafe, who had been helping Gina with the salad, donned a pair of oven mitts and took the lasagna out of the oven. The kitchen filled with the aroma of basil, oregano and fennel. "*Bellisimo*, Mama!" Rafe laughed and kissed Gina on the cheek. "This will be the best one yet."

"I'd like to think so." Gina shrugged apologetically. "But this was all I had left of last year's tomatoes. It's not the same when the tomatoes aren't fresh, and it's a long time till harvest. I refuse to use anyone's tomatoes but our own."

They sat at the huge kitchen table, which Gina had covered with a blue-and-white Italian print linen cloth and matching napkins. Mica put the salad on the table, while Gina served up the plates with lasagna and bread.

Rafe poured wine for everyone and then

offered a toast. "To Rowan's win. Our champion. And to Dad. This is your night, Papa." He lifted his eyes to the ceiling.

They all clinked glasses and then said a blessing.

AFTER DINNER, MICA helped Gina clean up the dishes and put the food away while Rafe walked Olivia down to the stable. "I figured you'd want to congratulate Rowan yourself," he said, putting his hand on the small of her back.

Olivia slowed her pace and then stopped. It was now or never. "Rafe, could I talk to you about something?"

"Sure," he replied, pausing beside her.

The sun was down and the solar garden lights had come on. They had just stepped out of the puddles of golden light that fell from the windows of the big house, and they were still far from the glow of the stable.

She lifted her eyes to his. "This is pretty serious."

"Is it as serious as what we discussed on Saturday? Because I've been thinking—"

"No," she cut him off. "It has nothing to do with that." She glanced away, wondering how to say what she needed to say. "I have some news to tell you. Really good news, actually. For me. This is something I've been working toward for a long time. All my life, really."

"This is about your photography?"

"Uh-huh." She clasped and unclasped her hands. Then she crossed her arms over her chest and squeezed her arms. This was harder than she'd imagined. When she'd rehearsed her speech in front of the mirror, it had seemed to roll off her tongue, but now, looking into his eyes, which were so dreamy and filled with the kind of caring she'd always hoped to find in a man, she lost her nerve.

But she couldn't back out now. Taking a deep breath, she said, "I don't know exactly how I did it, but I finally had the courage to send my work out to some publishers. Magazines, mostly. I got a lot of rejections. It was amazing how fast they turned me down."

He put his hands on her shoulders. "It's okay. You keep at it. Someone is bound to see what I see."

"What's that?"

He grinned widely. "That you're the best photographer on the planet."

"Well, one magazine thinks I may have what it takes. They gave me a test assignment of sorts and they liked my work. In fact, they called before I came to dinner. They want to hire me."

Rafe didn't react immediately, but then his eyes lit up like bonfires. "That's great, Olivia! We have another victory to celebrate."

She chewed her bottom lip and sucked in a breath. He probably assumed the publication was local. He was simply happy for her achievement. But was it possible that she meant enough to him that her aspirations were important to him, as well? For much of her life, she'd been closed off. She'd kept a lot of her deep troubles and feelings to herself. She hadn't wanted to bother anyone with her phobias or sorrows. People had their own problems. They didn't need to be burdened with more. She hadn't allowed anyone to get close to her.

Except Rafe.

She'd told him things she hadn't expressed even to her mother. Of course she hadn't wanted to hurt Julia, but digging down, she realized she'd feared rejection. She'd been afraid people wouldn't accept her, being the daughter of an addict. The offspring of someone so flawed and diseased who he'd abandoned his family. Olivia had assumed that people would think she was as weak as her father.

And had her father been weak? Or had he been strong to leave them? In his way, had he saved them from further pain?

Olivia's head throbbed with anguish as each conclusion led to another question still unanswered, still tormenting her.

"Rafe, there's something else. About the job. It's in Louisville."

"Louisville." He said the syllables precisely, as if forcing them to register in his head.

"I have to move there." Olivia felt as if her insides had slipped out of her. She was cold. Numb. Hollow.

Rafe's smile dropped off his face like melting wax. "Move?"

"Yeah." Her mouth was dry and gritty. She continued, "The magazine is overburdened with the Kentucky Derby coming up. The editor, Albert Allen Simmons, was so shorthanded, he handled my interview himself. After the Derby, they're sending me on a shoot in New Mexico. Another in California." She was frantic to find her earlier excitement, but failed.

"Move? Out of Indian Lake?"

"Yeah." Now was the time to tell him the worst part. "The name of the magazine is *Lexington Trophy*. It's new and they do a lot of features on horses and racing. Covers. Albert wants to use my shots for the cover."

"What shots?" Rafe dropped his hands and shoved them into his pockets.

Olivia forced herself to form the words. "The ones I took of Rowan in the winner's circle. Albert hasn't seen my photographs from Saturday—"

"Saturday? The Illinois Derby he just won?" Rafe shook his head and then raked his fingers through his hair. "Let me get this straight. You're telling me you're moving out of town. For good. To Louisville. And you're going to be using photographs of *my* horse to snag this job?"

She reached out for him, but he recoiled. "Rafe. That promise I made you shouldn't make any difference anymore. Rowan's pictures are everywhere now. He won in Illinois. Albert could buy shots from any stringer there—"

"Fine! Let him!" Rafe turned to walk away but then paused. He stuck his face right next to hers, his anger spilling over. "I don't care if Rowan's photograph is on all this guy's covers, Olivia."

"You don't? Then why are you so mad at me?

"You don't get it?"

"No, Rafe. I don't. I think you're being selfish and unreasonable."

"Me? Unreasonable?" he barked and pointed at the stable. "That horse was my dream. *Is* my dream. All I see here, Olivia, is you using Rowan to make your dreams a reality. Because of my devotion to him and my desires, you're able to step out of our lives."

Olivia realized she had broken his trust in her. She felt his pain as sharp as a dagger to her heart. The rift between them was quickly forming a gulf and only she could stop it. She scrambled for a solution. "Rafe, I'll tell him that Rowan is off-limits. That he can have anything else but his pictures. If he thinks I'm good enough, there will be other shoots in the future."

"Olivia." His voice was softer now. "I want you to be ambitious and test-drive your talent. You deserve that. You really do. I'd be the first one to tell you that you should take this chance. It's just, this is a shock. Moving away is a big deal."

"I know."

"Does this sudden decision have to do with your father by any chance?" He splayed his hands. "Look, I know it's difficult to heal those wounds, and I think you believe you're not hurting my feelings when you avoid talking about it. But it still hurts. We tiptoe around it, but it's the elephant in the room. I think because you couldn't trust him, you can't trust me. That's why you used Rowan's photos when I asked you not to. I wasn't the priority. I'm trying to understand you, Olivia, but all I feel is betrayed. You wanted this shot at your career, and by getting close to me, you got more access to Rowan. You were able to take more photos of him. Bottom line is that our relationship didn't tip the scales in my favor. So, in the end, maybe we just can't be together."

"Rafe, that's not true!" she said defensively, feeling the burn of her defection. She'd lost him. And she was desolate.

"Yeah…" He chewed his bottom lip and glanced into the distance. "I'm afraid it is. So, I'll tell you what, Olivia. You go to Louisville and you get your dream. Go on those great shoots you mentioned. Grab fame. But count me out of your plan." His voice was steady and brittle. He'd put his hands on his hips as he spoke, but his knuckles were white, as if he was using all his strength to steady himself. "In the end, Rowan and I served our purpose for you, didn't we?"

An eerie sensation flooded through Olivia, as if death had just laid his hands on her. "What are you talking about?"

"You got you what you needed out of us, didn't you? I guess you can always say we gave you this shot at the big time."

He spun on his heel and waved over his shoulder. "Good night, Olivia. Have a good trip." He stalked away and never looked back.

CHAPTER TWENTY-SIX

TEN DAYS IN Louisville had felt like a month. Olivia slugged back a bitter-tasting chain-brand cappuccino, wishing for even a sip of Maddie's brew. She hadn't slept more than five hours a night since she'd driven into town with her van piled high with clothes, linens, kitchen utensils and her inflatable bed. She felt she'd barely seen the inside of her own apartment, much less unpacked a single suitcase or duffel bag. All she'd done was work.

Albert had not only assigned her to two journalists, Lucrezia and Bart, but he'd also given her a shopping list of photographs he wanted taken over the next three weeks. He'd handed her a Garmin, an iPad and an old-fashioned street map. "You need to learn the city but fast," he'd said, shoving a thick manila file of photographs of Thoroughbreds into her hand. "We have less than two weeks till D-day. That's why I needed you here so quickly."

"The Derby, you mean."

"That's right. Morning, noon and night you'll be shooting anything and everything related to the Derby. We'll run interviews with the owners for months. Most of these horses will go on to summer and fall races. I want to know about their futures. I want to know if they're bringing up another horse for next year. Do they have stablemates? You will be everywhere they are until the Derby is over."

"Got it."

"Lucrezia is doing pieces on these first nine horses. Bart has the rest. He's an old pro at this. I gave him more ground to cover because he can do it."

"And I'm assigned to both of them? I appreciate your confidence in me."

Albert's face had registered a ghost of a smile. "You're young, Olivia. Lots of energy. Until the Derby is over, I'm depending on your youth just as much as your talent."

"I see," she'd replied, wondering if that was a compliment. "I'll get on it."

Olivia's desk was a small, drab army-green metal unit parked in a distant corner of the office. In her first hour on the job, Olivia had realized she couldn't use the rehabilitated six-year-old laptop she'd been given and volunteered her own computer. She was able to edit her photographs both at work and at home using her trusty laptop. It had worked out beautifully because Olivia could use it at her desk, in her car, at her apartment and in the coffee shop at the corner.

No matter how busy she'd been or how many hundreds of shots she'd taken and submitted each day, not an hour passed that she didn't look at her cell phone hoping to see a call, text or email from Rafe.

But there was nothing. It was almost as if she was dead to him.

Her mother, on the other hand, had communicated at least once a day. Julia had been just as surprised as Rafe that Olivia had won the job, but her reaction had been much different. Surprisingly, Julia wasn't concerned about replacing Olivia, which hurt Olivia's feelings more than she cared to admit. She'd been her mother's right arm since the first days of the deli. They were the Two Musketeers, or so Olivia had thought.

"Goodness, Olivia," Julia had said. "It's nearly summer—half the graduating class from the high school will come knocking for a summer job. I'll pick one or two and train them. If they're good enough and show interest, I could always move them into the catering, as well. I'll figure it out. Besides, this is the moment you've always dreamed about." She had caressed Olivia's cheek, but there was only joy and pride in Julia's eyes.

"Gee. I thought you'd be all teary-eyed and beg me not to go."

"I envy you this move. I've always dreamed of Florida. I wouldn't move there permanently, of course. Just for the winters. Louise Railton closes every December and comes back in April and she's like a new woman. She's met so many friends." She'd looked down at her hands and then back up at Olivia. This time Olivia saw a sheen of tears, but they weren't for her. They were for Julia's own lost dreams. "Maybe someday."

"You keep hoping, Mom. Something will turn up that can make that happen if you really want it."

Julia had smiled warmly. "You're absolutely right. You never lost faith that this would happen. I'll do the same."

IT WAS THREE days and counting to the Kentucky Derby, and the city was overflowing with visitors, trainers, owners and horses. Olivia was astounded at the hustle and bustle. It was as if the residents were preparing for the triumphant return of a hero. In a way, she supposed, they were.

The streets were clogged with florists' trucks delivering floods of roses to hotels, restaurants and offices. Invitations to Derby parties, both private and for charity, sat in stacks at the reception desk in the *Trophy* office. Actors, famous musicians, politicians and sports stars had booked every hotel suite.

Private homes played host to Hollywood celebrities and socialites from all over the country. Five-star restaurants were packed. Long lines ringed the streets around nightclubs where top-selling rock bands had been booked for over a year.

Albert stood over Olivia at her desk, tapping his watch. "What are doing here?"

"Editing the photos for Lucrezia's article on Just in Time." She pulled up a photograph of the chestnut-colored Thoroughbred. "What do you think?"

"Great-looking horse." He peered at the shot. "I'm not sure I want to use it."

"What? Why not?"

"Olivia, I know you're working hard, but

these photos are missing something. They're just not as good as the ones you submitted with your résumé."

"Rowan, you mean."

"Is that his name? Anyway, I don't know what it is. An essence. A spirit. Just in Time has done well this year, but I'm not picking him to win."

"You think you can pick the winners?" she asked, studying the image.

"The winners should be standout horses."

"But I won't know that until they actually run the race."

Albert shook his head as if he was trying to reason with an imbecile. This was the second time in three days that Albert had criticized her photographs without giving her a clear explanation of what she was doing wrong.

"Albert, please tell me what you're not seeing here and I'll give it to you," she said, hating that she had to plead. She was exhausted, but she wasn't desperate. Still, she couldn't work for the man if he didn't give her guidelines.

"You should know from looking at these horses which one will be the favorite."

"I could check the oddsmakers in Vegas," she mumbled sarcastically. But she thought she understood what he was saying. "You want me to find the ones that have heart, not just good lines and track records."

He snapped his fingers. "Exactly."

I thought I was doing that.

"Albert, by the time these horses make it to the Derby, they are *all* the best in the country. Every one of them is spectacular."

He leaned in close until their noses nearly touched and his eyes pinned hers. "And it takes a very gifted photographer to single out the very best from that elite pack. I thought you were that person."

"I am," she assured him. With a jolt, Olivia realized Albert was right. She did know how to see to the heart of a horse, but since her move to Louisville, everything about her work, her thinking, her own spirit, was out of whack.

It was as if the void that had opened up on her last night with Rafe had shut down her ability to connect with animals…or with anything. Was she forcing her heart not to feel the pain of their separation? Was she doing exactly what she'd done when her father had abandoned her? Stuffing her heartbreak into an iron locker and praying it would never escape?

Albert straightened and turned on his heel.

He took two steps and then said over his shoulder, "You've got a gig at the Brown Hotel in one hour with Owen and Sylvia Huet. Owners of Sideshow."

"Okay."

"Make sure you give me shots that *Town & Country* and *Horse & Hound* will cry over."

OLIVIA SAT ON a gold brocade sofa in the opulent lobby of the historic Brown Hotel in downtown Louisville listening to Owen and Sylvia Huet carry on about their adventures in Thoroughbred racing. Owen was fifty-six years old and looked every minute of it, his face tanned and weathered from the Florida sun. He was trim and broad-shouldered, and looked like a working man who did not leave the training and riding to others, but chose instead to live his life through his horse.

He reminded her of Rafe, or what he'd be like in twenty years, and she felt hollowness in her heart that threatened to swallow her. She glanced at her cell phone. Still nothing from Rafe.

She raised her camera to her eye so that no one would recognize the sheen in her eyes for what it was.

Frightening, how stingingly painful it was to miss someone.

Lucrezia, who was only a year out of the University of Louisville, barraged the Huets with questions that seemed inane to Olivia, but which the older couple indulged.

Olivia rose from the sofa and took her photographs as surreptitiously as possible, trying to capture those split-second moments that flattered both Owen and Sylvia and did not reveal their suffering at Lucrezia's inexperienced hands.

"And what are your aspirations for, uh…" Lucrezia looked at her notes and scrambled for the horse's name. "Sideshow?"

To win, obviously, Olivia thought with exasperation.

Both Owen and Sylvia gaped at the young reporter before answering stiffly.

Olivia continued taking pictures as Lucrezia went through her list of questions, which the Huets graciously entertained.

The interview was so painful, Olivia finally interrupted Lucrezia, who slung her a killing glare. "My boss would like some photographs of you and Sideshow. How about if I follow you over there now? After you finish your drinks, of course," Olivia said sweetly.

The relief on both Owen's and Sylvia's faces was blisteringly apparent. "Great!" they said in unison, setting down their half-finished cocktails. "You can ride with us, Olivia," Sylvia offered with a tone of urgency. Olivia realized how anxious they were for the interview to be over.

Lucrezia bounced to her feet and announced, "Actually, Olivia won't be going to the stables with us." She whipped out a white sheet of paper from the monogrammed leather folder she carried—probably a graduation gift from her parents.

Olivia nearly chided herself for her catty thoughts. Nearly. Lucrezia was gloating. This couldn't be good.

Lucrezia shoved the paper at Olivia. "Albert wants you to continue shooting the owners here at the Brown. He's sending another photographer to the stables."

Not photograph the horses?

Olivia was stunned. Albert was dead serious when he'd told her that her work had lost its spirit. Olivia smiled placidly, hoping the shock didn't register in her eyes. She had to find her edge again.

Lucrezia smiled at the Huets. "Albert wants the best for Sideshow. Olivia has only been on the job a few weeks and is just getting her bearings. We have a seasoned photographer, been around stables forever, Albert tells me." Her smile had turned into a leer. "Shall I follow you over there in my car?"

Lucrezia was beyond gloating, Olivia thought, but it didn't matter. Olivia was being taken down a peg because she'd lost something vital in her work.

Olivia had always viewed life and her subjects through her heart. The problem was that her heart was broken.

Olivia watched the Huets and Lucrezia leave the lobby, feeling as if the earth was quaking under her feet. She looked down at the expensive marble floor. Rock-solid.

Then she turned her gaze to the blank screen on her cell phone. What was this? Twenty times today, alone, she'd checked to see if Rafe had texted or called her. Never in her life had she spent so many minutes and hours wishing that her phone would ring. She would give anything to hear Rafe's voice.

"Olivia!" Bart shouted from across the hotel lobby, startling her out of her thoughts.

She whirled around and raised her arm in a wave. "Bart! I'm here." She rushed toward him and the next Derby entrant owner.

This is your dream come true, Olivia. What are you going to do with it?

RAFE CRUSHED HIS mother's homegrown mint in the bottom of a silver-plated mint-julep cup. He added a heaping tablespoon of powdered sugar and a jigger of his father's best Kentucky bourbon and stirred the mixture until the sugar dissolved. As he added crushed ice to the cup, he stared at the bourbon bottle.

The word *Kentucky* swam in his vision like a hologram: illuminated, vibrating and beckoning.

Rafe's father had often told him that you could count on one thing in life—irony.

It was ironic that Olivia, who had feared horse racing all her life, was now living at the epicenter of American horse racing. She was no doubt at the Derby today, covering the story for her new job. It was the one place in the world that Rafe had dreamed of being since he was a kid.

It was also ironic that he'd been partly responsible for putting her there right when he'd realized that what he wanted most in his life was Olivia.

Rafe wasn't sure if all that made him foolish or simply stupid.

Probably a bit of both.

He filled the cup with more crushed ice and placed a sprig of mint on top.

One thing was for sure: Olivia had made him think long, hard and deep about his life. His goals, intentions…even his integrity.

Three days ago he had telephoned John Galway, the owner of Mr. Blue, set up a meeting and driven out to his horse farm. Because of what Olivia had told him, Rafe had decided to give the Indian Lake Hospital Race trophy to Mr. Blue. Rafe might never know who really won, but with the win at the Illinois Derby to Rowan's credit, he felt the tally sheets should be fair and square. If there was an iota of doubt—ever—about the Indian Lake race, Rafe knew he couldn't keep something that wasn't rightfully his.

He could hear voices coming from the den, where the entire family had gathered to watch the race. Gabe and Liz had brought Sam. Maddie had arrived with four dozen chocolate-mint cupcakes and a very tired Nate, who'd worked past midnight the night before. Mrs. Beabots had driven out with Austin and Katia. Rafe noticed that no one mentioned Olivia or asked him if he'd been in touch with her. On the other hand, he knew that if any of them had spoken with her, they would have said something.

Gina had laid out a buffet of finger foods in the dining room. As cheerful as the event should have been, Rafe felt Olivia's absence more keenly than he had since she'd left.

He wondered if Olivia would have liked this party at all, since all the festivities centered on racing. The little Derby Day party was a tradition in the Barzonni household. Rafe could remember being no more than five years old and going out to the herb garden to pick the mint for the juleps. His father had loved the party and in those days, they'd invited friends from The Grange.

As she'd always done, Gina had drawn up a poster board with the names of all the horses running in the race. There were three crystal bowls on the sofa table with signs designating "Win," "Place" and "Show."

The bets were only a dollar each and it was great fun to root and cheer for one's favorite pick.

Rafe wondered how Olivia would feel about their at-home "betting." He would have liked to think that she would feel enough at ease to join in and toss a dollar in each bowl. But the fact was that he had no clue how she would respond because she wasn't in his life anymore.

Every day since she'd left, he'd thought that perhaps she might call him or text him, but she hadn't. He'd never been one to rifle through the mail, especially since he'd moved out to the coach house, but every night after coming in from the fields or from bedding down Rowan, he'd gone straight for the basket on the kitchen table where his mother tossed the mail.

There was nothing from Olivia.

By the end of the first week since her departure, even his mother had commented on his acerbic mood. Mica started calling him "Mr. Doom."

Oh, he'd been brave sending her away like he had. He'd meant it when he'd said he wanted her to pursue her dream. He just hadn't figured she'd cut him out of her life as if he was cancer. He'd thought he'd come to mean something to her. But the truth was, he was just someone she'd kissed a few times. A stepping-stone on the way to better things.

She'd never told him that she loved him. She'd never said she even cared about him.

He was guilty of reading emotions into her reactions to him that probably didn't exist.

He understood that she'd spent years keeping her emotions closed off because of her childhood trauma. He'd thought they'd both helped each other—him with his grief and her with her past.

Guess not.

Laughter poured out of the den as the television commentator described some of the outrageous hats the women were wearing at the Derby.

Rafe remembered Olivia's glorious hair and how it fell down her back in shimmering dark sheets. And the feel of her lips against his, the softness of her skin—

He grabbed the counter and hung his head between his outstretched arms. He wished someone had told him when he met Olivia that she was the kind of woman a man could never forget.

"Rafe?"

Chills swept across his back and down to his toes. It had finally happened. He'd lost his mind.

"Rafe."

Olivia's voice called his name like an ancient siren. If he looked up, he'd die or turn to stone or salt. Something dire. That he knew.

He gasped for air. He heard the sound of her heels against the tile floor. He knew that sound. Light, delicate steps, though purposeful and not at all timid.

"I knocked, but no one heard me," Olivia said.

He straightened and stared at her. He blinked, but the mirage remained. Irony number three. Just when you thought you had life all figured out, it sent you a curveball. He felt as if he'd been drinking, but the bourbon hadn't passed his lips.

"Olivia. I thought you were in Louisville."

"I was." She smiled.

He was confused. Today was Derby day. If she was working for a magazine that revolved around Thoroughbred racing, why was she here?

"I don't understand," he finally said. "Your new job is what you've always wanted. You moved there. You cut all ties to us here in Indian Lake. No phone calls. Not even a text. To anyone."

"I was overwhelmed with work," she began. "I can't tell you how many times I picked up the phone to call you—"

"But you were busy."

"I was, but truthfully, I was afraid you'd never talk to me again. You were so mad at me when I left."

He folded his arms across his chest, thinking it would keep his banging, thudding, galloping heart at bay. She was right; he'd been livid with her that night. Probably, he'd overreacted. Not probably. He did overreact. He was hurt, disappointed and shocked that she would leave town. Leave him behind. The fact that she'd even considered a life without him had sliced him to the core. He'd acted defensively. He might have even been guilty of wanting to hurt her back. Not a lot. But enough that she'd feel a sting while he felt as if he was dying inside.

But now, looking at her with those soft lights in her eyes, his heart melted. He didn't care what she said or did; he just wanted this moment to last—forever if he had his way.

"Mad? I suppose I was—then."

Olivia titled her head and peered up at him from beneath long, dark lashes. "And now?"

"Not so much," he replied in a low whisper. His eyes burned, but he didn't dare let her see that she had such an immense effect on him. "So, Olivia. Your job. How's that going?" he asked, hoping to distract from his sensitivity. He had to get ahold of himself. He vacillated between sadness and anger. Pain and revenge and then back to fear that he'd say something that would cause her to walk away. Again.

He wanted the illusion to stay.

"My job isn't quite what I thought it would be," she replied. "I love bonding with animals through my lens, and I was so sure that with all those magnificent horses in Kentucky for the Derby, I would take pictures like the world had never seen before. I know that sounds pompous, but it's what I'd dreamed for myself."

"What happened?"

"That's just it. Nothing happened. I looked in their eyes and everything was empty. I couldn't see them anymore. I realized when I looked objectively at my photos on the computer, they were heartless."

Rafe heard the sincerity in her voice and read the imploring expression on her face. "I see."

Rather than let him say anything further, she rushed on. "I realized I'd made the wrong choice going to Louisville, but it wasn't irrevocable. I could make other choices. I only just sent out my résumé and photographs. I jumped at the first offer. I don't know why I never considered freelance work before, but I think it's the right move. Working freelance would allow me to have that personal connection with the animals that I've always had. I miss that. I have to have that, Rafe."

"So what are you saying?"

"I quit that job yesterday."

"Quit—"

"And there's something else." She hesitated, then took a deep breath. "You see, I forgot something when I left, Rafe. I forgot to tell you that I love you."

Rafe's heart jump-started back to life, the shock was so intense. "You...you never told me that..."

She moved so close to him their lips nearly touched. "I was scared."

"You were?" He inhaled the fragrance of wildflowers and orchids. His hands were shaking, but he didn't dare touch her for fear he'd make the wrong move.

Her brown eyes plumbed his and he felt as if he'd levitated. He was anything but grounded.

She continued, "I didn't have to move out

of state to find what I've always wanted, Rafe. It was right here in my own backyard in Indian Lake. It was you. When you didn't contact me, I thought I'd lose my mind. Each day without you was interminable. The nights were unbearable, wondering if I'd ever see you again. Everything about me changed— and not for the better. I didn't know it was possible to miss someone as much as I missed you. I couldn't take it."

"So you're not just visiting, then?"

"No, Rafe." She smiled. "I've quit the job and come back home. Back to you, if you want me."

"Want you?"

"Do you, Rafe?"

Her eyes were filled with the promise he'd dreamed about. For the first time, those raw edges of fear were gone, smoothed into pure love.

He gathered her into his arms. "You're not afraid of me."

"I'm not," she whispered, sliding her arms around his strong back and putting her cheek against his chest. "Never again. I love you, Rafe. I want every minute you can give me. The only thing that frightens me now is being without you." She looked up at him. "I want to make dreams *with* you, Rafe."

He pulled her face toward his. "Olivia, since you left, I've been thinking about what I really want, as well. If the racing bothers you at all, then I can make changes, too."

"It's okay. I've come to grips with my father's addiction. It was his disease. Not mine. I had nothing to do with it, though I felt guilty all my life. And I was angry," she said sheepishly.

"I know that," he replied, feeling the pain his anger must have caused her when they parted. "I'm so sorry I hurt you, Olivia."

She put two fingers over his lips. "Shh. Don't. You have to know that I'm not all the way there yet, with my fears about gambling, but I'm so much better than I was. And I have you to thank for that. I can talk to you about anything."

"Anything?"

"Yes. Anything."

"Then I want you to think about this, because I've done a lot of soul-searching since you left. I've realized that I don't want to leave the farm. This land is so much a part of me, Olivia, I can hardly describe how much I love it. I also love my horses, as you do. I can't imagine a life without them in it. But I'm willing to give up racing because it causes you so much heartache. That's something I can't bear to see—even a glimmer of it hurts me, too. So I was thinking that I might start a dressage school. Right here at the farm."

"A school?"

"You said I was a good instructor," he countered defensively.

"The best, Rafe." She kissed his cheek. "I was terrified of riding a horse, and you made it magical. This is a wonderful idea. But are you really sure it would be enough for you? To give up racing Rowan? Because I don't want you to do it just for me."

He kissed her lips sweetly. "One thing I've always admired about you is your honesty, Olivia. And now I'm being honest with you. It's not just for you. It is what I want." He tapped his heart. "In here. I am this farm and my horses. And you."

"Oh, Rafe—"

"I love you, Olivia."

Then he kissed her, and his lips met hers with passion and wonderment. He couldn't get enough of her sweetness and her surrender. Her lips were pliant, soft and yet demanding. Enticing and promising him worlds he couldn't wait to explore. He knew as she kissed him back that she was truly his.

And that was all he needed to know.

* * * * *

YES! Please send me **The Montana Mavericks Collection** in Larger Print. This collection begins with 3 FREE books and 2 FREE gifts (gifts valued at approx. $20.00 retail) in the first shipment, along with the other first 4 books from the collection! If I do not cancel, I will receive 8 monthly shipments until I have the entire 51-book Montana Mavericks collection. I will receive 2 or 3 FREE books in each shipment and I will pay just $4.99 US/ $5.89 CDN for each of the other four books in each shipment, plus $2.99 for shipping and handling per shipment.*If I decide to keep the entire collection, I'll have paid for only 32 books, because 19 books are FREE! I understand that accepting the 3 free books and gifts places me under no obligation to buy anything. I can always return a shipment and cancel at any time. My free books and gifts are mine to keep no matter what I decide.

263 HCN 2404   463 HCN 2404

Name	(PLEASE PRINT)	
Address		Apt. #
City	State/Prov.	Zip/Postal Code

Signature (if under 18, a parent or guardian must sign)

Mail to the **Reader Service:**

IN U.S.A.: P.O. Box 1867, Buffalo, NY 14240-1867
IN CANADA: P.O. Box 609, Fort Erie, Ontario L2A 5X3